STACCATO

DEBORAH J LEDFORD

RICK —

I hope you enjoy the first book of my series.

Great to meet you at TFOB 2014.

Dagger Books
Published by Second Wind Publishing
Kernersville, North Carolina

Dagger Books
Second Wind Publishing, LLC
931-B South Main Street, Box 145
Kernersville, NC 27284

First Dagger Books edition published August, 2009.
Dagger Books, Running Angel, and all production design are trademarks of Second Wind Publishing, used under license.

For information regarding bulk purchases of this book, digital purchase and special discounts, please contact the publisher at www.secondwindpublishing.com

Cover and author photographer: Skip Feinstein
Original cover concept: Peter D. Esposito

Manufactured in the United States of America
ISBN 978-1-935171-17-1

This novel is dedicated, as always, to John.
Without you, I have no words.

1

Nobody decides to go mad. Tragedies occur—
forces of nature, emotional distress, sorrow for those
taken too soon, terror writhing below the skin.

Other elements drive people to madness—
smoldering rage, silent words that never stop
rambling in the mind, unrequited passion, even
merely following the path of destiny.

Fear also motivates insanity. If limits are pushed
to the extreme there are few other alternatives than
to face obstacles, or to flee from them.

I chose to flee. That was my undoing.

These are the events that drove me to the edge.

Three hours earlier Nicholas Kalman had discovered what he now knew to be his father's journal buried in a bookcase. After reading the leather bound book for the fourth time, each page now appeared as a separate snapshot locked in his mind, as did every piece of classical music he had studied since the age of five. For Nicholas, the capability of a photographic memory straddled the line of celebration and curse.

Now, he struggled with the realization that the words had been written by a man he had never known . . . and that these ominous passages were intended for him. Using his finger as a marker, he closed the book and studied the nondescript binding. Numbed by the words, he sat in an overstuffed red velvet chair and stared across the music room of his Uncle Alexander's ten thousand square foot mansion.

Ringing in his ears grew louder and he became aware that the Chopin had ceased flowing from the speakers concealed by tapestries of European landscapes hung along the walls.

Nicholas's mind dizzied from reading about the premonition of approaching doom, forewarning him of his own. Swallowing hard, he considered his father's fear. Then he realized the terror was real, filling his mouth with a copper taste. *This can't be true.* He wiped a trail of sweat from his temple with his sleeve, set the journal on the table beside him and forced himself to tear his eyes from it.

Compelled by the words, he found it impossible to re-shelve the book, or to dismiss the pages as utter fiction. He wondered what the written implications meant for him. Reading his father's recollections, he had fallen under their spell. His father warned of the seductive elements to be cautious of—things that had already ensnared Nicholas.

Looking around, he recognized what his father had described as cunning manipulations of deceiving comfort: first edition books exhibited within walnut cases surrounding him in a ritualistic circle, the ebony Steinway grand piano that sat regally upon a platform in the middle of the music room, exactly as the writings stated. The details even noted how flames from the fireplace bathed the Pakistani rug in an amber glow.

The visuals Nicholas discovered within the journal were vivid and concise, even the mention of the single malt Scotch he had been sipping. The liquor's bitter aftertaste urged him out of the chair. Baccarat tumbler in hand, he crossed the room to the bar and tossed the watered-down remains into the sink. He washed the crystal then polished the glass until it sparkled. He was careful to replace the tumbler in its original position equidistant from four others, then he angled the matching decanter directly in line with its crystal tray.

Cracking open a ginger ale from the mini refrigerator under the counter, he swallowed a mouthful. Refreshed by the cold, crisp drink, he went to the bookcase and placed two fingers in the crevice where he had found the journal, stuffed between thick editions of Elizabethan theatrical theory. *How did I not see it before tonight?*

Nicholas shuddered, feeling the ghost of his father join him. Though he did not know the final outcome of the man's life whose blood coursed through his own veins, Nicholas did know that his father, Charles Ian Hunt, like himself, had once been a celebrated world-class pianist.

As a boy, Nicholas had been told that at the time of his birth, his father's talents had been presented at renowned performance halls world-wide. Over the years, Nicholas had heard snippets of conversations between his Uncle Alexander and others about how Charles had deserted his wife and infant son, as well as his profession. His agent and managers had been horrified by his disappearance, but fellow competitors had celebrated the departure, at last rid of Charles's upstaging and the confident, sold-out perform-ances that brought audiences to their feet.

Walking in a fog to the Steinway, Nicholas trailed his fingers across the keys. Faint tones from the perfectly tuned instrument resonated throughout the room. He fought the temptation to sit at the keyboard, to lose himself and his new circumstance in a piece of music. *Focus. You can't pretend this away. It's part of you now.*

Nicholas's head throbbed with his heartbeat. *Should I mention this to Uncle Alexander?* Returning to settle back in the chair, he picked up the journal. Nicholas recognized how his father's past had mirrored his own life. He shared the man's unease as he flipped yellowed pages to a particularly troubling passage.

> *Nicholas, my son, if you ever find these words, I urge you to be careful.*
>
> *Beware of this man you call, Uncle. Although he will make promises of wealth and fame—the price will be that of your soul.*
>
> *It is a caution I did not heed. And now that he has finally found me, I am sure to never see you again.*
>
> *Watch over your mother, Nicholas. Keep her near you, or I fear she will simply disappear—lost to you forever.*

Nicholas thought of all the people over the years who had left his life without as much as a goodbye: several servants, various workers at the mansion, a tutor who disagreed with Alexander about his teaching methods . . . most of all, Nicholas's mother.

His stomach in knots, unable to deal with any more warnings, he slammed the journal shut. A sense of dread settled in his stomach. He realized that destiny and doom had found its way into his life—and into the very room his father had once known. His gaze went to the piano and he wondered if his father's fingers had touched those same ivory keys.

In a daze Nicholas left the music room, the journal clutched in his hand. He descended one flight of stairs, then walked along the second floor hallway of the mansion. When he reached his bedroom, he noticed light streaming from the crack at the floor.

Slipping inside, he eased the door shut and leaned against it. He scanned the room, its comforts calming his tense nerves. Flames licked in the fireplace, the duvet on the king-sized bed had been turned down, heavy drapes were drawn across the floor-to-ceiling windows. He pivoted his attention to the far end of the room. A slight smile lifted his lips.

Elaine Kalman sat in a plush wingback chair, feet tucked under her, dressed only in one of Nicholas's lavender dress shirts. He watched as she studied one of her ever-present college textbooks, occasionally making notations on a legal pad. He slid out of his loafers and walked to her.

She flipped back her curtain of long blonde hair and tucked a lock behind her ear. "Where have you been?" she asked in a stern voice followed by a stunning smile.

Nicholas bent down to kiss her full lips. "I hoped you would be here."

She tossed the book aside. "Just me and *Introduction to International Finance*."

"Well, now, I have something way more interesting for you to study." Nicholas held the gaze of her lazy gray eyes, then ran the tip of his tongue the length of her upturned neck.

4

"I've missed you," she purred, pulling him to her.

"It's late. Won't your mother be worried?"

"I told her I was pulling an all night study session with Olivia at her dorm."

"Who's Olivia?"

Elaine gave him a shrug and a coy smile. "Someone I made up. What's that?" she asked, pointing to the journal.

Nicholas hesitated, then settled on the floor and leaned his shoulder against her leg. "I found it in the music room. Practice wasn't going well. Uncle screamed at me as usual, 'In my opinion your timing is utterly without explanation,'" he said in a clipped European accent. "Then he stormed out all pissed off."

Elaine laughed as she gathered a handful of his curls and tugged playfully. "You sound exactly like him."

"I was sitting at the piano and this book caught my eye. How many years ago did your mother adopt me? Ten, right?"

She nodded and joined him on the floor.

"I've lived here ever since. Ten years in that very room. Six, seven, twelve, hours every day except when I'm on tour." He frowned at the book. "Strange that I only ran across this thing tonight. It must have been stuck in that bookshelf all that time." He tilted toward her and whispered, "It's like it was calling out to me."

"Are you going to tell me what *it* is?"

"My father's journal."

Elaine's eyes widened. "No way. How do you know?"

He opened the cover, turned to the first written page and pointed to the dedication: FOR MY SON, NICHOLAS RENFREW HUNT.

She traced a finger over the last word. "Hunt?"

"My real name."

"I never knew that."

"There's some pretty disturbing stuff in here," he said, closing the book.

"Like what?"

He hesitated, unsure of how much to reveal for fear of

alarming her. "It seems like a warning."

"A warning?"

"To beware of Alexander."

Elaine chuckled. "What does that mean?"

"Maybe I'm reading something into nothing. I don't know what to make of it yet."

Silence fell over them, neither taking their eyes off the journal.

"Do you want to read some of it to me?" Elaine asked in an uneasy voice.

Nicholas shook his head.

"Are you okay?"

His eyes locked on hers. "Honestly?"

"Of course." Taking his face in her hands, she said, "Always."

"I'm a little freaked." Troubled by the frown across Elaine's brow, Nicholas tossed the journal to the thick carpet and gave her his full attention. "Now I've worried you."

"No, it's okay, I just don't know what to think about this. What does he say about Alexander that's got you so freaked out?"

"Nothing." Nicholas sighed. "I want to forget about it for now. Forget about everything and everyone but you and me."

"I know what you need." She rose to sit on the chair they had been leaning against. Rubbing his shoulders, she quietly hummed a tune she had told him often ran through her head; a lullaby her mother sang when content.

He tipped his head back to look up at her. "That's nice." Elaine kissed his forehead. Finally able to relax, he exhaled and closed his eyes. "Are you staying here tonight?"

"If you want me to."

Nicholas turned around to face her. "It's not about want. It's about need. But if Alexander ever found out about us, he would flip out. I mean, it's a rush sneaking around behind his back, but it's dangerous, too."

Her smoldering eyes made him want her more. While they kissed, he reached for her shirt and found the top button, releasing one silver pearl stud after another. He leaned up to kiss the hollow of her neck.

Standing, he began to unbutton his shirt, prompting her to rise and help him. She pushed his roving hands away and he chuckled, struggling with his cuffs. He pulled the shirt off his shoulders and stood back to display his toned chest.

Eyes wide, hand to her mouth, Elaine gaped him. "God," she whispered, reaching out to touch his chest.

Nicholas looked down at what she gaped at: a golf ball-sized welt over his right pectoral, angry red, ringed with purple. He whipped the shirt back on, cursing himself for being so careless. His mind hijacked by passion, he had forgotten about the lashing he had suffered a few hours earlier.

Buttoning up, he brushed past her to sit on the bed. "Like I said, practice didn't go very well today."

"Alexander hit you?"

He replied with a weary shrug.

She went to him and knelt between his legs. Her voice quavered when she finally spoke. "I'm going to break that damned cane of his."

"He'll break it on me if I don't, as he says, 'Shape up to reach my maximum potential.'"

"We've got to get you out of here."

"What are you talking about?" Nicholas said in a defensive tone.

"There's no excuse for beating you. I know this isn't the first time either. You try to hide from me by undressing in the dark, but I feel you flinch sometimes when I touch you. Now I understand why you whimper if you turn a certain way. It's getting worse. Mother should have never allowed you to move in here. You should have stayed with us."

"Alexander wouldn't have allowed that. Anyway, I need to stay here." He avoided her probing stare. "I've got a performance tomorrow night. The tour's coming up and I need as much exposure in front of an audience as I can get before I go overseas. We're under a lot of pressure to perfect the Debussy."

Her voice raised an octave as she said, "He has no right to hit you. You need to leave that monster."

"And go where? I have no money. He's seen to that."

"That can't be. Your popularity grows each time you perform. And Mother said your fee last month with the Cleveland Orchestra was fifteen thousand dollars."

Nicholas nodded in agreement.

"How many concerts did you have last year? Thirty?"

"Thirty-seven. I know that sounds impressive, but I don't get anything but the allowance Alexander gives me, and a little cash when I travel. Didn't you notice when you went with me overseas those two times? Everything is taken care of in advance. We dine at the hotel restaurants where we stay, a driver is even provided. The promoter picks up anything else I need."

"But we go out—"

"And you always pay."

A look of dismay crossed Elaine's face. "I don't understand."

"He rationalizes, Elaine. Why would I need money? I live here, eat here. All I do is practice and study. The car is all I have and it's leased in his name. All my assets are frozen in trust until I turn twenty-one. 'Invested for my future' he says." *Eight months from now. An eternity.*

"You're an adult. He can't do that."

"He's the trustee. He can do whatever he wants."

"I have money."

"I can't ask you to help me with that." Sliding away from her touch, he went to the window. Blue light from the quarter moon's glow bathed the three-tiered fountain in the circular drive below.

"What he's doing isn't right," she muttered.

"What am I supposed to do if I leave? Get a job?"

"Keep performing. Why would that change?"

Nicholas snapped his attention back to her. "Without him? He wouldn't allow it. He'd ruin me first."

A passage from his father's journal came to his mind, warning him of Alexander's manipulation and devious ways.

8

How could he explain to Elaine his mentor had an evil streak that roiled below the skin? No words would ever convey Nicholas's thoughts. He returned to her, drawing her into his arms.

A sob caught in her throat. "Please come and stay with me and Mother. She would love it and we wouldn't have to hide any more."

"We can't go public," Nicholas snapped.

"Why not? We're not doing anything wrong. We aren't related. It shouldn't matter that we love each other."

"I agree, but it matters to him. It's all about appearances with Alexander. No one knows he's not really my uncle. He's told everyone in the industry that my talent is inherited directly from him." Nicholas sighed. "Anyway, I can't just walk away. I've worked too hard."

"And I love you too much to see him keep hurting you."

"I'll be all right." Stroking her hair, he closed his eyes and breathed in her scent of gardenias and rosewater. "I'm sorry I worried you."

"I think you'd better finish reading your father's journal. Maybe he has some advice to offer."

Nicholas nodded, having had the same thought. They held each other while the antique clock atop the mantel chimed eleven times. "We could go to the country house. If I play well tomorrow night he might let me stay away for a few days."

"No one goes there this time of year, do they?" She pulled away to look at him, excitement rising in her voice.

He shook his head.

"Let's do it. Right now." She rushed to the walk-in closet, threw open the door and rifled through the contents of tuxedos, designer shirts, tailored jackets and an array of dress shoes and sneakers.

"What are you doing?"

"Packing. Where's your duffel? The black leather one we found you in Prague."

Nicholas joined her in the closet and took her hand that clutched the supple leather bag. "I can't go now."

"Why not? It's the perfect plan. Everyone's asleep. We'll slip out and Uncle would never know."

"No, we need to do this right. Otherwise he'll be suspicious."

She pushed him away and planted a hand on her hip. "Okay, when?"

"Tomorrow night. Right after my performance. It's been booked for months. I've worked too hard to pull out. And it wouldn't be right."

"The consummate professional."

"Of course. Always," he said, reciting the phrase she often used.

She smiled, then rewarded him with a kiss. When he didn't reciprocate with his usual eagerness, she pulled away. "What's wrong? Are you okay? You look so sad."

"I can't stop thinking about my father's journal."

"Are you worried Alexander will be upset that you found it?"

"No. I don't think I should tell him. I keep going back to what I read. It's so . . . creepy. He wrote the journal a decade ago, but he mentions everything in the room, like nothing's ever changed. And the warnings are things like what to look out for, and to be careful of Alexander. I think—" Elaine stiffened and he halted his words, recognizing the same fear he had felt after reading his father's ominous passages.

"Go ahead, you can tell me," she said, her voice quavering.

"I think Alexander murdered my father."

She flinched, prompting him to wrap an arm around her. Tears welled in his eyes, her body wavered in a watery halo.

"He may have killed my mother, too."

2

Alexander Ambrus Kalman waited in the music room of his mansion for his niece, Elaine. Fifty-three years of living had discolored his corn-silk hair, but his sparkling aquamarine eyes remained focused, steeled, missing nothing. Afflicted since birth by a clubfoot, a brass tipped cane enabled him to move with relative ease. The hardwood stick, topped by a hand-carved ivory bust of a lion never left his side. Regal in appearance and stature, a black turtleneck accentuated his muscular upper body. He relished the fact that strangers found him intriguing, yet too aloof to approach.

Notes of Vladimir Horowitz's rendition of Rachmaninoff's Prelude in G, Opus 32, Number 5 filled the room, transporting Alexander to a melancholy cognizance.

Leaning on the cane, he tapped across the marble floor and surveyed the expansive vista from one of the twelve-foot-tall windows. The estate, perched high on the mountain-side, featured miles of an unobstructed landscape of the Great Smoky Mountains of western North Carolina. His view from the third floor looked out onto his acres of lush gardens and fountains where the sun fought to burn through the early morning fog. The panorama had been the reason he'd purchased the property to build his mansion thirteen years ago. The location reminded him of his youth spent in the mountainous Orseg region of Hungary.

Alexander's butler, Sampte, entered carrying a crystal vase full of blooming bougainvillea. Although Sampte stood well over six feet tall, he seemed to glide into the room. A charcoal morning coat hid his formidable build.

Sampte set the vase on a table near the window and said in a deep monotone, "Mistress Elaine is here as you requested."

Alexander loved the dichotomy of the delicate, burgundy flowers atop toxic, thorny stems. He caressed one of the fuchsia bracts. "Send her in."

Sampte retreated as quietly as he had entered.

Alexander's stomach fluttered in anticipation of his niece's arrival. As a child Elaine often visited Nicholas at the mansion, becoming the young boy's only true friend. As his niece matured into a young woman, Alexander found himself drawn to her beauty. Elaine's voice captivated him, her dulcet tones reminding him of a well-trained mezzo-soprano. Although her smile rarely fell upon him, his breath caught in his throat whenever he witnessed the curl of her exquisite lips.

At the sound of a knock, he squared his shoulders and turned to the door. "Yes, come in."

Elaine eased into the room, draped in a calf-length, brightly colored floral dress. Standing at the threshold, her eyes darted to meet his, then just as quickly she averted her gaze to look beyond him as she closed the door.

Alexander drew in a slow breath at the sight of her. *I must have her soon.* "You look lovely."

"What is it, Uncle Alexander? I'll be late for class."

Restraining his urges, he attempted a flippant approach. "I see that you stayed here last night."

She went to the window and gave him her back. "I fell asleep studying."

"And where did you sleep?"

"Why? Is it any business of yours?"

"I think your mother would be interested." He limped to stand a step behind her. "As would I." He closed his eyes and inhaled her floral fragrance.

Elaine replied with a shrug. Turning around, she flinched as she nearly bumped into him.

"You captivate me." When he reached out to touch her face, she stepped away, but not before he took a lock of her silken hair between his fingers.

Elaine's eyes widened. "What are you doing?"

"There's something I need to tell you."

She pulled her hair free. "I'm going now."

As she whirled from him, Alexander grabbed her bare arm and pivoted her to face him. "I'm not finished."

"I don't care what—"

"Let me speak. I've held my tongue for too long."

"Let go," she hissed.

He loosened his grasp and trailed his fingertips down the length of her arm. The feel of her silky smooth skin sparked his desire. "I've decided. It's time you moved in here."

A frown creased Elaine's brow, marring her beauty.

Alexander, amused by her response, puffed out his chest and announced. "With me."

It took a moment for her to speak. When she did, she stumbled over the words, "That's insane. You're my uncle. It's sick to even be thinking—"

"Don't think. Let me show you how your life will be with me."

Alexander entwined her hair in his fist and pulled her closer. "When I look at you, I hear Chopin."

Elaine's eyes grew wide. She recoiled and struggled to pull away. "Stop it, you freak."

"Freak? Freak, you say," Alexander raged.

She took hold of his wrist and attempted to free her hair. Her furious gaze locked with his and she said through clenched teeth, "Let go. Now, *Uncle*."

He released his grasp, mirroring her belligerent glare.

"I'm not one of your pupils, or a piece of music you can manipulate until it suits you. Every time I come here to visit Nicholas, you watch me." She scanned Alexander's body, her nose crinkling as though she smelled an unpleasant odor. "Leering at me. I feel your hot stare everywhere I turn. It's time you know . . . I—I love Nicholas. I'm with him. In every way. I would never even think of being with you."

Each searing word cut through Alexander. He leaned on the cane to steady himself. "How *dare* you deny me."

She folded her arms tight across her chest. "We're going away together. You'll have to find someone else to beat with your damned stick."

Alexander straightened his frame and towered over her. "Perhaps I should ask Sampte to step in here. Make you reconsider. He obeys me without question."

"Are you threatening me?"

"Take it as you may."

"You can't keep me away from Nicholas." Her voice remained firm, yet her eyes widened with apprehension. "Your scare tactics won't work on me. It's too late."

"You'll never take him from me—and you will be mine."

Voice steady and strong, she countered, "Consider us gone."

He closed the gap and pinned her against the wall, mere inches from her chest that rose and fell with rapid intakes of breath.

An abrupt knock prompted him to take a step back.

Timothy Sagan, Alexander's lesser pupil to Nicholas's talents, stepped into the room. Without a word, blue eyes glowing, a coy grin slid across the young man's face.

Elaine pressed a firm shoulder against Alexander's and freed herself. In an unsteady voice she said, "Stay away from me, you son of a bitch."

Timothy smirked at her as she ran past and slammed the door behind her.

Alexander limped to the window and looked down on the front path. After a moment, he heard another door slam and watched Elaine rush up the drive toward her car, colorful dress billowing after her. He watched her stumble into his gardener, Manuel Esteva. The man caught her and they spoke entirely too long for Alexander's liking. Manuel followed Elaine's gaze to the third floor. The two looked up at the music room window for a moment. She shook her head and pushed away from Manuel, got in her car and sped away.

Alexander waited until Elaine's silver Prius disappeared around the bend, then he turned his attention to Timothy. "You may begin."

Timothy nodded and mounted the two steps of the platform to sit behind the Steinway. He leafed through sheets

14

of music to Hummel's Sonata 5. Before he struck a single note, his hands hovered above the keyboard a full minute as he prepared to play.

Alexander settled in his red velvet chair and did his best to dismiss his longing for Elaine. He returned to the thought of how he had found Timothy performing in the minor touring circuit twelve years earlier. Impressed by the boy's memorization skills, and his fearless approach to the music, Alexander set out right away to secure the boy's talents. Timothy's nearly destitute parents reluctantly agreed to turn young Timmy over to Alexander's renowned tutelage.

Now twenty-two, Timothy's fair freckled skin and unruly red hair caused a hindrance, in Alexander's mind. The complete opposite of Nicholas's dark radiance. Alexander had often found himself strategizing how he would promote Timothy's non-traditional looks once he reached a higher level of competence, and when it came his time for exhibition.

"Don't rush the tempo this time. *Allegretto*. Play the piece as the timing is intended," Alexander said in a faraway tone. He flipped the switch to an antique metronome on the table beside him.

"She's upset you," Timothy said after a moment of studying his mentor.

"Your concern touches me."

"I try to be aware of everything you need from me."

"Then you must see that I face a troubling predicament." Alexander sighed. "There is a journey that must be made. A challenge at hand." He blazed an intense stare at Timothy. "Normally I would entrust this assignment to no one but Sampte. Nevertheless, perhaps you're better suited for this task. The matter involves my nephew, and Sampte is quite fond of him."

"Tell me what I can do," Timothy said without hesitation.

Alexander shook his head and waved his hand in a dismissive manner. Rising from his chair, he limped to the bar. "I must not burden you with my troubles," he said, splashing brandy into a snifter. "It is a family affair. You understand." Going back to sit in his chair, he motioned to the couch across from him.

Timothy rose from the piano bench and hurried to perch on the edge of the couch's cushion. Worry creased his brow as he bobbed his leg up and down. "You can trust me."

The older man watched Timothy become more eager as the seconds clicked off from the metronome. A drop of sweat ran from the younger man's sideburn to his jawbone. His evident anticipation amused Alexander.

"I haven't expressed recently how pleased I am with your progress. Your Liszt is near perfection and the Prokofiev needs little improvement. I know you have always felt jealous of Nicholas's talents in the past, and of the time I spend with him, but I need *you* now. Not Nicholas. It is your turn to prove your worth."

Timothy arced forward and Alexander knew he had piqued the young man's curiosity. He studied Timothy before continuing. "As you might have supposed, this concerns my niece. She is not an asset to Nicholas."

The pain of Elaine's involvement with Nicholas had immediately transcended to hatred for his prized pupil the moment she had spoken of their coupling. The thought of the two of them together as one sickened him. Now, he supposed, Timothy would suffice.

"Do you understand what I am saying?"

Timothy nodded.

"And what I require of you?"

"You want me to get rid of her."

Excellent. Alexander's fury again escalated when he recalled Elaine's snub. "It is too much to ask," he said, shaking his head.

"No," Timothy pleaded, nearly sliding off the seat. "Please, let me show you what I'm capable of."

Alexander took a sip of brandy and considered his pupil's offer. He knew Prokofiev was Timothy's most cherished composer, and always the unwavering pupil, the student had studied the master's works to exhaustion. Timothy needed only one more prompt from Alexander to accomplish the ultimate task required.

"Fine. Play the Toccata Opus Eleven. I want you to keep Prokofiev and his piece in mind as you compose what you are to do. Unleash all your talents and imagination."

Timothy crossed the room to the Steinway and again prepared to play.

Alexander went to him and placed a firm hand on his pupil's shoulder. Timothy's tense muscle relaxed under Alexander's palm. "As you well know by now, timing of this master's piece is as crucial as the execution."

Timothy angled his body to look up at Alexander and nodded, his eyes filling with tears.

Alexander raised the snifter. "To the challenge."

3

Nicholas found himself weary of the touring circuit. Though his passion for playing remained unquenched, and the rousing applause always provided a great high, when he returned to his empty hotel room, he missed sharing the accolades with Elaine.

While on the junior pianist circuit, Nicholas discovered the power he held over his audiences. As his mentor, Alexander made great effort to select the ideal pieces for Nicholas to awe the judges and audiences, and in turn, unnerve his competitors. Nicholas's confidence never wavered and as a result he rarely formed friendships with other musicians of his ranking. He enjoyed seeing his opponents squirm when the time came for judges to announce the winner. Rarely did he lose. Nicholas's envious colleagues shunned him because of his unsurpassed talent and systematic crushing of the competition.

Now two years into his professional career, he often found himself isolated. After a successful concert, he despised being alone. Although Alexander accompanied Nicholas on most of his travels, relishing the ovations as if they were for him, he often left Nicholas alone to join admirers after performances.

Stares in the dining room, at his table for one, kept Nicholas locked in his suite awaiting room service. During those long nights, Nicholas craved Elaine's company. Waking in the middle of the night, he desired her companionship as much as her body.

This night, at the university's Wilhoit Theatre twenty miles from Alexander's mansion, the words in Nicholas's father's journal tucked inside his tuxedo jacket rambled in his mind—as did, as always, thoughts of Elaine.

Four competitors were yet to perform, so Nicholas

decided to watch them from a different position. Walking along the offstage wings he marveled at the rigging system that consisted of twenty sets of lines. Most of the heavy stage drapes were at their highest position, which left the stage floor barren of all visuals but a grand piano and the performer sitting on the bench.

Nicholas looked up and spotted a man standing on the lowest catwalk, leaning against a railing. When the man nodded to him, Nicholas lifted his hand in greeting. Then he motioned for Nicholas to join him. Intrigued, Nicholas followed the length of the stage where he found a vertical ladder bolted to the back wall of the theatre. A circular cage enveloped the rungs. As he climbed upward, his head spun and his vision blurred. When he reached the landing of the first catwalk he swung his legs onto its platform. He pulled a handkerchief from his back pocket and wiped the grime from his hands.

Queasy from the height when he looked down, he squeezed his eyes shut. Steadying himself against the railing, he peeked out again, intrigued that he could view the performer sitting at the gleaming Steinway, as well as the full house of audience members.

With cautious footing, Nicholas approached the stagehand. "This is amazing. I've never been up here before."

"Been missing out. Best seat in the house." He clipped Nicholas on the shoulder. "Enjoy." He walked the length of the catwalk and disappeared into the shadows cast from the grid work pattern high above.

Appreciating the solitude, Nicholas thought about events of the night before. He smiled knowing he would soon be alone with Elaine. *Who knows? We may never go back.*

Remembering her excitement about their secret plan, he retraced his steps down the steep ladder, then into the darkness backstage. He tapped his breast pocket, comforted by the leather book.

From the wings, he rocked on the balls of his feet and waited for his turn to perform. Nicholas's patience ended after enduring a butchered Bach Concerto, No. 4 from an up-and-coming Russian. Unable to wait any longer, he eased to the stage manager's console and approached a stocky, older man wearing a headset, chewing on the stub of an unlit cigar.

"I'm pulling out," Nicholas told the man. "Would you tell the promoter for me?"

"You're shittin' me, right? You're up next."

"It's just an exhibition."

"Doesn't really count, right?" the stage manager said with a grin.

"Right."

"Still, your maestro's going to be pissed."

"Well, he's not here is he?" Nicholas winked and flashed the man an easy smile. "Give my slot to Sherry over there, will you?" He pointed to an anxious woman Nicholas's age playing an air keyboard. "She performs better when she doesn't have to wait so long."

The man pulled the slimy remains of the cigar from his mouth. "Why do you care?"

Nicholas rested his gaze on the pianist who had always placed second to his first place prize when they competed on the junior circuit. "She deserves it."

"Okay, kid. Good luck with the tour, huh?"

"Thanks."

Nicholas glanced at the performer on stage, then darted into the dressing room. He squinted when the brightly lit space hit his dilated eyes. He reached for his black leather duffel bag under the counter and took out the usual after-concert black wardrobe of slacks, turtleneck, socks, and Saucony running shoes. Looking at the clothes a moment he turned his attention back to his reflection of the sleek black tuxedo, tailored specifically for him during a tour in Parma, Italy.

He relished the feel of the soft giving cloth, and the way the cut of the jacket made him look. "*Stunning*," Elaine would say. Before he left that night, he had accessorized his lapel with a blood red rose from one of Alexander's prized bushes.

Sniffing the bud, he stuffed the change of clothes back into the satchel, then smoothed his sleeves. He knew Elaine would love that he had stayed dressed for her. He removed only the tie and put it in the duffel, zipped the bag shut and slung the strap across his shoulder.

He took one last satisfied look at himself in the row of mirrors surrounded by light bulbs that lined three of the walls and unhooked his black wool overcoat that hung from a rack. Anticipating the coming hours of passion and refuge, he rushed out the door.

4

Timothy Sagan stood outside the performers entrance at the rear of the Wilhoit Theatre, waiting for Nicholas to emerge. He had always been patient—an asset he knew would work in his favor when it became his time to tour in the world-class arena. As second chair, Timothy seethed inside when Alexander's favored pupil, Nicholas, received the bulk of their mentor's time and admiration. *Always after Nicholas.* He sneered, knowing if he had more attention from the maestro, he, too, could achieve greatness.

Timothy recalled the conversation with Alexander only hours earlier. He had felt his face flush when Alexander reprimanded him and thought, *This is my time. You're supposed to be attending to me now, not treating me like a novice.* When he had questioned Alexander, his mentor answered him with a glare so cold and intense Timothy had to turn away and hide his shame. Then moments later he startled when he felt a hand atop his shoulder, suddenly conflicted by Alexander's unaccustomed affection.

When Alexander instructed Timothy to rid him of his burden, he became aware that the task his maestro had composed was an opportunity not to be taken lightly. Most of all, he must not fail.

It filled him with a surge of hope that their relationship might grow beyond pupil to confidant. Love from Alexander was what Timothy craved most, and an emotion Alexander had never conveyed before that moment.

Over the years, in order to learn more about his mentor, Timothy had befriended others who once knew Alexander. During trips when Timothy traveled with Nicholas on tour, he listened silently to stories from conductors and promoters who still spoke of the greatness Alexander possessed as a pianist. Timothy listened, fascinated by the tales of

Alexander's fanfare-filled performances, always punctuated by rousing pieces and brilliant execution that thrilled all who beheld his talent. Audiences rarely witnessed such a young performer possess Alexander's command of music. These renowned men often told Timothy to consider Alexander's teaching a gift, and that he and Nicholas were privileged to be under his tutelage.

Alexander demanded world-class perfection at all times. Timothy now realized the depth and scope expected of him. *Prokofiev.* His mind spun with ideas of how to remedy his mentor's pain. Alexander and his servants were Timothy's only family and the mere thought of losing favor in Alexander's eyes terrified him.

For the first two years living in Alexander's mansion Timothy had been Alexander's sole pupil. Then Nicholas invaded their world and became the favorite student—and to Timothy's dismay—the favored child. The two boys rivaled each other for their mentor's attention from the moment Nicholas moved into the mansion.

Because of Nicholas's prowess, Alexander allowed Nicholas to practice at the Steinway in the music room six to eight hours every day and then remain in the cherished space to study composition and private schoolwork. Timothy, forced to endure training on his own, received virtually no tutelage from Alexander. He also had to settle for the Baldwin on the first floor, far from his mentor,.

Alexander often boasted of how it had taken only three years to guide young Nicholas to the height of the boy's capability, and that it took little prompting to keep him at the keyboard, practicing for hours without ceasing. In turn, the maestro had yet to utter a single encouraging word about Timothy's abilities. He still felt the sting of betrayal when Alexander decided to exhibit Nicholas as soon as the boy turned fourteen, instead of Timothy.

He worked as hard as Nicholas, but his efforts did not prove as fruitful, which caused great bouts of depression. His mastery of the piano proved *merely* near world-class standards. He had yet to achieve the caliber of a lead artist.

Nicholas excelled on all levels, whereas Timothy seemed to have remained stagnant, many times having to settle as opener for the featured pianist—more often than not, Nicholas Kalman.

Now that Nicholas had achieved fame and accolades, he was all promoters, exhibitors and audiences talked about. "It all changes tonight," Timothy muttered.

Now that his end of the task assigned by Alexander had been accomplished, Timothy decided Nicholas needed to clean up the mess. Nicholas had to be the one to get his precious hands dirty this time.

Let's see how pretty-boy handles real life, he thought as Nicholas emerged from the performers entrance, looking like a *GQ* cover model in his tuxedo and perfect hair. *Always so proud of yourself, aren't you? Well, we'll see about that once you find what I left for you.*

Timothy smiled with satisfaction as he noted Nicholas's disappointment.

"What the hell are you doing here?" Nicholas groaned.

Timothy scanned him head to toe then glanced at his watch. "You're early."

"Decided not to go on."

"What? You mean you didn't play?"

"I wasn't feeling the music tonight."

"Ah, man, the maestro's going to kill you."

Nicholas shuffled his feet and shrugged.

"And you didn't change. Alexander always wants us to wear black after a performance."

Nicholas tugged his lapel. "This is black."

"Why did you pull out?"

"I've got something more important planned."

Timothy's mouth dropped open. "More important? Does Alexander know?"

"Do you see him anywhere?" Nicholas asked, putting on his overcoat.

Timothy knew Alexander had not been happy with Nicholas's rendition of the Debussy and had refused to attend that evening's performance intended to promote

Nicholas's upcoming tour.

"Well, I'm real sorry but you'll have to postpone your plans." Timothy held out the powder blue envelope he had taken from his breast pocket.

"What's this?"

"From Alexander."

Nicholas snatched the envelope, then unfolded a matching blue sheet of paper. Timothy leaned forward, trying to look at the letter's contents.

Nicholas thinned his eyes. "Is this for you, or me?"

"Sorry. Go ahead."

Turning into the light flooding the side entrance, Nicholas read the note out loud. "Take the delivery to Henri Thibodaux. He is expecting you." He lowered the paper and mumbled, "Who the hell is Henri Thibodeaux?"

Timothy shrugged. He took a pair of black leather gloves from his coat pocket. "You'd better put these on. Alexander said not to touch her."

"What am I supposed to deliver?"

Timothy waited a beat before he answered. "I put it in your car."

Nicholas hesitated. "Look, like I said, I've got other plans. That's why I left early."

As Nicholas tried to brush past, Timothy blocked his path. "Other plans?"

"Yeah. Tell Alexander I'll make his delivery tomorrow. Maybe the day after."

"Right. You want me to tell him that?"

"Yes."

"No." Timothy shook the gloves until Nicholas grabbed them from him. "Map's on the back."

Nicholas flipped over the note and scanned the drawing. "This is way out of my way."

"It won't take long this time of night." He swept his arm the expanse of the full parking lot. "Everyone in the county seems to be here, waiting for a performance they're never going to see."

Nicholas held Timothy's glare, but did not take a step.

"You've already defied him once tonight," Timothy reminded with a tip of his head toward the theatre.

Nicholas slapped his thigh with the gloves, looking past Timothy.

"She'll wait," Timothy said in a stern voice. "I'll tell her you'll be late if you'd like."

"What are you talking about?"

"Elaine." Timothy smirked. "I know you've been screwing your cousin."

Nicholas took a threatening step closer. Timothy reared back. "Watch your mouth, asshole. And, she's not my cousin."

Timothy raised his hands in surrender. "Don't worry. I won't tell."

Nicholas shoved a glove on each hand. "Stay away from her."

Timothy chuckled as Nicholas turned and strode away. "Better get going. Henri Thibodaux's waiting. Careful now, no mistakes."

Suppressing the desire to follow his opponent, a sly grin crept to Timothy's lips.

5

Henri Thibodeaux, like his father before him, was the only private mortician for Swain County, North Carolina. His operation, located outside the city limits of Bryson City was remote and so low-bid that Henri also served as gravedigger at the cemetery adjacent to the property. He would enlist the assistance of a few schoolboys who weren't too revolted by the task. Often, he urged them into duty by chiding, *"I dare you,"* or if necessary, *"What a bunch of pussies!"* He'd make a game of it, overseeing the unearthing excursions in the dead of night. He would beguile the boys with risqué stories of women, and distant places made up of his own imagination. He seldom lacked enough troubled teens willing to help him. They seemed to like Henri, even though he spent most of his days with dead people.

Although his name sounded exotic, Henri had never ventured more than thirty miles from his home of graves and towering pines. And the women he claimed to know so much about, existed exclusively within his well-worn collection of pornography magazines.

Liquor made from his still, tucked deep in the woods behind the morgue, helped him deal with the dead spirits he swore haunted the grounds. Homegrown moonshine had been the largest staple of his diet the last several years, causing his memory to become clouded as the seasons crept by.

He shared his harsh brew with the group of boys in exchange for their strong backs. Although suspicious of Henri's oddness, the teens never betrayed him for fear of being laid to rest in the unmarked field where Henri told them an "unknown few" had been buried.

Ten years ago Henri received an anonymous call from a man requiring his services. The man spoke with a heavy accent Henri couldn't place. Times were lean and he had already buried most of the elderly citizens of the county at the time, so he reckoned, why not? He would have needed to close up shop soon if no more business came his way and he worried over what the community would do without his undertaking.

When the man quoted an ungodly amount of money for his services, Henri became wary of the situation. The caller told him to think the proposition over and hung up, leaving Henri stunned. He remained restless all night wondering if he should have taken the offer right away.

At dawn the next morning, by the time he had worked himself into a panic, convinced the man would not call him again, a messenger delivered a bulging sealed envelope. The deliveryman shifted one foot to the other, looking green from the odor of formaldehyde and disinfectant that wafted around the compound Henri could not even smell anymore. He figured the stench must be potent because no one voluntarily entered his place of business, with the exception of forced visits dearly departed families had no choice but to endure.

Eyes on the bundle, Henri signed for the package and dismissed the man with a grunt. He returned to his cracked Formica table and unwrapped the parcel. His jaw dropped as he stared at a thick wad of fifty-dollar bills. At first count, he thought there must be close to two thousand dollars stuffed inside. Henri's mouth dried up. He felt dizzy wondering where this little miracle had come from. Digging through the brown paper, he found a powder blue envelope with a hand-written note inside. Clutching a handful of money close to his chest, he read the fluid script.

> *I trust this will be enough to accomplish the task of disposal. My man will arrive shortly after midnight.*

The foreboding request concerned Henri, but he could not bring himself to return the money, even if there *had* been a return address written on the parcel.

Midnight came and went. Henri thought maybe he'd misunderstood. *Was I supposed to meet him somewhere?* He checked the note again, but no other details miraculously appeared. The man obviously knew where he lived, so he waited.

Henri dozed off around three o'clock. Soon after, his porch light exploded, the *pop* so loud he nearly fell off the couch. He stumbled to his front window to see who had trespassed on his property, but saw no one.

He flinched at an insistent knock. Hand trembling, he opened the front door a crack. Henri's eyes went wide as he took in the figure of a man more than a foot taller than him, standing in the shadows of his porch. Although wrapped in black plastic, Henri recognized the outline of a body draped over the man's shoulder.

"So, this is him? Or her?" Henri quavered.

The stranger did not respond.

"Okay, then." Henri brushed past the man and onto the path. "My shop is this way."

Standing at the cement building that served as his morgue, Henry glanced in both directions to make sure they were not being watched. He pulled a key from a rotting crevice of the doorjamb. Unbolting the lock, he waved the man inside. "I was worried you wouldn't come."

"Too many people around."

Henri recognized the same accent, but the voice sounded different than the man who had called. "Kids. Yeah, this place draws them. The graveyard and all."

He motioned to the stainless steel table in the middle of the room. The man carefully laid the body down. Withdrawing a twenty-dollar bill from his pocket, he handed the money to Henri. "I found it necessary to break your light." Then he turned and without another word walked out of the morgue.

"A man who always pays his debts. My father would have liked that about you," Henri called out after the man who had disappeared into the darkness.

He shut the door, secured the deadbolt, then settled his

nerves with a long pull from a jug he kept hidden in a cabinet. Five gulps later he set the container aside and took the few steps to his new assignment. He removed the thick plastic covering and stared at the corpse. Henri sighed, relieved that he didn't recognize the dead man.

Snapping on a pair of industrial plastic gloves, he tugged a rolling cart topped with surgical instruments closer. It had been nearly six months since he had performed an autopsy and he decided this anonymous man would be good practice for him. He always felt bad violating the people he had known, but he had no emotional ties to the stranger. He could cut into this body without remorse.

Focused now, he began to drain the fluids from the body and drained more from his jug while he waited. The moonshine loosened his taut muscles and soon his panic and unease lifted enough to notice heavy bruising on the man's upper arms.

Henri took up a scalpel and sliced a Y pattern from the man's clavicles to his groin, then pulled back the skin. After cutting away the ribcage, he removed the internal organs one by one. He noted that the man's liver weighed close to twelve pounds, and figured the man must have been a heavy drinker who died naturally from liver failure. The clear liquor from his still came to his mind and a warning flashed for him not to enjoy his own home brew too much.

The discovery made him feel more comfortable. At first he feared the man had been murdered and he would be faced with the burden of hiding a crime for the rest of his life.

As Henri finished with the procedure, something caught his eye. Dread filled the pit of his stomach. Aiming the light at the dead man's face, he lifted the corpse's head by the chin.

An indention on the victim's throat the size of a quarter had blued its impression in the skin. Although Henri tried to convince himself the man had died from a failed liver, experience told him otherwise.

"His windpipe's been crushed," he mumbled, horrified by his discovery. Now, the bruising on the man's arms made sense to him. *Someone must have held him down while another strangled him with something.*

Blood rushed from his head as he stumbled to a nearby stool. Sweat studded his brow. *Should I call the cops?* First, he thought of his beloved still. Then he remembered the package bursting with money, the hulking figure with a corpse draped over his shoulder as if it weighed nothing, the creepy voice on the phone. The man lying before him had met a murderous fate. Henri didn't dare tempt the same outcome.

He buried the anonymous man along with his extracted organs in an unmarked grave, far away from the dignified residents of his hallowed graveyard. He convinced himself he would learn to live with his part of the crime and decided that if his unknown client ever contacted him again he would fervently turn the man away.

As time went on, legitimate business grew worse. He couldn't refuse when the dollar amounts increased. Over the last ten years Henri had buried a dozen victims, delivered in the dead of night, in the unmarked field.

Now Henri alternated his drunken gaze from the picture window in the front room of his house, to the door, then to the telephone. Two hours ago he had received another call from the foreigner. A customer would be dropped off for Henri to attend to later that night. He eased the grimy drape open an inch and peered out at nothing but blackness.

Tipping the ever-present jug to his lips, he chugged until his eyes burned. He swiped a hand across his mouth and considered not answering the inevitable knock on the door calling him to service. But he needed the money and he knew he would not—could not—turn away the responsibility that had become so burdensome on his soul.

He settled on the couch, clutched the cool glass container to his chest, and waited. He uttered a prayer for forgiveness, apologized for the thousandth time to his dead father, and slid into a drunken slumber.

6

Nicholas jogged through the nearly full parking lot of the Wilhoit Theatre. Mist settled among the vehicles, muting their colors. Earlier that night, fearing scratches and dents in his prized jet black Porsche Targa, he had parked at the farthest space at the end of the row. Nearing his vehicle now, he glanced over his shoulder to see if Timothy followed.

He puzzled over Timothy's insistence that he wear the gloves. The ominous warning replayed in his mind. *Her? Did he say not to touch . . . her?*

Nicholas never liked Timothy. He annoyed Nicholas with his habits. The way Timothy would concentrate, sometimes up to three minutes before he laid a finger on the keyboard, or would sit on the edge of the bench eternally awaiting Alexander's approval after he concluded each composition. Even as a boy Timothy would do anything to please Alexander, which sickened Nicholas who felt mastering the piece to perfection should be the reward, not Alexander's fawning.

Reaching his vehicle, Nicholas noticed the alarm light wasn't flashing on the console. He tried the door handle and found the car unlocked. *Nothing is mine*, he thought bitterly. He looked back to challenge Timothy for breaking into his car, but saw no one else in the lot.

A dim glow from the dome light bathed the cramped interior in soft blue. He tossed the duffel bag into the miniscule rear compartment and realized the passenger seat had been shoved back to its farthest position. His attention went to an oversized, stuffed canvas laundry bag on the floor in front of the seat.

Intrigued, he slid behind the wheel and tugged at the thick muslin, then placed a gloved palm on top of the object. Feeling resilience, he jerked his hand away. *Oh my God, is it a body?*

Scrambling out of the car, he pulled Alexander's note out of his pocket. Rereading it, he wondered again about Henri Thibodeaux. Flipping the paper over, he traced the route leading to the unfamiliar location with his finger.

He craned his neck and looked for Timothy again. His heart pounded as he forced his breath to a slower pace.

Nicholas felt a sudden shift in his life. He stood still, counting his heartbeats, reminding himself to breathe. Fearful, horrified, yet intrigued, he knew he must look in the bag.

He strode to the passenger side, searching both directions to be certain no one watched him. Fog enveloped the cars giving them the appearance of hulking beasts. He heard nothing but the buzz from an overhead light. Glancing at his watch, he presumed half an hour remained before the concert would end. There would be no intrusions.

Opening the passenger door, the faint light lit the cloth just enough to make out the body's outline. Bending into the car, he unwound the knot that tied the sack shut.

Swallowing his nerves, he pulled the bag down over the body's head. Long strands of hair emerged. He realized it was a woman and fought down the bile rising in his throat.

Why would someone kill her? Why would Alexander put my career in jeopardy? If I get caught with a dead body I'll be arrested. The thought of Timothy and his ominous words of warning to be careful entered Nicholas's spinning mind. *That bastard's got to be involved.*

The woman's mass of tangled, blonde hair cascaded over her face. The top of the dress she wore, made of soft cloth with a colorful flower print pattern, looked familiar. A breath halted in his chest.

No. It can't be . . .

He didn't have the courage to look at her closely, so he repositioned the body, then dragged the cloth sack beyond her shoulders.

The sweet scent of gardenias and rosewater hit him with blunt force. His gut churned, a lump formed in his throat, strangling his whimper.

Mind racing, he swept the hair from the corpse's face. He cupped her head in his hands and bent inches from her. Blood slammed to his brain, ringing in his ears deafened him. He managed to utter a guttural growl.

God, no, not Elaine. The one person he trusted completely. She, who had unselfishly relished his triumphs and filled his days and nights with excitement and passion.

He could do nothing but stare at her beautiful, porcelain face, now turned ashen, expressionless. She had been his salvation. He mourned every time they were apart, rejoiced once they reunited. He would never see her again, be with her, love her.

Nicholas wrapped his shaking arms around Elaine's body and rocked her. Tears coursed down his cheeks. He mumbled her name again and again. After a long time, he lifted her from the tumble on the floor, swept the bag from her body and crumpled the cloth into a ball at her feet. Placing her carefully in a seated position on the passenger seat, he smoothed her hair and took her limp head in his hands. He kissed his lover's waxen forehead and released her limp body. Pulling the seat belt tight, he snapped her securely in place.

His entire body shook as he shut the door, then paced in front of the car and raked his hands through his hair. Thoughts of retribution filled his raging mind. Vows of revenge rocked the core of his being. He opened his arms and lifted his head to the misty sky. A wail of anguish emitted from deep inside him, rising in intensity until he expelled no more sound. He thrust himself forward and crashed his fists down on the hood of the Porsche.

The cacophony of sound echoed throughout the parking lot, mixing with his strangled sobs.

7

Timothy sat in the black Mercedes-Benz S-class sedan Sampte used to run errands and chauffeur Alexander. Hidden from view, he had parked behind a row of ancient oak trees across from the mouth of the Wilhoit Theatre's parking lot entrance.

He cranked up the volume to the sound system when Liszt's *Mephisto Waltz* eased toward the crescendo eight minutes and two seconds into the piece. The music aroused him as he lit a cigarette and reveled in the knowing of what must be Nicholas's undoing right this moment.

It took the time to finish the entire smoke before Timothy saw Nicholas's Porsche gun toward him and fishtail out of the lot and then onto the slick road.

I wish I could have been there to see his face when he found her. God, I would have loved that.

He smiled a wicked grin, fired up the engine and tossed the butt out the window.

Nicholas's vehicle remained at the stop sign up the street a full minute. Then the engine gunned and the left blinker flashed on and off.

Timothy frowned. The instructions on the note were clearly to drive south. The car's indicator blinked Nicholas's intent to turn the opposite direction.

He leaned closer to the windshield and a trail of oily sweat skidded down the middle of his back. "Where the hell are you going?"

* * *

As the Porsche rumbled its readiness at the stop sign, questions raced through Nicholas's frantic mind. *Where can I take Elaine where she'll be safe? I can't go to the police, they'll think I killed her*. The thought of law enforcement's involvement before he had a clear explanation of Elaine's demise terrified him.

He mentally skipped from one possible location to another. It was automatic for him to turn right out of the parking lot instead of left as Alexander instructed in the note Timothy had given him. Right, headed toward home. He broke the instinct to turn that way.

Why would Alexander want me to take her to Thibodeaux's? Who is this man anyway? Maybe I should go there. But that's what Alexander wants. Did Alexander think I wouldn't look in the bag? Be like Timothy, never questioning his demands? Maybe this man Thibodeaux has something to do with Elaine's death. Maybe it's a trap.

Another thought horrified him. *Maybe I'm next.*

A passage from his father's journal slammed to his mind.

> *I always believed I chose the life I'd led. Although my decisions may not have been figured out completely, I thought they were mine to make. Now I see how wrong that observation was. Actually, everything to this very day has been carefully laid out by some overpowering force. Every move and thought I have made has led me to this spot, watching this very plan slowly evolve and blossom into my soul.*

Nicholas felt certain his father must have faced a predicament paralleling his own right now. Stopped at a crossroads, Nicholas pondered his decision. Placing a hand on Elaine's shoulder, he wept at her coldness. Then he remembered their plan to go to the country home. As a child, he often felt it was the only place he had ever been truly safe. He slid the car into first gear and turned onto the narrow two-lane highway.

From time to time, he glanced at the lifeless body next to him as he drove the winding, desolate mountain road. Tears filled his eyes, blurring the road ahead.

Clutching the steering wheel, his fury surged. He forced Elaine from his thoughts and concocted a plan.

8

Timothy anticipated that the chore of disposing of Elaine would elevate him in Alexander's esteem—that he would become the favored pupil as well as the single person Alexander could rely upon to take care of whatever needed to be accomplished. No matter how unpleasant the request. He had worried at first over the task regarding Elaine, but with shrewd deliberation, what evolved turned out to be so simple.

Only two hours earlier, Timothy merely went to Elaine's dorm room and explained to her how Nicholas had taken ill and that he needed her right away. He recalled how worried she became, rushing after Timothy to his car. Her insistent questions did not cease until he delivered her to Alexander's mansion.

Now, as Timothy drove the powerful Mercedes along the weaving mountain road after Nicholas, he remembered the words his mentor would often chide him with. *"Fingering and memorization mean nothing without passion."*

Whenever he dared to protest, Alexander would insist he stretch his imagination. *"Your mind lives in a box, Timothy. You must open this box in order to embrace any talent you possess."*

When Timothy came up with the idea to let Nicholas dispose of Elaine, Timothy trembled with excitement—convinced Alexander would find the plan to be brilliant, a composition all his own. He glowed with pride, no longer locked within the box.

Soon after he had come to live with and learn from Alexander, he discovered how manipulative the older man could be. That he knew all about mind games. His mentor often professed great knowledge of what it took to win in competition and life.

Timothy felt snubbed whenever Alexander reveled over how uncommon Nicholas's amazing dexterity and memorization skills were in a virtually untrained ten-year-old. Timothy had been jealous of Nicholas at first sight. The younger, sharp featured, dark-haired boy showed more natural talent, and Timothy seethed with envy.

Alexander provided Nicholas with a piano long before he convinced the boy's mother to transfer guardianship to Alexander's sister, Aranka. From the first day Nicholas stepped into the mansion, Timothy's needs became secondary.

The first year Timothy came to live with Alexander, he overheard a conductor friend of Alexander's inquire about Nicholas's mother.

"Whatever became of Teresa Hunt?" asked the smug Swede.

"Ah yes, Charles Hunt's elusive wife," Alexander had said.

"I recall her being refined and, oh, so aloof. I don't believe she's ever deigned to attend a single conductor's soirees. She's quite unsuited to be a performer's wife, wouldn't you agree?"

"Absolutely. She refuses to mingle with Charles's contemporaries and fans. Even refuses to join him on tour."

"Disgraceful."

"Indeed. I've no idea of her whereabouts." Alexander said, lifting his snifter of brandy.

Alexander did not tell this man that with Charles gone, he had forged a relationship with Teresa. Timothy knew this after catching the two embracing in a dark stairwell of the mansion. His maestro's murmurs of passion, replied by her moans, had aroused Timothy as he imagined the caresses on his own skin.

He had discovered from another of Alexander's acquaintances that Alexander even considered making his relationship with Teresa legal. But Timothy knew the truth after overhearing Alexander tell Sampte he didn't want the woman. He only wanted the boy.

"Teresa will remain in Nicholas's life only until the boy is comfortable living here," Timothy overheard Alexander tell Aranka. "It's best to distract him from her presence when she is here. She will need things and I will provide them, but be aware, her time is short with him. She has discussed leaving once she's unburdened from the boy. Start preparing Nicholas for her departure."

Timothy had learned that Teresa's long-lost husband, Charles Ian Hunt, left what most people thought a fortune to her. But over the years Teresa had developed expensive tastes in furniture, clothing, and other luxuries. She spent the remainder of Charles's earnings with flourish. Soon, her carelessness led her into Alexander's firm grasp. Once Alexander and Teresa's liaison was established, Alexander tended to Nicholas's needs. Alexander assured Teresa that any earnings Nicholas received from his competitions and exhibitions would remain in a personal trust fund, established for his training and the cultivation of his talents.

Alexander proved an exemplary provider. With Teresa's penchant for nice things, it took little prompting to tempt her to his bed. Once this had been accomplished, Alexander began mentoring Nicholas. Soon, Alexander entered young Nicholas into the most elite juvenile competitions on the touring circuit. Timothy believed in his heart, though his tutelage was all but forgotten, that Alexander had not abandoned him.

Although Timothy cherished any time his maestro gave him, he feared the man as well. Their sessions captivated Timothy, leaving him full of delight and wonder at the depth and knowledge of music the man possessed. He also looked forward to the occasional duets he shared with Nicholas. His confidence soared when he capably matched Nicholas's phrasing and fingering. He thrilled at showing off these talents to Alexander. The biggest drawback during these practices had been the outrage the maestro often exhibited.

"You claim your desire to be the best of the best?" Alexander would ask. Calm questions would escalate to shouting, punctuated by the shattering of a glass thrown

across the room, or a vase exploding due to a swift blow from his cane. His rage rising to a crescendo, he would roar, "*Prove it to me!*"

Alexander often used harsh words and was not always fair in the assessment of Timothy's skills, and yet, Timothy knew that with every instruction, he grew as a performer and a man. Alexander never allowed failure to enter Timothy's mind.

Both boys often lived with their mentor's wrath. At times his rages lasted days. Timothy dealt with Alexander's mood swings as best he could. If Nicholas could be unflinching during one of Alexander's flailing tantrums, so could he. At least he could try.

Timothy's composition of tonight's fate would prove his devotion—that he was capable of anything his mentor demanded. He reached for the stereo and turned up the volume on Rachmaninoff's Sonata No. 2, Op. 36., sweeping away any apprehension. He smiled, relishing the music and the superior position he now held over Nicholas.

Puzzled by Nicholas's disobeying the instructions on the blue note paper Timothy had forged, he decided not to take any chances. Careful not to advance too close, he raced up the mountainous highway and chased Nicholas's Porsche.

After a few more miles, Timothy realized Nicholas must be headed for Alexander's country house, but he had never driven to the secluded location and had no idea where the turnoff was. He no longer spotted flashes of red taillights through the trees.

He sped along the treacherous road and cursed himself for losing Nicholas. Screeching to a halt, he performed a three-point turn and backtracked to where he thought he had lost sight of the Porsche.

He glanced at the GPS unit built into the dash. He figured Sampte probably had the directions loaded into the device, but Timothy had no idea how to operate the contraption.

Inching ahead, he scanned both sides of the road, but found no break in the thick forest where there could be a tributary.

He noticed a cut in the shoulder of the two-lane wide enough to park and rolled to a stop. Overgrowth of enormous kudzu-covered towering pines loomed above.

He slapped the steering wheel over and over, his curses deafening him inside the confines of the Mercedes. Spent, frustrated and pissed off, all he could do was hope Nicholas would eventually come back this way.

In case luck turned in his favor, he unrolled the window to hear the rumble of the Porsche. A blast of cold air stung his left cheek. Although dressed in layers of clothing and wrapped in an oilcloth duster, Timothy shivered as he inhaled the air pungent with sap. He beat his arms with cold fingers and regretted giving Nicholas his gloves.

Hands shaking, he lit a cigarette, then pulled the silver flask hidden in his jacket and took a swig. Both vices were forbidden by the strict Alexander, and Timothy felt a little guilty. Nevertheless, he took another sip.

The liquor burned a hot trail from his throat to his stomach, immediately settling his nerves. He felt content. And patient. He thinned his lips and convinced himself Nicholas would appear again soon. All he had to do was wait. Not a problem. He'd been doing that very thing for years. He could wait all night if necessary.

9

Nicholas had maneuvered from the highway onto a dirt road almost completely obstructed by overgrowth. He had driven the same route many times during his secret excursions in the sports car.

He drove along the narrow, rutted tree-lined drive that led to Alexander's country home. Frost crystallized on an open field. Eerie fog filtered through the bare limbs hanging low along the roadway.

Nicholas's nerves calmed slightly as the outline of the house grew closer. The two-story house, settled on fifty remote acres deep in the forest surrounded by smells of pine and juniper, conjured memories of childhood summers he and Elaine had shared exploring the grounds.

The landscape looked different with oak trees barren of leaves. Everything appeared bigger and somewhat foreboding.

Taking the final curve, he turned into the circular driveway and parked close to the front steps of the house. His attention fell on Elaine and fresh tears burned his eyes.

Gathering courage, he reached for a flashlight tucked behind the seat and climbed out of the car. He studied the structure where, as children, he and Elaine spent every hour of daylight hiding in the rustic rooms and playing in the surrounding forest.

His ease evaporated as horrible feelings flooded over him. Ever since discovering the awful secrets in his father's journal his life had been damned. And the horror of finding Elaine's dead body cemented his dread. His next objective would be to orchestrate the questions he would ask Alexander. He knew he should probably go to the police instead, but he needed to get the answers he hoped would calm his screaming soul from the mentor he also called

Uncle.

Convinced of his decision to keep Elaine in this familiar, safe place until he confronted his mentor, he ran up the steps to the porch and reached into a crumbling terra cotta urn full of crusted potting soil. Cursing the inhibitive feel of the gloves, he fished a key from the pot and wiped the brass against his thigh, stuck it into the lock, opened the front door, then hurried back to the car.

He took a deep breath and let it out slowly as he opened the door. Lifting Elaine from the seat, he was startled by how heavy she seemed. He remembered the saying: dead weight. Pushing the thought aside, he stumbled up the steps to the front porch. He also noticed that her limbs seemed to be stiffening. A morbid forensics television show he once watched at his aunt Aranka's house came to his mind. He recalled the doctor stating it normally took seven to ten hours for a body to fall into complete rigor. Having no idea how long Elaine had been dead, he knew he needed to move quickly.

He also knew he wouldn't be able to carry her far in his arms, so he eased her atop his shoulder and balanced her weight. Shuffling into the foyer, he reached for the flashlight in his rear pocket and snapped it on, bathing the room in its halogen beam. He noticed that everything remained the same as when he had helped Sampte winterize the estate six months earlier. White sheets covered the furniture. Thick drapes were drawn shut. The surroundings seemed uninviting, yet comforting at the same time.

As he approached the staircase at the far end of the entry, he heard only his heartbeat thudding in his ears and his feet grating on the wooden steps. His breath rasped, causing a faint cloud to drift from his mouth. He chose not to think of these distractions, or of Elaine's cumbersome body. "First finish this task, then think of the next," he told himself.

Reaching the top step, muscles straining, he staggered down the long narrow hallway to the last door. He turned the doorknob to the bedroom that had been his whenever he visited. Puffs of clouds expelled from his mouth as he entered the freezing room.

He scanned the sparse furnishings with the flashlight. A large leather trunk sat at the foot of a king-size, four-poster bed. An immense, walnut armoire stood against the far wall.

A three-quarter moon cast eerie shadows from a massive tree branch outside the window. White silk sheers on the windows billowed into the room. Shards of broken glass were scattered on the floor below the window ledge, its jagged edges glinting in the moonlight. A lifeless form lay in the middle of the clutter.

Easing closer, Nicholas barely recognized the bloated body of a dead raccoon. Revulsion rose up in his chest. He winced at the sight and stuffed his nose and mouth into the crook of his arm to lessen the stench.

Side-stepping the animal, he carried Elaine to the antique armoire. An elaborately scrolled brass key protruded from the lock. He turned the antique key and opened the full-length double doors.

He gaped at the man reflected in the mirrors hanging inside both doors, looking frantic and harried, burdened with a woman's body draped over his shoulder. The shock of his own vision threw him back into reality. The otherworldly circumstances that surrounded him were his alone to deal with.

Staring at the image that looked like the ghost of himself, he struggled with what he knew he must do. He placed Elaine into the empty cabinet, gently arranging her in a seated position. He smoothed her dress and brushed the hair from her face, tears flowing as he caressed her cheek.

He went to the bed and swept off the thin coverlet, then tucked the throw protectively around her and bid his beloved goodbye.

Hands trembling, he closed the double doors of the armoire, locked the cabinet, then tucked the antique key under his glove until it settled into the palm of his sweating hand.

Nicholas shuddered, his mind racing as he backed away from the cabinet that now entombed Elaine. Bumping into·

the opposite wall, he slid down the smooth surface to sit on the cold hardwood floor.

The raccoon caught his attention and a memory came to him of the summer he had turned thirteen—the first time he had been exposed to death and killing.

Alexander had awakened him late one full-moon night and asked if he wanted to accompany him and Timothy hunting. Nicholas puzzled over the invitation. He didn't even know his uncle hunted. He assumed the stuffed animals displayed throughout the country home were for show.

Excited to be included, Nicholas said yes and pulled on the neatly folded clothes at the foot of his bed. Running past Elaine's door, he wondered if he should brag to her. No, he decided he better wait until later. He'd never killed anything before and he didn't want to look like a coward if he couldn't go through with it.

Nicholas met Alexander and Timothy outside. Dressed head to toe in black, boots laced to their knees, they both carried crossbows. Timothy petted his weapon like he would a kitten, a spooky grin curving his mouth. Apprehensive about weapons, Nicholas waved away Alexander's offer of one for himself.

Nicholas followed the two into the blackest part of the dense woods beyond the country house. Always surprised by how fast Alexander moved given his extreme limp, Nicholas struggled to keep up.

Alexander and Timothy communicated in a silent short-hand, using only movements from their crossbows and nods of the head.

Timothy proved proficient with his weapon and marked three kills that night, Alexander, five. Nicholas wondered why they didn't take any of the possums and raccoons with them. Instead, they left the carcasses to rot in the next day's hot summer sun. He thought the point of hunting was for food.

It sickened him, knowing Alexander found the act of killing to be sport. He ran from the two and fell to his knees at the edge of the clearing. Timothy's laughter rumbled under the sounds of Nicholas's retching.

Alexander and Timothy joined the panting Nicholas and rested, taking sips from their canteens. Nicholas batted away Alexander's offer for a drink.

The call of a great horned owl echoed in the stillness, a noise so loud Nicholas shuddered. In one fluid movement, Alexander pulled out a semi-automatic pistol from a shoulder holster hidden by his coat. Its shining barrel and pearl-handle grip glowing in the moonlight captivated Nicholas.

"My father commissioned this gun from the finest gunsmith in West Germany," Alexander told Nicholas in a low voice. "He presented it to me as a gift when I was your age." The way Alexander caressed the etched barrel with his fingertip made Nicholas shiver, not from the cold. "Someday this will be yours."

Alexander took a shooter's stance, sweeping one of the pines with his drawn pistol. He trained the gun to where the bird perched on a high branch, surveying them.

Nicholas wanted to call out, warn the owl. He thought surely it had to be bad luck to kill something so regal, so ominous, but he did not utter a sound.

Alexander took aim and pulled the trigger. The thunderous hollow crack reminded Nicholas of the sound a pine tree made right before swooshing to the ground after it had been sawed. The explosion drove sleeping birds out of their nests. Small animals scurried in the underbrush.

The owl, large as a small child, tumbled from the sky and thudded on the ground.

Timothy raised his fists in victory and whooped in excitement. Nicholas's hands flew to his ringing ears. He shut his eyes, blocking out the horror.

As Alexander strode to admire his kill, he noticed Nicholas didn't follow. "You're one of us now," Alexander said, his voice echoing in the eerie night air.

"I didn't kill anything," Nicholas said, his entire body trembling.

Alexander tucked the pistol back into its holster. "It isn't always in the doing."

Alexander's ominous words rang in Nicholas mind as he shook himself out of the memory. He sat in the same position on the floor across from the armoire for a long while, his mind and strength spent. Eyes locked to the closed cabinet, he got up and crossed the room. Placing a hand on the cabinet's door, he patted it several times. Then he ran through the doorway, down the hall and leapt down the stairs two at a time. He raced to the front door and burst through it.

The brisk air revived him and brought his senses alive. Filling his lungs until they burned, he raked shaking hands through his hair.

Knowing he must be careful not to make any mistakes now, he replayed his movements and noted them to memory. He took the key from the front door's lock and replaced it in the flowerpot.

Going to his car, he felt reluctant to leave. He looked up at the second story window of the room where he prayed Elaine would be safe. He clenched his fists and again vowed to avenge her death.

He slipped behind the wheel and slammed the door shut, struggling to keep his terror in check. Recognizing a floral fragrance clinging to his clothes, he drew his lapel to his nose and breathed Elaine's scent deep into his lungs. Fresh pain stabbed his heart.

Focusing his efforts on stilling his trembling hands, he fired the Porsche's engine, took one more look at the house, threw the car in gear and fled into the still night.

Racing down the winding road, he muttered, "You want to play games, Uncle? Okay, we'll play games."

10

Nicholas maneuvered the tight curves of the desolate highway. He swept his glove-covered hand across his face to clear his vision blurred by tears and sweat.

The sharp sting of the armoire's antique key under the glove cut into his palm, keeping the thought of Elaine fresh in his mind. He remembered her smiles intended only for him. Looks shared, knowing their meaning without words. The light dancing in her gray eyes, gleaming like silver pearls. The last vision of her in the armoire obliterated all of his pleasant feelings. He clutched the steering wheel and accelerated to a speed that made him feel queasy.

He took the switchback curves well over the speed limit, the Porsche roaring past the pines lining one side of the highway. The engine's rumble bounced off the rushing current of the Nantahala river far below.

He worked over in his mind what he would say when he encountered his mentor. The thought of Alexander masterminding the tragedy of Elaine's death entered Nicholas's mind again. He understood Timothy putting Nicholas's career in jeopardy in order to eliminate a threat—but what would Alexander gain?

Could Alexander have found out about Elaine and him? They were always so careful, never daring to venture near Alexander's personal wing on the third floor. They even deemed the kitchen off limits when they were together. Elaine never stayed overnight. *Until last night*, Nicholas remembered with dread.

He put aside his uncle's possible involvement and focused his rage on Timothy. After all, his rival put Elaine's body in the car. Certainly, Timothy would do anything to acquire advantage in Alexander's eyes. It must have been Timothy. With this knowledge burning in his mind, he turned up the volume on the CD player. A classic Gustav Holst piece burst from the speakers. The *vivace* tempo caught him by surprise. He thought, how appropriate the title of the composition: *Mars, The Bringer Of War.*

Downshifting, he concentrated on the road's tricky curves. Out of nowhere, another pair of headlights approached the rear of Nicholas's car. The high beams reflected and winked in the rearview and side mirrors. He slowed, squinting to see the road ahead.

The bright lights burned white dots into his pupils, and swayed in the air in front of him. Annoyed, Nicholas pushed the window-down button, stuck his arm out the window and covered the side-view mirror. The glare in his rearview made it difficult to see the road ahead. His vehicle drifted into the oncoming lane.

A car approaching from the opposite direction, blaring its horn, aimed itself directly in Nicholas's path.

"Jesus!"

He banked the wheel hard and hit the brakes. Two wheels slid in the roadside gravel. The Porsche came to a halt alongside the guardrail. The driver continued to blast his horn as he sped past. The car behind Nicholas veered around him, raced ahead, and disappeared beyond the bend.

He took deep breaths, forcing himself to relax. Pulling back onto the highway, he kept a prudent speed as he rounded the next curve. Grateful for a straightaway, his nerves settled a bit.

Another car came around the bend, hi-beams blazing. The driver veered into Nicholas's lane and barreled toward the Porsche. Nicholas gasped and flashed his high beams.

The two cars played chicken from one lane to the other, racing head-on toward each other. Nicholas swerved to the shoulder and skidded in the loose scree.

Nicholas's eyes flicked to the rearview mirror. The other vehicle zoomed past and continued up the highway, its taillights a red blur.

The Porsche fishtailed in the dirt, momentarily paralleling the guardrail, then crashed through the barrier before it nosedived off the road. The car slammed against a rock and the airbags exploded, then deflated seconds later as the vehicle continued its descent.

His screams filled the tiny compartment as the car careened down the steep embankment, ripping saplings and ground cover from their roots. The Porsche struck a boulder, the impact causing the driver's door to pop open. Having forgotten to fasten his seatbelt, Nicholas tumbled out.

At last, the Porsche came to a halt at the river's edge. The front tires sank into the quagmire, the grill and front-end crushed, windshield shattered. Puzzle pieces of glass from the burst passenger's window tinkled as they scattered onto the seat. Nothing but silence followed.

11

Minutes later, Timothy snapped twigs underfoot and struggled through overgrowth, following the Porsche's path of destruction. He struggled through the forest's thick growth, down the treacherous embankment. Halfway to the river's edge, he swept a flashlight over the area and settled the beam of light on the destroyed vehicle below. He smiled when the Porsche lurched, then slid into the raging Nantahala River. Taken into the current, the car floated downstream. After less than a minute the dark mass disappeared from the light of the moon.

After bidding a silent *adieu* to his despised opponent, Timothy fought his way up the steep slope. Reaching the idling Mercedes, his distorted reflection in the dark tinted window caught him by surprise. The psychotic glint in his eye excited him. Adrenaline raced through his body as he struggled to calm his rushed breathing.

As Timothy pulled onto the road, his only regret was not being able to revel in the sight of Nicholas's lifeless face, as he had Elaine's. He so wanted to witness Nicholas's corpse sitting in the car next to his beloved Elaine.

His mission now accomplished, Timothy couldn't wait to receive the proud welcome Alexander would issue him. But Timothy's elation soon plummeted. He needed to provide proof that Elaine had been disposed of—Alexander would demand that. Unfortunately, everything had gone down river with the car, including Elaine. Now he could only hope that neither Alexander, nor Sampte, would contact Henri Thibodeaux to confirm delivery of Elaine's body. He would have to convince them that the task had been completed. He knew if he couldn't pull off his persuasion, he too would wind up as dead as the two lovers.

*   *   *

Thrown from the Porsche, Nicholas lie motionless in a heap, settled atop a pile of dead pine needles and leaves, barely aware of his surroundings. The roar of the river surged no more than twenty feet below. Taking inventory of his wounds, he felt a warm path of blood trickle down the length of his face.

The distinct smell of pinesap awakened his senses. Half cognizant, his thoughts wandered. Flashes of memories snapped in his mind: the scar that zigzagged the inside of Elaine's left ankle, the feel of cool piano keys on his fingertips as he played Chopin's Waltz in C-sharp Minor No. 2, the essence of ancient sheet music. Elaine's smile.

12

Alexander's endless evening came and went. As he had sternly taught the virtue of obedience to his two boys, he had not been alarmed by Timothy's disappearance without a word of progress throughout the night. He took pleasure in being Maestro and knew Timothy's task mustn't be measured in time. Therefore, he waited alone in his music room.

The phone rang shortly after midnight, rousing Alexander from his musing.

"Dammit, Kalman, why didn't Nicholas perform tonight?" the voice barked across the line. "I had a house full of high dollar patrons and let me tell you, they were not at all amused. He may be the best pianist I've ever booked, but this is beyond unprofessional."

"Whatever are you talking about?" Alexander asked.

"Your boy! Why did he leave early? Do you realize the financial jeopardy you've put me in if refunds are demanded for the tickets?"

Alexander pondered the man's disturbing revelation a moment. "My apologies, Ashton. We've been attending to poor Nicholas for hours. A bout of food poisoning. Something you left for him to nibble on in your greenroom, no doubt."

"Sick? I only heard he'd left without explanation. This looks bad, Kalman. Very bad." The man on the other line stumbled over his words. "I've been here hours calming some of the audience members you promised Nicholas would greet."

"Offer them an exclusive performance by my protégé at my private residence if you must."

A long silence followed, then the promoter responded, "That's quite generous of you, Maestro. I'm sure they'll all accept."

"Fine then." Alexander hung up before the other man could say another irritating word.

Sampte entered carrying a covered tray. "You should eat, Master."

"Anything from Timothy?" he asked, ignoring Sampte's urging.

Sampte set the tray on the table next to Alexander's chair. "Nothing. Shall I go looking for him?"

"I've been informed that Nicholas did not perform tonight. Do you know anything of this?"

"No, sir. Zardos dressed him in his tuxedo. I assumed—"

"Send for him immediately."

"He's not here." Sampte stiffened. "Do you think he knows about Elaine?"

Always with your worries. So typical of our Hungarian heritage, Alexander thought, but answered Sampte with silence.

His mind turned to the past. Once Alexander's father had begun living comfortably in America, he employed "foreigners" because he had been told they would be forever grateful as long as they were kept well fed and boarded, but to be careful not to pay them enough money so they may decide to bring their meddlesome families from the old countries.

"Foreigner," in his father's regard, defined anyone not living in America for more than one full generation. Alexander always thought this odd since his elder had not been able to secure passage to the United States for his family until Alexander had turned eight-years-old.

In the old country, Alexander's father learned of a prominent music promoter visiting from the United States. He had lured the man to attend a concert where Alexander performed. The reception of delighted, normally reserved audience members, and even dispassionate judge's reactions to young Alexander impressed the promoter. Everyone, it seemed, found the lovely flaxen-haired boy appealing, not only to listen to, but to watch as well. "Such innocence," they proclaimed. Tears filled women's eyes as they watched the crippled boy stagger and limp toward the piano.

Before the show that night Alexander's father had whispered in his ear before taking the stage, "*Stumble before you reach the bench.*"

He did as his father instructed. The patrons gasped as Alexander lurched toward the Bösendorfer, then recovered as he reached the bench. He bowed with flourish and seated himself regally at the grand piano. He heard titters of laughter from the crowd, amused by his little legs swaying, unable to reach the pedals. Their amusement ended when he began to play.

The promoter saw a glimmer of financial promise and signed a deal with Alexander's father that very night.

Many years after his father passed away Alexander found out from Sampte that his father had threatened the promoter's life if he did not find a way to bring Alexander to America to perform. When Alexander heard this bit of information, he merely smiled.

"*Why does this amuse you?*" Sampte had asked when he told Alexander of the revelation.

Alexander answered with a swipe of his cane to the insubordinate servant's shoulder.

In the years that followed, Sampte had not dared to mention the past again.

A curious grin now settled upon Alexander's face as he remembered his father's devious, yet effective, ways. Alexander laid a light hand on Sampte's forearm.

His servant's eyebrows knitted together. "It would have been better left to me."

"It's time Timothy proved his worth."

"Is there anything I can do?"

"Make yourself available to clean up his mess."

Sampte nodded then left Alexander to his waiting. He ignored the tray of food, only leaving his chair to replenish the brandy glass again and again until daylight broke.

13

Mid-morning the following day, Timothy stood in the open doorway of Alexander's music room. Silently he watched his mentor sitting in his favorite chair, staring across the room at nothing. A snifter of brandy in his hand rested on the overstuffed arm.

Timothy smoothed his hair and shirt, then knocked once and entered the room. He did not expect to be met with a piercing glare.

"I've been waiting to hear word all night," Alexander snapped. "Where have you been?"

Alexander's ruddy complexion and rumpled clothing alerted Timothy that the man had been drinking heavily. He cautioned himself to be careful. "I'm sorry. I didn't mean to worry you."

Alexander dismissed the apology with a wave of his hand.

Timothy squared his shoulders and said in a confident tone, "It's done."

A shudder swept over Alexander's body. The brandy sloshed out of the snifter and seeped into the red velvet material of the chair, mimicking a bloodstain.

Timothy waited for a response, but received no words at all. *I did what you asked. What more do you want from me?* Thoughts of what to do next whirled through his mind. *Please him. Play something. Make him proud.* He crossed the room to the Steinway, sat down, and began to play Prokofiev's Toccata Opus 11.

In Timothy's periphery, he saw Alexander struggle out of his chair and walk toward him. He swayed and leaned heavily on his cane. As he drew closer, Timothy's playing became more *maestoso,* rousing. His confidence grew with each bar. Timothy's fingers glided across the keys. He felt the music become one with his soul as never before. The platform under him creaked and he sensed his maestro's presence behind him.

Alexander's hands on his shoulders made Timothy sway. Passion filled him as he felt certain to be rewarded with Alexander's exclusive attention. Never again would there be the need to share.

Hot air blew against Timothy's neck as Alexander whispered, "I'm pleased you are safely home. Unfortunately, I can wait no longer for Nicholas. I must sleep." The stench of stale pipe smoke and brandy reeked from his clothing and hot breath. "We will speak. Soon."

Timothy turned in time to see his master nearly teeter off the step.

"Compose your performance carefully," Alexander warned, his words drifting behind him as he weaved out of the music room.

14

Nicholas drifted in and out of awareness throughout the morning. With fuzzy eyesight, he looked for, but did not see his Porsche. Waking occasionally, he urged his battered body along the path the car had cleared after careening down the embankment. Broken brush, loosened rocks, and saplings ripped from the earth impeded his movement.

He clung to overgrowth and pulled himself up the nearly vertical incline. With every inch gained, pain racked his ribs and left ankle. A gash that ran from his right temple to his chin re-opened and bled whenever he grimaced. His clothes and body were filthy, his tongue swollen from thirst.

Although his overcoat impeded his flow, he dared not abandon it. He crept up the steep wall of the ravine, encouraged by the sound of an occasional passing car far above. Exhaustion overtook him often, forcing him to rest.

He had not been so close to nature since the night "hunting" with Alexander and Timothy. He heard faint rustling nearby and imagined teems of creatures hidden beneath the underbrush. Remembering warnings of snakes near water, he pushed frightening thoughts from his mind.

Nicholas remained still, just shy of passing out again as memories of Elaine flooded his bleary mind. Her soft blonde hair, straight back and dancer's legs brought his torture alive. Her scent of gardenias and rosewater filled his mind, but was quickly erased by the smell of moldy dirt encrusted in his nostrils.

Regretfully, he remembered how they were often separated because his touring conflicted with her college schedule. Alexander, unaware of their relationship, allowed Elaine to accompany Nicholas on two occasions when he had fallen ill or too troubled by pain in his legs to travel: first to Milan, then three months ago to Prague.

Nicholas had thrilled at Elaine's delight in being lavished with perks due to his international stature. Although Alexander secured two accommodations, Elaine's bed would never be slept in, her room never entered.

During both trips, they stayed in his luxurious suite at the finest hotels. Massive cut flower arrangements met them upon their arrival, fresh exotic fruits burst from intricate baskets. Beluga caviar and Cristal champagne awaited their mere request.

He had traveled to both countries numerous times and longed to share his knowledge of the ancient cities with his love, but they rarely seemed to even get out of the room until a panicked promoter pounded on the door, fearing Nicholas would be late for his performance.

A spike of pain seared his ribs, bringing him back to the present. Words from his father's journal wavered into his mind and he concentrated, visualizing the journal's page.

Nicholas, you turn four years old today. Three years ago I left the not-so-happy home I created with your mother. I couldn't bear to hear the plans of her future based on my success any longer. I tired of being forced to endure her cold urgings to tour more cities overseas, demand more money for my performances, play at only the most regal venues around the world.

I wondered more and more why she wanted me away so much of the time. I suppose I always knew it had something to do with Alexander.

So, I left. I didn't leave her destitute. After all, I also left my life's blood—you—in her care.

She had sufficient funds at her disposal. Many would even call it wealth. I fled, content that my son would never suffer hardship. When I left, I disappeared with little more than the clothes I wore that day and took off down the long barren road to anonymity without even a photograph of you.

This, I regret. The vision of your face fades,

leaving an unquenchable sadness.

Nicholas pushed the words away. Fighting kudzu and thick, tangled underbrush, he dragged his body farther up the steep hazard. After resting, he tried again and nearly passed out. He realized if he didn't make it to the highway he'd have to spend another night in the cold.

The dread and fear of being undiscovered propelled him forward. His mind numb from the pain, he worried that his ankle might be broken. He feared most for his hands whenever he glanced at the gloves, now shredded from climbing the jagged slope. Struggling to focus, he stared at his broken nails and bloody finger pads. *Will I ever be able to play again?*

Hours earlier, he had heard cars passing. Now, only a few occasional vehicles went by. Sampte often warned him about navigating the treacherous road at night and he knew that soon, no one would be driving by.

Unable to see his destination, let alone reach it, he decided to rest until morning. He scooped pine needles and dead leaves from the forest's floor over him until exhaustion overtook him. He drifted off, thinking of Elaine sitting in the chair in his room, clad only in his lavender shirt, her long hair sweeping aside, her lilting voice saying his name, her touch, the taste of her on his tongue.

His vowed retribution for her murder kept him from giving up.

15

Aranka Kalman had dialed all of Elaine's friends and classmates she knew of, but no one had heard from her daughter. Although Elaine rarely stayed at her dorm room, choosing instead to sleep at home, Aranka hoped her roommate would know where she might be. She did not. When her instructors informed Aranka that their student had missed classes for two days, she became frantic.

Her mind spinning with the worst situations her daughter might be facing, Aranka decided to ignore Alexander's insistence that neither Elaine, nor Nicholas for that matter, had been to the mansion in days.

Driving toward her brother's main residence, she dialed Nicholas's private line again. After repeated ringing, she tried his cell phone, but the call rolled immediately over to his pleasant recorded voice and she left yet another message. Each instruction for him to return her call had elevated in intensity.

She said through gritted teeth, "Nicholas Renfrew Kalman, this is Aranka. For the fifth time. You must phone me immediately and tell me where Elaine is." She took a deep breath and let it out slowly. "Tell her I'm not angry, but she needs to come home. Please, Nicholas, this is not right, or proper. You know this. Phone me."

She clicked off the line, but continued to hold the phone. Shaking her head, Aranka thought of the events that had transpired over the last two years.

Although Elaine's grades and standing qualified her to attend any Ivy League institution she wished, she had opted instead to attend the local university. When Aranka received notification of Elaine's acceptance to the traditional college, she had confronted her daughter.

"I'm not going anywhere, Momma," Elaine declared.

"Why not Wharton or Yale, darling? International Banking is not something you merely pick up. It must be taught."

"And you'll teach me when the time comes." Elaine rushed to her mother, throwing her arms around her. "Don't fight me on this. You'll lose. This is where I belong."

At her daughter's last utterance, Aranka knew her daughter was in love. The possibility of Elaine and Nicholas's romantic involvement never occurred to Aranka before. She feared the consequences if Alexander were to find out about their relationship. Aranka knew Alexander would forbid it, allowing nothing to stand in the way of his protégé's training.

She remembered how her brother had convinced Nicholas's mother it would be best if the boy stayed with him after Alexander tired of his courtship with her. With promises of continued wealth and assurances that she would be well cared for, Teresa had relinquished the ten-year-old to Alexander and Aranka's care. Alexander made it clear that the woman would have no further involvement in her son's life.

As the mother of a young daughter, Aranka couldn't believe the woman's nonchalance. How could anyone give away their child for money? She often wondered if Teresa even thought about her son, regretted her decision to abandon him, wondered if he was all right—even knew of Nicholas's success as an adult.

The adoption went smoothly. There were promises of greatness in Nicholas's hands. That, and Alexander's declaration of funding for their efforts, swayed the adoption board. Teresa Hunt offered no resistance, and though there were inquiries, no trace of the boy's father could be found in order to negate the petition.

It was agreed between Aranka and Alexander that she would take Nicholas into her home at first, and the adoption papers would state her as the adoptive parent. However, guardianship transferred immediately to Alexander after the last home-visit from the authorities were accomplished.

Alexander insisted Nicholas no longer be called by his father's name, Hunt. "He is a Kalman now," Alexander had said. "With this name he will receive respect. Charles Hunt was not an honorable man, Nicholas would be haunted by his birth name."

Aranka regretted letting the boy go. She often worried over young Nicholas's unstable upbringing and knew his life would become solely dedicated to music—and, to Alexander.

She had grieved over her brother's lost youth, all too aware of his endless practice sessions, grueling travel schedule and constant exhibitions. Most disheartening of all must have been never being good enough in their father's eyes. She feared the same fate for Nicholas. The past repeating itself, to Nicholas's detriment, weighed heavily on her mind.

Aranka stopped at the closed double gates that forbade entry to Alexander's mansion. She punched in the security code, waited for the filigree fence to whir open, then pulled up to the front steps.

She exited her vehicle and scanned every window, searching for her daughter's face. Her mouth dried up as she formulated what she would say to her brother. To arrive like this, without an appointment or so much as a phone call, on top of being unprepared was a mistake, but she needed her brother to realize the urgency to find Elaine.

Before she could form a single coherent thought, the door opened to reveal the Hungarian man that, although had been with Alexander forty-five years, she didn't know at all. As always, Sampte merely bowed, stepped aside and swept out his arm for her to enter.

Sampte offered her no words as she followed him up the left staircase. She ignored the snubbing and turned her thoughts to how much she appreciated the fact that Elaine and Nicholas had taken to one another right away; the girl, fascinated by the boy's talent; the boy, envious of the experiences the girl enjoyed outside the confines of wealth and the piano. Aranka was aware of Nicholas's fear that he would never be witness to a so-called "normal" life. He learned of childhood through Elaine's eyes.

Standing at the music room door she took a deep breath and let it out slowly. She spotted him sitting at the small table on the balcony, surveying his domain. Straightening her skirt, she joined her brother.

"I wasn't expecting you," he said.

"You must tell me where Elaine is, Alexander."

"I assure you, I don't know." He pointed to the chair beside him. "Have tea with me."

Unwavering, she remained standing. "I don't want tea. Is Nicholas traveling? Are they together?"

"Perhaps."

Her anger increased at his callous tone. "Perhaps? That's all you have to offer? You may not care where our children are, but I assure you, I do."

"They're hardly children. They can do as they please."

"I don't want her staying here overnight, but I know how close they've become." Watching him sip calmly from his bone china cup unnerved her. "Does this not concern you?"

"Why would it?" he asked, seeming taken aback.

"Love occurs when we least expect it. Or want it."

Alexander clinked the cup hard into its saucer and shoved his chair back. He fumbled for his cane and limped to the balcony railing. "Love. What does a boy know of love?"

"Perhaps it's only her then."

"They're siblings," Alexander roared.

"No. They are not, much as you would like them to be. They share the Kalman name innocently."

"Go home now, Aranka," he said, his face reddening. "I have a lesson to prepare."

"Yes, back to your precious music." Aranka reached for her bag. "Just assure me she isn't here."

"She is not here."

"Fine. I'm going to the police."

Alexander whirled to face her. "Why would you do such a thing?"

"Andras," she countered, hoping the endearment their

father called her brother would soften him, "she is my daughter. All that I have. I will do anything to find her."

"Do as you must." Alexander dismissed her with a flip of his wrist. He stormed off the patio and into the music room. The cane's brass tip striking the marble floor resounded throughout the cavernous area.

Aranka heard the tapping long after Alexander departed, keeping metronome-time with the staccato of her heartbeat.

16

Twenty miles from Alexander's mansion, activity bustled within the original county courthouse, now a substation for the Swain County Sheriff's office. Deep in the Smoky Mountains, the county encompassed five hundred and twenty-eight square miles, twelve of them bisected by the mighty Nantahala River. Its sheriff and twenty-three deputies protected and served nearly thirteen thousand residents.

The second floor housed the sheriff's office and his squad of deputies. The space buzzed with the energy of male and female officers, both in and out of uniform. Styrofoam cups and half-eaten pastries littered industrial metal desks. Scorched coffee permeated the air. A dozen work areas stood in an erratic configuration within the large room.

Officers of differing ages and ethnicities worked their cases on computer keyboards. A few old-timers pecked on electric typewriters. Some conversed with irate offenders or fielded phone calls.

Along the far wall, deputies Steve Hawk and Kenneth Stiles sat across from each other.

Hawk's smooth, cocoa-colored forehead furrowed as he concentrated on an issue of *Psychology Today*. He felt the publication gave him an edge when questioning the offenders who passed through the precinct, usually belligerent juveniles accused of defacing property, or feuding neighbors. He occasionally marked entries on the pages with a yellow highlighter.

Stiles, ten years older than Hawk, his blue eyes known to catch the minutest detail or flaw in an offender's demeanor, flipped through a manila folder and studied the notations. "I don't blame this guy for taking off. If I had five kids and shrew-of-a-wife like his, I'd be missing, too." He rubbed a hand over his non-existent beard.

"I'll be glad when we land a case worthy of our substantial talents," Hawk offered. "Like a serial killer or mass poisoning."

Stiles chuckled. "Not likely in this county."

Their bear-sized sheriff, Nathaniel Sands, approached them, manila file in hand. "Hawk, you're up," he said, tossing the folder atop the deputy's desk. "Give what you've got going to Stiles. This is priority one. Don't screw it up," Sands warned. "It's sure to be a high visibility case if it's not resolved quick."

Hawk nodded as he opened the file.

"If I didn't have a meeting with the governor in an hour I'd be handling it myself."

"No need to worry, Sheriff."

"Study up. She'll be here in about five minutes."

Hawk swallowed hard and shot a look at his partner.

After the sheriff went back to his office, Stiles said, "He's goin' fishin' with the mayor."

"Yeah, I figured it was something like that." Hawk scanned to mid-page of the document, then his stomach stirred. "This is it, Kenny. We've got our cure for boredom right here. Listen up. Missing woman, twenty years old, five-ten, blonde, gray eyes."

Stiles got up and went to look over Hawk's shoulder. "Gone how long?"

"Two days."

"Who reported it?"

Hawk turned to the next page. "The mother. Aranka Bela Kalman, one twenty-nine Vargo Canyon."

"The banker over at Carolina Trust?"

"Must be."

They both looked up when the room went quiet. A woman dressed in a tailored blue dress, clutching a leather handbag had entered the station. Her porcelain face seemed never to have met sunlight. Her cautious eyes darted around.

Hawk had never seen his boss move so fast to greet anyone. Sheriff Sands motioned for Hawk to follow as he escorted the woman toward a private room.

"You ready?" Stiles said.

With a purposeful stroke of his hand, Hawk smoothed the buzz haircut that denied any possibility of an unruly Afro.

"Don't screw it up," Stiles mimicked in a flawless impression of their boss.

Letting out a nervous chuckle, Hawk slid the knot of his tie up under his collar, then grabbed the file and a note pad.

"Pretty as a picture," Stiles called after him.

Hawk stifled a grin and followed Sands into the cramped interrogation room and stood inside the door.

"Ms. Kalman, this is Deputy Steven Hawk. I've assigned him to your case," Sands said, seating her at the table. "He's the best investigator I've got. He's highly capable and I assure you, he'll find your daughter."

"How do you do, ma'am," Hawk said, shaking her delicate hand.

"I hope you don't think I'm jumping to conclusions," the woman said. "Elaine has never been involved in anything before that would cause me to worry. She'd certainly never go anywhere for this long without assuring me she's all right."

Sheriff Sands slipped out of the room and closed the door behind him.

"Ms. Kalman, before we begin, could you verify the information I have here about your daughter?" She nodded and he turned to the cover sheet on the initial report. "She's a student at Western Carolina University in Cullowhee?"

"Yes. Elaine is in her third year, but she'll be testing out early, graduating with full honors in finance."

"Maybe she's involved in something that would take her away from school? A trip you didn't know about?"

"No, that's not possible. I'm sure it's nothing to do with school. I've spoken to her instructors and the friends I know of."

"Well, ma'am, where do you think she is?"

"With Nicholas, I presume."

Hawk opened his note pad and began writing the details.

"What is Nicholas's last name?"

"Kalman. The same as ours. Nicholas lives with my brother, Alexander."

"So, you never married?"

"My husband left after Elaine's fifth birthday. It was my brother's suggestion that Elaine and I revert to the family name."

Hawk leaned forward, drawn to the woman's soothing, refined voice tinged with an accent he couldn't place. "I see. And your brother's full name?"

"Alexander Ambrus Kalman. I asked him if Elaine may have unexpectedly gone on tour with Nicholas, but he repeatedly told me no."

"On tour?"

"Nicholas is a professional concert pianist. He travels the world." She crossed her hands and placed them atop the scuffed wooden tabletop.

"Is he touring now?"

"According to Alexander, not until next month."

"So, you think they're together."

"It is possible. Elaine did accompany Nicholas on two tours in Europe, but I've checked her room and her passport is where she always keeps it, and none of our luggage is missing."

Aranka looked weary as she edged forward in the chair. "Elaine and Nicholas grew up together. She's only three months younger than him. Nicholas was ten when I adopted him."

"They're not related?"

"No. He was the son of one of Alexander's colleagues. When the man disappeared, his mother found it impossible to provide for him. Alexander insisted we step in to care for the boy."

"But he lives with your brother?"

"Yes. Even at ten years of age, Nicholas showed proficiency at the piano. He immediately .became Alexander's pupil. Soon after the adoption became final, my brother decided it would be best if he lived with him."

Aranka settled into the chair and stared at her hands. "Nicholas had tutors growing up, but Elaine attended public school. I wanted her to have a normal childhood."

Hawk put down his pen and listened intently.

"Alexander exhibited Nicholas in competitions from the time he turned twelve. Elaine was the only stable child Nicholas knew. They spent every one of her school breaks together. They didn't see each other much during Elaine's high school years, but the summer after her graduation, they were inseparable."

"That was three years ago?"

Aranka answered with a nod. "She spent all her free time with him. I encouraged their friendship, though I missed her terribly when she was gone." Tears filled the woman's eyes. She fumbled in her purse, extracted a crisp handkerchief the precise shade of her outfit and dabbed her eyes and nose. Then she pulled out a glamorous black and white headshot of a young woman from the bag. "This is Elaine."

Hawk studied the picture. "She's very beautiful." Leaning in close, he asked softly, "Ms. Kalman, do you think your daughter and Nicholas could be involved in a sexual relationship?"

Lowering her eyes, Aranka answered, "Yes."

"Yes, they could? Or yes, they are?"

"I know my daughter has feelings for him."

After nearly an hour of Hawk's questions, followed by Aranka's detailed answers, Hawk said, "Well, Ma'am. I think that's all I need to know for us to get started."

She expelled a deep breath, took up her bag and headed for the door.

"One more thing, ma'am. What does your brother think?"

Aranka's jaw muscles tightened. "You'd have to ask him. Though I doubt he would tell you."

"Why is that?"

"He's quite private, and frankly, would find the intrusion an insult." Then she stepped from the room.

Her ominous answer a mystery to Hawk, he proceeded to write out a preliminary list of what he needed to accomplish.

A spark of excitement stirred in his chest, certain this would not be the average investigation.

17

Alexander reveled in Timothy's newfound confidence as his student performed a flawless Franz Liszt Liebestraum No. 3 on the Steinway. He was satisfied that his protégé had chosen this composition, knowing it was Alexander's favorite, written by his beloved Hungarian countryman. *At last, he's committed this piece to memory.*

Lost in the music, Alexander stood at the curve of the piano smoking a pipe filled with smooth Italian Brebbia tobacco. He kept time by tapping a long finger upon his hardwood cane's ivory handle, a contented smile on his lips.

Alexander ached to ask Timothy what had transpired the night before, but he patiently waited until the younger man offered the words. Alexander knew this mind-game worked heavily on Timothy's psyche.

"That'll do for now. I have something for you, then we must speak of Nicholas," Alexander said, displaying a performance program. "Although I'm not certain you are ready, everything has been arranged."

Mouth agape, Timothy stared at the playbill that featured his picture on the cover.

"You will be pleased by what I've decided you will play."

Timothy's hand trembled as he took the program and opened the first page. "Prokofiev?"

"Do not disappoint me."

Timothy frowned as he studied the announcement. "In three days?"

"We'd best get started. Begin at the twelfth bar of the Seventh."

Timothy laid the program on the piano's lid, picture down. Hands hovering above the keyboard, he prepared for a full minute before his fingers touched the keys. Two bars into the composition, he rushed his fingering.

Alexander issued him an admonishing glare.

"I'm sorry. I—p-p-please, let me start again."

"Clear your mind." Alexander stifled his rising anger as he went to his chair. "I have no desire to hear merely the execution. You must focus."

Sampte entered, carrying an ornate tea set on a silver tray. As Sampte bent to serve him, Alexander, melancholic from the music, wondered if his companion ever missed the rich countryside of their homeland, as he often did.

The only other servant on Alexander's household staff also hailed from Hungary. Zardos, thirty-eight years Sampte's junior, appeared at the doorway.

"What is it?" Alexander snapped, disturbed by yet another interruption.

"Sir, a police officer is here. He requests a meeting with you."

Timothy's hands halted on the keyboard.

Alexander whirled to Timothy. "Do not stop until you are instructed to do so. Ever."

Timothy turned back to the keys and continued to play.

"This man is here now?" Alexander asked.

Zardos nodded.

"Leave now, Timothy. We will speak of Nicholas the moment he is gone." Timothy looked up at him, his face drained of color. "Pray the officer's visit is not due to your transgressions."

Timothy nodded and rushed out of the music room, playbill clutched in his hand.

18

A dozen years ago Hawk had watched from afar Alexander Kalman's mansion being built. First, the blasting of a plateau on the ridge, foundation poured, interior walls erected, trusses settled, tiles laid on the roof, the arrival of truckloads of stone. When construction was completed he had driven his parents to the mammoth structure. His mother clucked her tongue in amazement as she rocked his infant sister, Annie. Dad did his best to calculate how much such a place would cost to build, but gave up when it came to estimating the price tag on the fieldstone that covered the entire complex. They sat and stared in awe through the fancy ironwork of the closed gates, imagining what treasures could be found behind those huge double-doors beyond the front porch.

He never imagined setting foot inside, but now here he was, standing in the foyer, staring up at enormous tapestries that hung from brass rods along thirty-foot-high, walnut-paneled walls. Dual staircases along opposite sides of the entry raised three stories. Regal oil paintings lined the incline to the top of the stairs. The magnificent spindles of the banisters were as big around as Hawk's thighs and buffed to a blinding gleam. Shining pinkish marble columns in the middle of the entryway matched the sea of flooring. A flower arrangement the size of a small car sat on the table in the middle of the open area.

When he had been ushered into the house by a young man dressed in a long black jacket, Hawk had been met by the faint sound of elaborate piano music, but now he only heard a grandfather clock near the front door tick off the seconds.

A few minutes later, the servant who had introduced himself as Zardos reappeared and hurried down from the top staircase.

"This way, if you would, sir," he said.

Hawk met him on the second floor and followed him back up to the third. Reaching the last step, Hawk noticed a man of formidable size tuck inside the darkness of another room. Hawk stopped for a moment, unsure of the vision, but he didn't see any other movement, or hear a single thing. He hurried to catch up with Zardos who had turned down a long corridor. Standing in front of a closed door, the servant knocked once, opened the door and ushered Hawk inside with an open hand. Without saying another word, Zardos hustled back down the hall.

Why is he so nervous? Hawk wondered.

When Hawk entered the room, an older, light-haired man rose from a chair. Although he leaned on a cane, Hawk thought he seemed quite fit. Walking to him, Hawk extended his hand.

"I am Alexander Kalman. What may I do for you, officer?"

"Deputy Steven Hawk, Mr. Kalman. I need a moment of your time."

"Of course. Please, make yourself comfortable," Alexander said, motioning to the couch. "May I offer you anything?"

"No, thank you. This shouldn't take long," Hawk replied, sitting ramrod straight on the edge of the seat.

"What may I do for you, Deputy . . ., Hawk, is it?"

"Yes, sir. I spoke with your sister earlier today. Turns out, your niece has been missing for two days. We're trying to locate her. Ms. Kalman mentioned you might be of some assistance."

At the sound of a knock, Alexander's lips thinned and the muscles at his jaws bulged. The door opened to reveal a red-haired man in his twenties. Behind him, a Latin man, dressed in khaki work clothes stood, head down, wringing the brim of a straw hat in his hands.

Alexander reared back in his chair at the sight of the men. "Would you excuse me a moment, Deputy?" He asked, then limped quickly to the door.

In the doorway, all the men spoke Spanish in hushed, yet animated tones. After a short exchange Alexander raised a hand, halting the Latino mid-sentence. Alexander said a few harsh words causing the other man to back up, his eyes going wide. The Latino glanced at the deputy and nodded once, then rushed away. Alexander said a phrase to the red-haired man in yet another foreign language.

Why aren't they speaking English?

The young man flinched when Alexander laid a hand on his shoulder. He said a few more words, then closed the door and returned to his chair.

"Please excuse the interruption. Manuel Esteva is my gardener. He said as he walked past your vehicle the angels spoke to him. He has confessed to three short shots of wine when he had sworn to the Madonna he would refrain. He believes that since the message came from your vehicle, you are his confessor. He has come to accept his penance." Alexander gave Hawk a tight smile. "I suspect he heard a voice coming from your car radio."

Hawk grinned. "You speak Spanish fluently?"

"With so much travel I'm forced to endure, I find it beneficial to have a command of many foreign languages. Do you speak Spanish?"

"No. I'm afraid not."

Alexander seemed to relax after Hawk's revelation. "Actually, I'm well versed in a number of languages. And although music needs no translation, I have taught my pupils the benefits of studying the mindset of the classical masters in their mother tongue."

"Are you talking about Nicholas?"

"Of course."

"I understand he's a pretty good piano player."

Alexander chuckled. "Actually, Nicholas Kalman is a world-class pianist. He is my top pupil. He's won the gold medal at the Vladimir Horowitz International, and many other junior events. Since he turned professional he's performed at the most elite theatres around the world."

"Who was the young man with Esteva?" Hawk noticed that Alexander's demeanor became a little colder.

"Timothy Sagan. He is also my pupil."

"He lives here, too?"

"Yes."

"I'd like to have a word with him."

Alexander tapped the head of his cane with a long finger. "Whatever for?"

"I'd like to know his whereabouts the past forty-eight hours."

"He's been here with me for days. We're preparing for his first solo performance."

"So, you're his alibi?"

"Has there been a crime committed?"

"Not that I'm aware of. I'm just asking questions at this point."

"What is the purpose of your visit?"

"Your sister is very concerned about your niece."

"Yes, well I don't feel there's any reason for alarm. It's not as though she's a minor. And, this has happened before."

"When was that?"

"During Nicholas's last tour. I found myself unable to travel with him and Elaine graciously accepted his invitation. They were away for twelve days on two separate occasions." Alexander took a sip from his china cup, his hand still, gaze cool and even. "You see, unbeknownst to me, it seems Nicholas and Elaine had been in a relationship for quite some time. This . . . coupling has caused my sister a great deal of embarrassment, as I'm sure you can imagine. Though they are not blood relations, there is a stigma that would certainly surround them if their . . . tryst were to become common knowledge."

"Nicholas was adopted by your sister, right?"

"Yes, but shortly after, he came to live here with me and to study." Alexander shuffled in his seat. "It seems my sister has told you a great deal. Why is this matter so intriguing?"

"Well, they're not related, so why would anyone suffer any embarrassment? Except for you, I suppose." Hawk noted the flare of Alexander's nose. "Are you close to your niece and nephew?"

"Nicholas is like a son to me."

"And he's not on tour?"

"Not presently. I assure you, this is a great deal of concern for nothing consequential."

"Where is Nicholas, Mr. Kalman?"

"I do not know, Deputy. I assume he is with my niece. They're not children. Frankly, I don't know why my sister is making such a fuss. She's wasting your time and will be quite embarrassed when they show up in a few days time."

"You own a black Porsche Targa, Mr. Kalman," Hawk stated.

Alexander stopped tapping his cane. "You know quite a lot about me."

"The car, sir."

"Of course. Yes, I lease a Porsche but Nicholas drives it."

"Is the vehicle here?"

"No. I'm sure Nicholas has it."

Hawk made a final notation, closed his pad and stood. "That's all I have for now."

"Fine then. If there's anything else you need—"

"A photograph of your nephew would be helpful."

"Of course." Alexander limped to the piano. He flipped through a stack of sheet music and extracted a program.

In the professional black and white photograph, Nicholas Kalman, dressed in a tuxedo, leaned in a relaxed pose against a grand piano. He wore a wide, appealing smile.

"Impressive photo," Hawk said.

"Yes. His allure is widely appreciated, as you can imagine."

"I'll be in touch," Hawk said, waving the program in the air.

"I'll call for my servant."

"Don't bother, I can find my way out." Hawk strode to the door and closed it behind him before Alexander had the chance to protest.

Hawk took the stairs as quick as he could manage. The

conversation buzzed in his head as he made a beeline for the front door, hoping to get off the grounds before he forgot anything crucial. He vowed to remember every detail so that he could recount his observations to Stiles. He prayed the micro-cassette recorder in the glove compartment had fresh batteries.

Making a mental list of elements he needed to investigate further, he saw the ominous man he had encountered earlier seem to glide to the front door. He blocked Hawk from exiting. They stared at each other, each holding their ground.

Without a word, the man bowed, reached behind him and opened the door.

Hawk gave him a terse nod and moved onto the porch thinking, *These are the oddest people I've ever met.*

19

After the deputy's departure, Alexander replayed their conversation in his mind, searching for any details he should not have revealed. He had been drinking far too much and sleep had all but eluded him ever since Nicholas's departure. The more he thought about the deputy's pointed questions, the angrier he became.

Moments later, a light knock pulled him from his musings. When Timothy entered, Alexander rushed to him. *At last, some answers.* "Assure me all is well," he said, piercing Timothy with his eyes.

"I'm sure it is. Nicholas took care of it."

"Nicholas?" Alexander asked, leaning close enough to smell Timothy's nervous sweat. "That was not your instruction."

Timothy stood a little taller. "Don't worry. They won't bother you anymore."

"What are you talking about?"

"Elaine and Nicholas."

"Elaine, yes, but where is Nicholas?"

Timothy stifled a grin. "I suspect he and his crashed Porsche have floated halfway to Georgia by now."

Alexander labored for breath. *My Nicholas dead? Impossible.* "You were to take care of Elaine. I meant Nicholas no harm."

"I sent him to deliver her to Henri Thibodeaux."

"Why would he do that?" Alexander cried out.

"I gave him a note, supposedly from you, telling him to take her there."

"I did not want that. Never, ever would I have wanted Nicholas to be involved in this." Alexander struggled to push down his fury, fighting the urge to strike Timothy. "Tell me precisely what you've done."

"I put her in his car and waited for him at the theatre." Timothy stumbled over his words. "Then I gave him your note—I mean the one I wrote that was supposed to have been from you. Then I followed him. The note said to go to Thibodeaux's—I think he went to the country house, bu-bu-but I didn't know where it was. So, I pulled off and waited for him. A while later, he drove by, and I followed him again." In a hushed, guilty tone Timothy finished, "Then I saw a car going right for him. It forced him off the highway."

Alexander reached out and squeezed Timothy's bicep in a vice-like grip. "What exactly did you see?"

"Only his taillights falling over the edge. His car went down the embankment. I tried to reach him, but by the time I got there, the Porsche had slid into the water. All I could do was watch it float away. He was inside. She was, too."

"And when were you going to tell me?"

"I thought it would be better not to say anything. That way when the authorities came—"

"That was not your decision to make." Alexander thumped his cane on the floor, replaying the details Timothy had provided. "You know for certain both were in the car?"

Timothy jerked, a look of dismay on his face. "Of course. I assumed he would be going to Thibodeaux's after he went to the country house."

"Think Timothy. Why would he have gone to my country house?"

"I don't know. I'm sure he was pretty upset when he found Elaine's body in his car. Maybe he wasn't thinking straight and went there to figure things out. I wanted to make sure he wasn't going to do anything to you. That's the reason I followed him. I was surprised as hell when he lost control of his car."

Timothy did not hold his mentor's gaze. Alexander knew Timothy lied. He did his best to suppress the rage building inside. "I will ask you only once more." Alexander took a step forward. Timothy retreated a step. Eyes blazing into Timothy's, he asked, "Why the country house?"

Timothy thought a moment, blinking rapidly. "Well . . . I'm pretty sure she was in the car, but I guess . . . maybe she could be there . . ."

"But you do not know for certain."

Timothy stammered, "Well, no. Like I said, I waited down the road. I knew he'd have to come back down the mountain—"

With the aid of his cane, Alexander pushed away and turned from his pupil's wide-eyed fear. "Once again, you have failed me."

After a moment, Alexander whirled back around. With swift concise movements, he raised his cane and delivered a blow atop Timothy's shoulder, then to his crouched back. Timothy slumped to the floor.

Alexander swept a hand through his tousled hair. "That deputy mustn't find Elaine."

Timothy nodded, rising from the floor to face Alexander, his cheeks red, streaked with tears.

Alexander, mere inches from Timothy, held the incompetent boy's stare. "Do not disappoint me again. Do you understand?"

Timothy nodded.

"Rectify this immense blunder of yours. Go now!"

20

Lying in the filth of the embankment, tangled in kudzu and dead brush, Nicholas drew the tattered overcoat around him. Although the garment's armpits were now torn, as the temperature dropped, he felt grateful for its protection. Knowing he needed to stay as lucid as possible, he visualized a page from his father's journal.

> *Now I sit on the front porch of a modest cabin where I spend much of my day swaying in an ancient rocking chair. No expectations, plans, or dreams. I find that I've become an old man before my time.*
>
> *And, that I miss you desperately, Nicholas. My melancholy has reached such depths that I decided to steal this little book. Hopefully I'll be able to sleep easier with the troubling thoughts off my mind and onto these pages. Don't know if it will work. Maybe tonight I will. Nicholas, I pray these words of warning don't find you too late.*
>
> *And, that my efforts won't die unread.*

Nicholas did his best to push aside his father's troubling words. Music filling his mind, he imagined the notes to Schubert's Sonata in B-flat Major. Yet, no matter how hard he concentrated, his father's words of caution interrupted his mental playing.

As the sun passed the ridge, turning shapes to shadows, anxiety nestled in the pit of his stomach. Nicholas's fears turned from his inability to punish Elaine's killer to dying alone on the mountainside, both of their bodies never to be found.

21

Darkness had fallen by the time Hawk reached the sheriff's station.

"You look like crap," Stiles told him.

"Long day," Hawk said, crossing the squad room. He poured a cup of scorched-smelling coffee, then went to sit at his desk.

"I've been waitin' on you."

"Living vicariously through me again?"

"What can I say? Sheriff's got me cleanin' up log sheets from a week back. Can't even make out most of the handwriting. Gotta say, yours is especially bad."

Hawk laughed, grateful for the light banter.

"Boss has been sniffin' around. Asked half a dozen times if you'd called in. Where you been?"

"All over. First, at the university checking out Elaine Kalman's friends and teachers, then off to Aranka's brother's mansion."

"Yeah? What was it like?" Stiles asked, leaning toward Hawk.

"Like *Gone With the Wind*, only bigger."

"I've heard the guy has more money than his sister."

"Don't doubt it." Hawk shuffled through his stack of messages. "You took a call from Shelly in records?"

"Yep. She ran Alexander Kalman through the computer system for you." Stiles tapped his pencil on his desk and looked at Hawk. "Shelly's pretty cute."

Hawk frowned, wondering where Stiles was headed. "I guess so, yeah."

"Not as cute as Inola Walela, though." Hawk leveled a glare of warning, but Stiles didn't appear to be finished. "Don't pretend you're not interested in her. I see how you light up every time you run into her."

Stiles was right, Hawk had noticed Inola Walela, the only female cop on the Bryson City police force. She was captivating, beautiful, smart, tough, exactly what he hoped to find in a woman. He didn't know what intrigued him more, the fact that she was part Cherokee who had excelled professsionally despite growing up with her grandmother on the local reservation, or that she had rebuffed his advances every time he so much as tried to ask her on a date. The challenge made him even more interested in her.

"Leave my non-existent love life alone, partner," Hawk warned. "Get back to what Shelly found out."

"The guy's clean. Not even a parkin' ticket. In fact, there's no record of a driver's license. Never even been fingerprinted." Stiles read from a note pad. "And, he's rich. Owns houses all over the place."

"Interesting. He didn't offer that bit of information."

"Says here he's got the one you went to, that's his primary residence. Another one in Swain County, listed as a country home. An apartment in New York, and a place across the water in London."

"Why wouldn't he tell me that? Wouldn't he think they might be staying at one of his other homes?"

"Got somethin' to hide maybe. Hey, I got a question for you."

"What's that?"

"Why's a big shot, internationally known, piano man livin' in podunk North Carolina?"

Hawk frowned and jotted down Stiles's remark on his note pad. "That is a good question." Settling back in his seat he sipped the coffee, wincing at its bitter taste. "Alexander Kalman's got a fellow the same age as the missing girl living with him. Nicholas Kalman. Apparently, they're very close."

"They're blood kin?"

"No. Aranka adopted Nicholas when he was a kid, but Alexander got his hands on him soon after. Even gave him his last name."

Stiles tore off his sheet of paper and handed it to Hawk who put the notes inside the Kalman file.

"Do you think maybe the two are together?" Stiles asked.

"Could be. If Kalman's got several residences maybe they're playing house at one of them. Kalman did say something strange though. He spoke of Nicholas and Elaine's relationship in the past tense. That they 'had' been in a relationship. Like they broke up, even though he's confident they're together."

Remembering something, Hawk flipped through his note pad to recall the entry. "And, he said *if* I find her, they would be together." He puzzled over the odd statement again.

"Too late to do anything else tonight. Let's grab a beer. You're buyin', big shot investigator," Stiles joked, reaching for his rain slicker.

The phone rang and Stiles picked up the handset. Listening, he held up a finger for Hawk to wait. "Thanks. I'll let him know." Stiles replaced the receiver. "They've pulled a black Porsche Targa out of the Nanty. Registration lists Alexander Kalman as the owner."

Hawk stared at him. "Was Nicholas Kalman inside?"

"No details available. Come on, I'll ride with you."

"You sure? It's gettin' late. Becky may worry."

Stiles rushed after Hawk. "She's sleepin' by now. Anyway, like you always say, I love to live vicariously through you."

*   *   *

A North Carolina state trooper stood beside his cruiser staring up at the forbidding closed gate to Alexander Kalman's estate. He pushed a button on the brick column and waited. Twirling a plastic-covered Stetson in his hands, he looked into the camera mounted above him.

After a full minute, an angry voice crackled from the speaker. "Are you aware of the time?"

"Sorry, but I need to speak to Mr. Alexander Kalman."

"He's not to be disturbed."

"Disturb him. This is a police matter," the officer barked. He had spent the last stretch of his watch in a car with an unsatisfactory heater and had chugged the dregs of cold coffee from his thermos hours ago.

After a long silence, the gate began to creep open.

In his rush to meet the trooper, Alexander hadn't even shut the front door. He stood on his porch as the cruiser parked in the circular drive. His grief over Nicholas had troubled him throughout the evening. He'd been restless and far from sleep when Sampte came to the music room, announcing the caller.

Alexander knew the visit must have something to do with Nicholas. Standing on the porch, he began composing his performance. He gave an impatient wave to the officer when he slid out of the cruiser.

"Mr. Kalman?"

Alexander nodded. "Yes, yes, what is it? Has something happened?"

"Sir, I need to confirm that you're the owner of a black Porsche Targa. License plate, one-four-oh-nine, H?"

"Yes. Obviously you know that."

"I'm here to notify you that your car's been located."

Alexander limped a step closer. "What do you mean located? My vehicle wasn't reported stolen. Where was it found?"

"In the Nantahala River, sir. You didn't report it missing?"

"No. My nephew, Nicholas Kalman, drives that vehicle."

The trooper replied with a shrug.

"Is he all right?"

"I can't tell you that, sir."

"Why will you not tell me?" Alexander shouted.

"All I know is, they found the car."

"I'll dress," Alexander said, pivoting on his cane.

"Not necessary. They won't let no one near the crash site."

"Well, I'm not expected to wait here, am I?"

"Yes, sir. I'm afraid so," the trooper said, hurrying back to his cruiser. "I'm headed there now. You'll be notified when we get more details."

"I insist on accompanying you. I'll have my man bring around the car."

"They'll just turn you away. Best if you stay put." He slammed his car door shut before Alexander could say anything else.

*　　*　　*

In the darkness of his music room Alexander settled into his velvet chair. Bartók's *Hungarian Swineherd's Dance,* blaring from the sophisticated sound system did little to calm his nerves.

At first seething over Timothy's bumbling of his instruction, Alexander's frustration turned to rage. *How dare they forbid me from seeing the crash site.* He sipped from the snifter of brandy on the table beside him. Alexander felt numb, empty of emotion, and more alone than ever before. The thought of all his efforts as a mentor filled him with sorrow. *Everything lost. Now the Kalman name will never again achieve greatness.*

His gaze went to the stack of Nicholas's photographs, newspaper clippings, and glowing concert reviews that attested to their ten years together, scattered on the table beside him.

More articles were strewn on the floor at his feet. He reached for the framed photograph of Elaine he had brought from his bedroom. Standing outside, her mother's barn in the background, she wore a simple dress. Blonde hair flowing in the breeze, she smiled easily at the camera. He caressed the frame. *Why couldn't she have responded to my desire for her? I would have given her everything.*

Thoughts of her with Nicholas quashed his passion. He cursed Elaine and the love Nicholas and he shared for her. At the music's crescendo, he reached for the brandy snifter and flung it across the room. Fine cut crystal exploded into shards against the fireplace.

He covered his face as a scream burst from deep in his

chest.

*　*　*

Timothy had not moved from his position at the window of his bedroom in hours. From the time he watched the trooper's headlights sweep across his ceiling, he'd sat in the straight-back chair, tipped back, feet on the window ledge, staring out at the darkness.

He had looked forward to becoming comfortable in his position as Alexander's primary pupil. He imagined how he would revel in the attention, but now his situation had taken a terrifying turn and he no longer felt confident of his future.

He had barely slept since returning from the river incident, becoming aroused every time he replayed the event in his mind, making him feel rejuvenated and more alive than ever before. Then Alexander had erupted in a terrifying fury. Now Timothy feared for his own life. He rubbed his still-aching shoulder.

When the officer had stepped from his car to speak with Alexander, Timothy slipped onto the landing. He overheard the cop say they had found Nicholas's car, apparently without him, or Elaine, inside. The news had drained Timothy of every emotion but dread. Not knowing what to do next, he dressed and awaited instructions in case any were to come.

The remote to the sound system in his room sat on the windowsill in front of him. When the compilation of Bach's *Variations* on the CD finished, he prompted the disc to play again. Repeatedly throughout the night, Timothy listened, the dim display of the player his only illumination.

The single possession Timothy had from his childhood was a small plastic combat soldier. His only source of comfort, he kept the memento with him at all times. Over the years, the face had been worn down and the rifle barrel had long since shorn off.

Sheet music for the Prokofiev he would perform in only three nights lay splayed out on his lap. One hand tapped out the fingering of the musical piece now nearly committed to memory, the other cradled the faded toy soldier.

Though the pain from Alexander's thrashing had diminished, Timothy's shame had not. He had failed again, and his apprehension filled him with unsettling doom.

22

Hawk and Stiles arrived to a scene bathed in generator-driven white-blue spotlights. County vehicles were parked on U.S. Highway 74, resembling a young boy's scattered toys. The cruisers' revolving red and blue lights added to the eerie glow.

One hundred yards below the roadway, officers milled about on the muddy bank of the Nantahala River. They searched the area around the crushed vehicle, barely recognizable as a black Porsche. The sports car sat precariously on the riverbank, suspended by a cable attached to the rear of a tow truck.

White-capped ripples rushed past, glinting in the moon's light. It had been hours since the Porsche had been discovered, but the scene still buzzed with activity

"Jesus, look at all those guys," Hawk said. "Must be the most excitement they've seen all year."

A uniformed officer, his entire body covered in a clear raincoat, broke away from the group and approached Hawk and Stiles. "Trooper Jerry Wilkes," he said, with an upward snap of his head. "Been expectin' you."

"I'm Deputy Hawk, this is Stiles. Any survivors?"

"No bodies inside." Wilkes turned and pointed to the tow truck perched at the shoulder of the highway. "They pulled the vehicle from the river about an hour ago. May have to chop it up. Can't seem to get the dang thing up the embankment." The three watched the futile effort to budge the car, tow cable taut.

Wilkes handed Hawk a plastic bag stuffed with the vehicle's registration booklet, a gold key ring, and a black leather wallet.

"Found a duffel bag tucked in the rear compartment. Some clothes and that wallet inside. Driver's license is issued to a Nicholas Renfrew Kalman."

"Anything else?" Stiles asked.

"Empty canvas bag on the floor of the front seat. Looks like a laundry sack. It's bagged and tagged in case there's any evidence. Soakin' wet, though. Doubtful they'll find any residue. Got it in my trunk."

"Who found the car?"

"Old timer," Wilkes said, pointing to a weathered man dressed in hunter's camouflage, surrounded by three troopers. A shotgun, broken open at the barrel, was nestled in the crook of the white-haired man's arm.

Hawk nodded toward the old man. "What's with the shotgun?"

"Says he was out checkin' on his crop."

"Crop of what?"

"Ginseng," Wilkes answered.

"Ginseng?" Hawk and Stiles asked in unison.

"Big money around here if you know what to look for."

"This isn't private property," Hawk said.

"Nope, Carolina forestland, but he says the plants are his. He found 'em. Staked his claim. Waitin' on them to mature before he digs up the roots to harvest."

"Think he'd shoot someone for it?" Stiles asked.

"He'll say no."

"What do you think?" Hawk said. "Any trouble before?"

"Oh, yeah. Not from him, though. Like I said, big money. This guy ran moonshine in his prime. Pretty proud about it."

"Been tellin' tales, huh?" Stiles asked.

Wilkes chuckled. "Diggin' his own grave."

Hawk hitched his head toward the Porsche. "Think it's a dump?"

"Can't really tell without knowin' the point of impact. River's runnin' pretty high and rough from the rains last week. Car could've carried for miles. Come sunrise we'll start lookin' for skid marks and trashed guard rails."

Wilkes held up a finger and eased away from the deputies to rejoin his group of men. "Farrow, Mellon, take your teams and work in opposite directions. Bag whatever you find for the deputies."

After they snapped on latex gloves, Stiles spread the soaked contents of the evidence bag out on a nearby cruiser's hood and sifted through the limp items.

Hawk picked up the wallet and examined its contents. "Picture and info matches the driver's license. It's Nicholas's." He found no credit cards or cash in the billfold. The only other item, a smaller version of the headshot photograph of Elaine Kalman, Aranka had provided. "Proves we're lookin' for the right people."

Stiles took the ownership packet and leafed through its soggy pages. "Lease is in Alexander Kalman's name, all right."

"If this is a dump it'd be a pretty damned elaborate plan just to cover someone's tracks," Stiles offered.

At the sound of an engine's roar, Hawk looked up to witness blue smoke belching from the tailpipe of the tow truck. Tires spinning, emitting more fumes, the disheveled driver cursed and urged his beast to perform.

"Could take a while," Hawk said. "Let's go check it out."

"Damn. I'm gonna mess up my pretty boots," Stiles grumbled.

They eased down the steep embankment, skirting saplings and slick rocks until they reached the Porsche mired in the muck on the river's edge.

"Airbags are popped," Hawk said, pointing to the compartment. "Probably went off at first impact and deflated before the car reached the river."

"Lotta' damage." Stiles examined the driver's door. "Door could have popped open, I reckon."

"Great. First no Elaine, now no Nicholas. Guess we've got two cases on our hands."

"What *we*? I'm here for the ride," Stiles said, grinning.

"Thanks for your support."

Hawk watched Wilkes pick his way down the ravine with the ease of an experienced hiker.

"Got a mess here, don't we?" Wilkes said.

"Someone definitely could have been in the vehicle

during the accident," Hawk answered.

Wilkes pointed downriver. "There's a nursing home about three miles down the highway, but it doesn't have a care facility. They take their emergencies to the county hospital."

"That's eight miles up-river," Hawk said.

"About that. Other side of the ridge. We've already checked with them. Most of their injuries over the last couple days have been walk-ins. Stitches, bee stings. Couple huntin' incidents and so forth. A few motor vehicle accidents. Mostly nothing serious, except one DOA. Heart attack, they think brought on after a car wreck."

"Possible victim from this crash?" Stiles asked, sounding hopeful.

Wilkes reached inside his slicker and pulled out a note pad, then flipped a few pages. "You lookin' for someone in his mid-fifties?"

"Not even close," Stiles said, kneeling to check out the undercarriage of the Porsche. "Any vehicles reported missin' around here?"

"Nope, checked that out, too."

"You stayin' on scene?" Hawk asked the trooper.

"You bet. Came on duty right before the vehicle was spotted."

"Forest is pretty thick through here. Mobile phones probably don't work, do they?"

"Nope. No service until you're up or down the mountain."

"Radio our dispatch and they'll contact us." Hawk took a business card from his breast pocket and handed it to Wilkes. "Be sure to let us know if anything else turns up."

"You bet," Wilkes said, taking the card.

"Looks like a long drive back for us," Stiles replied.

"Come daylight, have your divers search the riverbanks four miles downstream and two miles upstream," Hawk instructed. "Good work, Wilkes. Stay in touch," he said, shaking the trooper's hand.

"Let me know if we can do anything else now, you

hear?" Wilkes eyed the deputies head to toe. "There's a real nice bed and breakfast down the road a piece in case you wanna stay close by. Hot shower's probably callin' out to you about now."

"He means we stink," Stiles said.

"We've definitely put in our sixteen hours today," Hawk agreed.

"Naw, we better get back," Stiles said.

"Be seein' you then." Wilkes tapped the brim of his hat, ascended the bank, and disappeared into the trees.

The deputies followed the path Wilkes had blazed up the escarpment to their cruiser.

"What're you gonna tell the sheriff?" Stiles asked, trailing behind Hawk. "He'll be after you for answers in a few hours."

"I don't know," Hawk said frowning. "I think maybe I should talk to the uncle again before I'm forced to resign due to my incompetence."

"Gonna have to burn this uniform," Stiles said, sniffing his shirt.

Hawk ignored his partner's grumbles and leaned against their sedan. "If Nicholas and Elaine survived that crash, it'd be a miracle. Unless this is some sorta set-up we've walked into. If it is, they're probably holed up somewhere all nice and cozy."

Stiles kicked mud from his boots. "Lotta' cabins around here. Most of 'em are vacation homes. Vacant during the off-season."

"I'll have Wilkes check that out. First thing on the list is to check out Kalman's other properties," Hawk said more to himself than Stiles. "I think his other house isn't too far from here."

The deputies slid into their vehicle. As Hawk brought the engine to life a thought came to him. "A bed and breakfast would be pretty romantic."

"And private," Stiles agreed.

Hawk zigzagged around the jumble of cruisers. "Gotta make a list of everything to cover."

Stiles shook his head in sympathy. "You're gonna be up all night, aren't you, partner?"

"Could be a long list."

23

Throughout the night Nicholas had made an effort to inch onto the shoulder of the highway. At daybreak he tucked into a fetal position at the side of the road. He floated in and out of consciousness, occasionally lifting his head to look down the barren two-lane.

Please, someone, find me now.

Brahms playing in a constant loop in his mind, he did his best to stay awake. Relieved by the journal still inside his jacket pocket, he thought of his father's words scribbled in the diary. He urged himself to hang on a little longer.

His palm felt raw from clutching the armoire key inside the glove, but he didn't try to take the covering off for fear of losing the slender brass object.

A vision of Elaine's dead body flashed before his eyes. Nausea flooded over him and he dry-heaved. Exhausted, he settled his head on the ground and waited.

*   *   *

Jessica Taft had endured an endless night in a cramped, ancient cabin deep in the woods. A classmate had offered to let her stay at a cousin's place so Jessica could get away from her distractions and finish the mid-semester paper for her theatrical set design class.

She had spent most of the last semester working in the scene shop of the university's Wilhoit theatre, and after the latest production closed she realized if she weren't more careful, she would flunk the subject she worked so hard to major in. She jumped at the chance to get out of town.

When Jessica arrived at the cabin yesterday morning she felt full of ambition. Motivated by the prospect of no inter-ruptions, and free from the usual noise at her apartment complex, she spread out her notes and reference books on the worn table in the one-bedroom abode. Thirsty for the promised, exquisite creek water piped into the cabin, she remembered she needed to turn on the water first. Following the instructions her friend had scribbled on the back of a restaurant receipt, Jessica found the valve, but no tool to turn it. Luckily, she kept a gallon of spring water in the trunk for her often-steaming, decade-old Ford Taurus's radiator.

Power proved to be another problem. At dusk she went to find the breaker panel, but when she shoved the lever, nothing lit up. She scurried to build a dismal fire in the inadequate fireplace. The need to toss another log into the opening every twenty minutes became a tedious task.

"Talk about roughing it," she had mumbled.

She had looked forward to frying the fresh smallmouth bass and collard greens purchased at the local market on her way to the cabin. She eyed the useless cooler, knowing a long, hungry night awaited her.

Hours passed and she tired of feeding the flames. She wrapped up in musty quilts in front of the dwindling embers. Darkness led to fear. She clutched the flashlight she had retrieved from her car and swept the bright beam toward every creak.

Trembling from the cold, she considered heading back down the mountain, but remembered her friend's insistent warnings not to attempt the treacherous road at night. The hairpin turns were too dangerous, not to mention the sheer drop to the roaring Nantahala River a few feet from the highway's shoulder. On the drive up, she noticed that except for along the most dangerous bends, the road had no guardrails.

As dawn lightened the room she finally fell asleep, but soon after a flurry of bird squawks awakened her. She couldn't pack her gear quickly enough. Usually careful with the expensive reference books and her neatly rolled blueprints, she tossed everything in a jumble to the back seat of her idling, coughing car.

She eased onto the highway and heard an ominous,

buzzing roar. She tensed, as the noise grew louder behind her. Alternating her vision from the road ahead to her rear-view mirror, she looked for what caused the sound.

Nowhere to turn off, she slowed her car to a crawl. As she came out of a tight curve, a fluorescent yellow motorcycle, mounted by a form dressed entirely in black leather, materialized behind her. Another followed. They swayed back and forth impatient to pass, gunning their powerful engines. It seemed an endless time before Jessica hit a straightaway. As they roared past, she thought the bikes and riders looked as one, their bodies draped along the gas tanks, heads hidden in alien-looking helmets.

Heart thudding, Jessica took a few quick breaths before accelerating to a safe speed. A flash of movement caught the corner of her eye. A deer darted from across the opposite side of the road and stopped mid-lane. She squealed to a halt, inches from hitting the doe. The stock-still animal stared at her a moment, then burst through the brush and vanished.

"I have got to get off this mountain," she said, clutching the steering wheel.

Jessica figured she must be halfway down the mountain when, turning a bend, she noticed the same two motorcycles parked on the shoulder ahead. Helmets in their hands, the riders were crouched over something.

One of the men ran to the middle of the road and waved her down. She stopped and rolled down her window a couple inches as he ran up to her.

"There's a man lying on the road. Can you help?"

She struggled to see beyond the other man who remained kneeling, but all she could make out were a pair of shoes pointing at the sky.

"The guy's in bad shape," the motorcyclist said, eyes wide, breathing rushed.

Pulling as far off the road as possible, Jessica hurried from the car and followed the cyclist. Stepping closer, she saw the outline of a man, nearly camouflaged by dirt, dried pine needles, dead leaves.

She leaned in closer and placed a cautious hand on his

neck. Feeling a faint pulse, she put her ear near his face. A low gurgle escaped from the man's mouth. His eyes blinked open. He raised his head a little and looked up at her, then he squeezed his eyes shut, his head falling back onto the ground.

"Thank God, he's alive." She pulled a cell phone from her jacket. "Can you hear me? Hang in there. I'm going to get you help."

The face of her phone announced: NO SERVICE. "We can go to Mars, but I can't get cell service in these damned mountains." She shoved the phone back into her pocket.

She placed a hand on the man's back and said, "What's your name? Can you tell me your name?" He remained still. "Has he said anything?"

Both cyclists shook their heads.

"Let's put him in my car." She ran back to her vehicle, and stopped parallel to the group. The riders draped the injured man's arms over their necks, trashed dress shoes scraping the blacktop as they carried him to the car.

She swept her belongings to the floor and the cyclists settled the man onto the back seat. Tucking her jacket around him, she asked the bikers, "Which way is it to the county hospital?"

"Other side of the ridge. Back up the mountain."

"Great," Jessica muttered.

"Good luck," one of them said. They put their helmets back on and mounted the bikes. Engines revved, and in a colorful flash they were gone.

"I'll get you to the hospital." Jessica told her passenger. "Just hang on."

After three attempts, she turned the Taurus around and headed back up the mountain. Purpose gave her the confidence to battle the curves once again.

24

Deputy Hawk followed Zardos up the stairways of Alexander Kalman's mansion. He ran a caffeine-shaky hand across his face, regretting he hadn't achieved a smoother shave. He felt weary from yesterday's long hours that had stretched well into the night. Questions about the Elaine Kalman case plagued him and he had finally fallen into a fitful sleep. Now, only four hours later, he took the steps in a haze.

Hawk had spent most of his childhood in the same county. His mother and younger sister still lived in the only house he had ever known, located in a secluded neighborhood bordered by a forest of trees at the edge of Bryson City. Despite his pleas for his mother to accept the money he offered so they could move into a newer house, his mama always refused. So instead, he lavished her with gifts: her first dishwasher, a vacuum cleaner, and a fifty-two inch, high definition digital television set. It tickled Hawk when-ever she commented about how the people on her TV looked just like real life. *"Look at those colors, Steven. Like we're right there,"* she would tell him, amazed.

After high school Hawk accepted a psychology scholarship to the University of Massachusetts at Amherst. His grade point average proved exemplary, as were his extracurricular activities and status on campus. He excelled in debate and political science. During his illustrious three years of attendance his professors raved that he would be a proficient psychologist. The words of praise soon turned to disappointed gossip when Hawk decided to quit the "Yankee" college. He missed the people of his community too much. He yearned for their calm ways and easy smiles. But most of all, he had missed his mother and younger sister.

Standing in the music room doorway, Hawk was again taken aback by the lavish surroundings of Alexander Kalman's mansion. Hawk thought of his family's simple lifestyle as he entered. His eyes settled first on the lush upholstered furniture and expensive-looking pieces of art sitting on tables and hanging on the walls, then the piano, shining under its own special spotlight. He wondered what such extravagant belongings would cost. The sight of Alexander dining at an outside table drew him from his curiosity.

Zardos extended his arm toward the patio, but did not escort him there. Instead he rushed off, leaving Hawk to announce himself.

Stepping onto the terrace, Hawk's breath caught as he marveled at the vista. Ageless oak, maple, and pine trees flanked each side of the secluded property. Hawk thought the vision even smelled green as he spotted flashes of passing cars along the Interstate, miles away.

Hawk licked his lips as he watched Sampte pouring orange juice from a glass pitcher.

"Good morning, Mr. Kalman," Hawk said. "Incredible view you've got. Don't believe I've ever seen our mountains looking so spectacular."

"At last. I've been waiting for word all night," Alexander said, tossing his napkin next to his plate. He waved Hawk to a chair opposite him. "Tell me more of this accident."

"Unfortunately, there's nothing much to report." Hawk swept the hat from his head and slid it on the seat next to him. "I'm sorry about the early hour, but I've got a full day ahead."

"Ah, yes, the ongoing search for my niece. Sampte, coffee for the deputy. Would you join me for breakfast?"

"Just coffee, thanks." He eyed the pitcher. "And some of that juice if you don't mind."

Sampte nodded and poured fresh brew into a delicate china cup, then juice into a tall crystal glass.

Hawk dipped his head in thanks. "Actually, because of the circumstances last night, our search has extended to include your nephew."

"Well, that's absurd. You can't be searching for someone who hasn't been reported missing."

"The crash is suspicious. There's no body. In all probability, the driver was ejected."

Alexander dabbed his mouth with the napkin as he gave Sampte a puzzled look. "No bodies you say?"

Hawk noted to himself that Alexander had referred to more than one body, so he ran with it. "Since no bodies have been recovered, we've been checking out all the bed and breakfast resorts and summer cabins, but so far no one seems to have seen Elaine or Nicholas. We've also contacted the closest hospital to where we recovered the vehicle, and a nursing home facility nearby. Unfortunately, there haven't been any admissions matching your niece or nephew's description."

Alexander sat back in his chair, giving Hawk his full attention. "What may I assist you with?"

"Well, sir, I'd like to ask you some personal questions."

"Have I become an element of your little investigation?"

"You're a piece of the puzzle."

"I see."

Hawk shifted in his seat. "You might prefer this to be a private conversation," he said, avoiding Sampte's gaze.

Alexander and Hawk stared at each other a moment. Then Alexander raised his hand and dismissed the servant with a wave.

Sampte stepped inside the music room, but Hawk figured he would still be able to hear every word of the "private" conversation. Hawk removed a pen and notepad from his breast pocket. "Mr. Kalman, I understand you were at one time an acclaimed pianist."

Alexander sipped from his cup and watched Hawk with a steady gaze before he began. "I was born with a clubbed foot. Unfortunately, numerous surgeries were unsuccessful. While other boys played soccer, I found solace in the piano, which never mocked me. I began at a very young age and advanced quite rapidly. Many prodigies are exploited by the age of twelve. I was at ten."

Hawk waited for the man to continue, but he merely folded his napkin into a precise square and placed the fabric next to his plate. He thought this would be all the information Alexander was willing to reveal, but after a long pause he continued.

"My mentor, who was also my father, cultivated me into an appealing curiosity to booking managers. By the time I reached fifteen I had toured all of Europe. Even East Germany. I was the Golden Boy of the pianist circuit. The mere mention of my name promised sold-out houses, adoring crowds, gold medals everywhere I performed. By the time I turned nineteen my child prodigy status had expired. Although I toured well into my thirties, I didn't fare well as an adult performer. I had merely been a novelty." Alexander cleared his throat. He looked down at his coffee.

"Is your nephew, Nicholas, a novelty?"

Alexander chuckled. "Quite the opposite. His allure grows as he matures. Female audiences adore him. Men want to be him."

"How long have you been his teacher?" Hawk asked.

"Nearly eleven years."

"So you know him pretty well," Hawk stated.

Alexander drained his juice glass. "I know everything about him."

"Except where he's been the last couple days." Hawk sipped his juice, studying the man who shifted in his seat and avoided direct eye contact. "About the Porsche. Was it for your personal use?"

"No. Actually I acquired the vehicle for Nicholas. He tours so much my wish is for him to relish his downtime. It is merely a plaything I purchased as a reward for his accomplishments. Naturally, I hoped the enticement would also keep him here with me."

"I assume Nicholas gets paid for these performances. Couldn't he buy his own car?"

"Not that it's any of your business, but his compensations are held in trust so that he doesn't mishandle the funds."

Hawk flipped through a few pages on his pad. "I understand you own more houses than this one."

A tight smile crossed Alexander's lips. "It seems you know quite a lot about me."

"It's routine to run a check on all parties involved in a missing persons case."

"I see. Yes, I own a number of properties, including an apartment in New York City and a flat in London. We rarely stay at either. They were purchased for investment purposes. I choose to reside here, therefore, so does Nicholas."

Hawk remembered Stiles's question as to why Alexander decided to live in the heart of the Smoky Mountains rather than anywhere else. "Why did you decide to move here, Mr. Kalman?"

"Nicholas is a celebrity in the industry. We live here so that he may concentrate on the work. In anonymity. Although we've resided here over a decade, we're still considered outsiders, therefore no one bothers us. This is precisely why I chose this location."

Hawk nodded, figuring the answer was as good as Alexander would ever give. "With your permission, I'd like to have the authorities check your out-of-state properties. I'll need you to provide me with addresses and phone numbers of your contacts."

"I cannot imagine that Nicholas or Elaine would be at either of them. I would have been apprised of their arrival. The Manhattan apartment has a doorman and strict security. I would have been notified of anyone requesting entry. And there is no accessibility to the London flat without the manager being summoned."

"And the other house?"

"My country house? I suppose that is a possibility. There's no need for a caretaker since that residence is vacant most of the time. My gardener tends to the grounds every four or five weeks."

"It's located in Swain County, right?"

"Yes. Not far off Highway seventy-four."

"The seventy-four, you say?"

"Is that relevant?"

"Well, your vehicle was pulled out of the Nantahala River along that highway."

"Of course I wasn't aware of that as no one felt it necessary to inform me."

"Mr. Kalman, I need to take a look at that property." Hawk reached for his hat and slid out of his chair. "Now."

"I'll contact *Señor* Esteva with instructions to meet us at there right away." Alexander snapped his fingers, catching Sampte's attention.

Hawk marveled at how fast the servant appeared beside them. It seemed everyone did exactly as Alexander commanded, without question or delay.

He wondered if Elaine and Nicholas had been the first to defy the imposing man in complete charge of every thing and every person around him. And if they did, had they made a fatal mistake?

25

Timothy told himself all would be well. Now that Alexander had convinced him Nicholas must have left Elaine at the country house, he plotted his next move. Come daylight he would go there and find where Nicholas must have hidden her. Take her to Thibodeaux. Be done with it. Then as morning came, he cursed the sight of the police cruiser rounding the drive, thwarting his carefully laid plans. When he recognized the officer to be the same deputy who arrived unannounced yesterday, Timothy's mood plummeted even lower.

Before he could decide what to do next, Sampte burst into the bedroom, cordless phone to his ear. "Alexander has given us orders. We must go."

Timothy stared at him, shocked by the urgent actions of the normally sedate servant.

Sampte waved his free hand at Timothy. "Come. Come!"

He rose so fast the chair tumbled to the floor.

"Esteva, this is Sampte," he yelled into the phone. "You must go to Master Kalman's country house, immediately."

Sampte snapped his fingers and Timothy lunged for his jacket hanging on the back of the door.

"See that everything is in order, Esteva. You are to report anything amiss only to me. Do you understand? We will meet you there shortly."

*   *   *

Sampte had maneuvered the Mercedes along the mountain road as fast as he dared, but now became trapped behind a tarnished Ford Taurus that refused to travel beyond twenty miles per hour.

"Pass the damned car, would you?" Timothy demanded.

Sampte gritted his teeth and strangled the steering wheel to keep from striking the young man. "Enough! I know this road far better than you."

Impatiently waiting to pass the vehicle ahead, Sampte tailgated the sputtering four-door. A few minutes earlier they had nearly collided into two motorcycles as they came out of a blind curve and he remained unnerved. Then he had nearly driven off the shoulder of the highway searching for where Timothy thought he had seen Nicholas go off the road.

At the first opportunity Sampte floored the accelerator, passed the Ford, and sped through the winding turns.

Reaching the turnoff to Alexander's country home, the sedan fishtailed onto the soft dirt road. Before Sampte had even pulled to a stop in the drive, Timothy jumped from the vehicle.

"How much time do you think we have?" Timothy asked.

"Half an hour at most. Alexander will stall and feign being lost." Sampte dug a hand in the pot on the porch and withdrew a key. Brushing the brass clean, he shoved it in the lock, then rushed through the front door.

Timothy pushed in after him. "Find Esteva and see where he's already searched. Maybe he's found something."

Sampte grabbed his sleeve. "Hurry," he said, knowing a near-frantic look flashed in his eyes. "We must find her before that deputy arrives."

26

Jessica burst through the emergency room entrance of the county hospital. "Help me! I've got someone in my car. I think he's dying."

The registration attendant sloshed coffee onto her log sheet. The triage nurse rushed to Jessica and waved for an orderly to grab a nearby gurney. They lifted the injured man from the car and laid him on the rolling bed, then bolted through the emergency room double doors.

A wave of nurses, a resident, and two interns swarmed the patient being wheeled into an empty bay. Examination immediately underway, hands flew across the patient's body, all choreographed to silent music.

Jessica eased toward the curtain and watched, awe-struck, clutching a lock of her hair.

"Get Doctor Everett in here," someone shouted.

"Check stats."

"Full trauma panel."

"One liter saline wide open."

"IV push."

"BP sixty over forty. Respiration forty, rapid and shallow. One fifty heartbeat. Temp ninety-six."

Numerous pairs of scissors slit away the filthy overcoat, tuxedo jacket, then shirt.

A nurse expertly inserted an intravenous line into a vein in his arm.

"Side head supports. Don't know what we've got here, yet."

They washed away the grime and dried blood from his face. A woman dressed in blue scrubs sheared away remains of tattered gloves. A tarnished antique key slid out of the scissors' cut and tumbled from the patient's left hand, landing on the hard flooring with a *tink*. The nurse retrieved the key and stuffed it inside a clear plastic bag. The impression of the key's outline had cut its shape into the patient's raw palm. She unsnapped the scuffed watchband and put it in with the key.

An orderly handed the nurse the jacket and she slipped her hand in one of the pockets. Withdrawing a leather book the size of a man's hand, she set it aside and searched the other inside pocket. The nurse pulled out a powder blue envelope and a gold writing pen. Within the trouser pockets she removed a silver money clip holding a thin fold of bills. She tucked the belongings into the plastic bag, zipped the container closed, then with a black marker she wrote the current date, the initials J.D. and the number seventy-eight.

An attendant made notations on a chart, another secured leads from a cardiac monitor to the man's well-built chest.

"Warming blanket."

"Type and cross for blood."

"Acute swelling to the left ankle," answered by, "X-ray on that."

"Multiple contusions and lacerations to the head. Call in the plastic surgeon for the facial lac."

A man wearing a white lab coat who Jessica thought looked younger than her checked the patient's eyes with a penlight. "Pupils slow but reactive."

Now clean, the man's face appeared bloodless white, as was the skin on his limbs, revealed when the clothes were cut away. Knees scraped raw, his torso and legs were covered in bruises and puncture wounds. He appeared lifeless with the exception of the slight rise and fall of his chest.

"Is he going to be okay?" Jessica asked a nearby nurse, her eyes never leaving the man.

The nurse laid a hand on Jessica's shoulder. "We'll do everything we can for your friend."

"Yes. Do everything." The man wasn't a friend, nevertheless, Jessica felt responsible for him now. "Save him."

27

Timothy ran from room to room on the upper floor of Alexander's country house. Crazed, he searched for Elaine in every closet and under each bed. Sweeping knuckles across his eyes to clear the sweat that had coursed into them, he blinked to clear his blurred vision of the walls as he rushed past. A cloying, sweet smell grew stronger as he advanced down the narrow corridor.

The first thing he noticed upon entering the last bedroom down the hall was the freezing temperature. His gaze slid to a broken window, a scatter of glass on the floor, a bloated dead carcass of a raccoon swarming with maggots. He covered his nose and mouth as he walked to the animal and nudged the corpse with his shoe.

Drawn to the cedar chest at the foot of the bed, he opened the lid to find it empty. The armoire across the room caught his attention. He tugged the delicate knobs, but the doors didn't budge.

Hearing the crunch of gravel outside, Timothy rushed to the window. His heart thudded at the sight of Hawk's cruiser pulling into the drive.

"Sampte! They're here!"

Sampte hurried from the front porch to open the passenger door for Alexander as the deputy's cruiser came to a halt.

"Why didn't you wait to go in until I got here?" Hawk snapped, looking at the open front door.

"I'm sorry," Sampte said. "I thought perhaps—"

"Never mind," Hawk barked. "Is your man Esteva here yet?"

"In the basement, turning on the power," Sampte answered. "There is no one here. Everything is precisely the same as when we left last summer."

"Mr. Kalman, I assume I have your permission to enter the premises," the deputy stated. He breezed past Alexander and into the house without waiting for an answer.

Alexander quietly asked Sampte, "Where is Timothy?"

Sampte motioned with his head to the upstairs windows.

"Did you find her?"

Sampte shook his head.

"Esteva?" Alexander asked.

"He's been throughout the house, but found nothing," Sampte whispered.

"You're certain?"

"I believe him."

Alexander held Sampte's gaze for a moment before limping up the front steps one at a time.

"I want everyone to stay in the front room until I take a look around," Hawk ordered.

The red-haired young man Hawk recognized from Alexander's mansion rushed into the room. Out of breath, cheeks blazing, his wide eyes scanned the men.

In one quick movement, Hawk's hand went to his side and rested on the butt of his Glock.

"Whoa," Timothy shouted, raising his hands in the air.

"Okay, everybody relax," Hawk snapped. He turned his back toward the wall in order to view the entire room.

"This is my pupil, Timothy," Alexander said, going to the young man and draping a protective arm across his shoulder. "He means you no harm."

The Latin man Hawk also recognized from Alexander's mansion stepped into the room—someone else to worry about. Hawk's annoyance grew.

The man, his skin nearly as dark as his own, locked his gaze on Hawk's badge, then dropped to the gun.

Hawk commanded, "Stay where you are."

"It's all right, Manuel." Alexander waved the trembling man closer. "He's my gardener, Manuel Esteva."

Dressed in crisply ironed khaki work clothes and sturdy

boots, Esteva edged toward the group, his eyes darting from one man to the other.

"Have you been anywhere else besides the basement?" Hawk asked Manuel.

Esteva looked at Alexander.

"He's not here to take you away, Manuel. There is no need to worry. This deputy needs your assistance. Your status will not be in jeopardy. Isn't that correct, deputy?"

Hawk nodded and the gardener blew out a relieved sigh. He pointed to the staircase. "Come with me, Esteva. Everyone else stay down here."

Alexander spoke a few insistent words in Spanish to Esteva who nodded, head bowed. "No *la migra*?"

"No. Don't worry, you're not in any trouble," Hawk said, urging him up the stairs.

Walking down the hall with Esteva, Hawk stuck his head in the first open door and scanned the room. Taking another step, he stopped, sniffed the air, and pinched his nose. "What is that smell?"

"I find a broken window," Esteva said. "And a dead raccoon."

"Where?"

Esteva hustled to the farthest bedroom. From inside the doorway, he pointed toward the floor under the window.

Hawk shouldered past Manuel, into the room. "Freezin' in here." His eyes fell on the raccoon and he knelt over the dead body. "Must've fallen from the tree."

"I clean up, now. Okay? Master Kalman no like mess."

"Yeah, sure, okay."

Esteva hurried out of the room.

Boots crunching glass underfoot, Hawk walked to the window. Pushing aside the curtain, he saw a tree limb that ran the width of the window, a few inches from the glass.

He heard the muffled sounds of a heated argument brewing downstairs and eased onto the landing to listen.

Sampte's stomach roiled as he watched Alexander attempt to hold down his rage.

"Madness. This is madness," his master hissed in a lowered voice, accentuating each word with the thump of his cane upon the braided rug.

"She could be anywhere in this place," Timothy said, his fearful gaze never leaving the stick.

The boy had failed. The chore had not been one for an over-eager child. Again, Sampte wished his master had left the crucial task to him. In an attempt to defer Alexander's wrath on Timothy, he offered, "She may not be here at all."

Alexander continued to glare at Timothy. "Yes. No one seems to know where either of them are."

"That's good, though. It gives us time—"

"There is no *us* in this matter, Timothy," Alexander said. "This is your mess. If you'd have followed my orders I would not be faced with this fiasco."

Timothy lowered his head. "I don't know what you expect me to do."

The mentor lifted the pupil's chin with the lion's head of his cane and met Timothy's glistening eyes. "You owe me your life and everything in it." He stepped to within inches of Timothy's trembling body. "Correct this matter."

Alexander turned to Sampte and said, "He's not worth the fifty thousand dollars I paid for him." He shuffled out the front door, slamming it after him.

Tears swam in Timothy's eyes.

Sampte creased his brows and gave the boy a sympathetic pat on the shoulder, then trailed after his master.

Hawk moved from the shadows at the top of the stairs. Though he had not been able to make out all the words the men exchanged, he sensed by the tone of the conversation they knew more about Elaine than they were telling him.

He decided to set his sights on Timothy. He assumed the vulnerability with Alexander might work against the kid.

More than once during his investigation, Hawk had considered the possibility that Elaine and Nicholas were innocently lying in one another's arms, unaware of worrying her mother. Now, he wondered if they were playing everyone for fools, merely hiding somewhere, taking pleasure in tormenting their Uncle Alexander Kalman.

28

At fifty-two, Dr. Calbert Everett had burned out as a thoracic surgeon at Sloan-Kettering in New York City. Finally taking the wise recommendation he often gave to his patients, he found a small community in North Carolina and retired from the perilous life of drive-by shootings and overdoses.

After pulling what must have been his ten-thousandth small-mouth bass out of the river, walking distance from his forest-hidden cabin, he became stir-crazy.

He ventured to the quaint yet immaculate county hospital with volunteering in mind and was bitten by the healing bug once again. Three years from the time he first walked through the doors, he found contentment in treating patients in the laidback manner Southerners preferred.

Everett's young assistant, Ellie, eager and pleasant as always, sat across from him in the cramped office writing down his instructions.

"Be sure to remind me to go over the budget to be certain we're still on track this quarter. The county's nearly broke. We don't want to spread ourselves too thin before we're out of the winter season."

Ellie nodded. "Are you going to check on the John Doe?"

"I'll head there right now." Everett pulled on a white lab coat with his name embroidered above the pocket. "Is the woman who brought him in still around?"

"Yes." She checked her notes. "Her name is Jessica Taft. She refuses to leave."

"There's dedication for you," Everett said, bustling from his office into the hospital's corridor.

Ellie chased after him, holding an armful of charts. "She's in the upstairs waiting room."

Calling over his shoulder, Everett said, "Very good. See you soon."

Everett bid everyone he passed a pleasant greeting. Reaching the stairwell, he took two steps at a time up to the second floor.

At the waiting room's registration desk, he beamed at the elderly nurse behind the glass. "Hello, Louise." Everett nodded toward a woman dozing in a chair, an open textbook in her lap. "Is that the young lady who brought our patient in?"

"Yes, Doctor. He's stabilized. They're about to send him up to a private room."

"Wonderful. I'll let her know. Thank you, Louise."

Everett went to Jessica and stood before her. "Excuse me. Miss?"

The young woman blinked several times and looked at him with a blank expression.

"I'm Dr. Everett, the head of emergency medicine. I understand you brought our patient in."

"Yes, I did." She set the book onto the seat next to her, then rose to meet his handshake. "I came around a bend and there he was." Her eyes found the floor. Nibbling her bottom lip, she crossed her arms tight against her chest. "I really thought he was dead."

"It's a good thing you found him when you did. Looks like his accident occurred a couple days ago."

Jessica's hand went to her mouth, her face creased with worry.

"He hasn't regained consciousness yet, and that's a concern. We'll know more once he's awake and can speak. We're about to move him to his own room. He's recovering as well as we can hope."

"What a relief."

Everett patted her hand, then took a note pad and pen from his lab coat pocket. "Do you know what his name is?"

"No. I've never seen him before. You don't know?"

"We didn't find any identification on him. I thought perhaps he might have said something during your heroic efforts to get him here." She blushed and looked away. "Don't worry, we'll find out. There's really no need for you to stay."

"Well . . . I'd like to see him before I leave if you think that would be okay. I kind of feel responsible for him. Know what I mean?"

"Of course," Everett said, touched by her concern and devotion to a complete stranger. Then again, the young man would now be scarred for life. When he stabilized, he would need someone to care about him. Everett smiled at the lovely young woman. "I'm sure he would like that."

29

Nicholas awoke in a haze. Disoriented, he looked around at the sterile surroundings of a small room. *Where the hell am I?* The pain reminded him. Looking down, he saw the faded hospital gown and the thin blanket draped over him, bathed in an unpleasant bluish tone from the fluorescent fixture over his head.

When he attempted to raise his leg and swivel from the bed, he winced and uttered groans of pain. He wriggled his nose, feeling something stuck inside his nostrils. Cool, dry air hissed as he pulled at a thin line of plastic. Eyes tracking the conduit settled on his chest, he startled at a needle attached to another tube inserted into the vein below his bicep. His gaze followed that line of conduit and saw that it was attached to a bag half-filled with clear liquid, hanging from a pole next to the bed.

A flashback of him sitting inside the careening Porsche raced through his mind. Sweat began to stipple his forehead, and he urged his fear to subside.

Lifting his hands, he panicked at the sight of them wrapped in gauze. He attempted a piano fingering position. Pain shot through his hands. His dry eyes stung with tears. *I've already lost Elaine, now my ability to play, too?*

He rubbed the bristles of beard, the gauze catching on its growth. He gently patted a bandage wound around his head and over his right eye.

Thoughts of Elaine flashed in Nicholas's mind. *Thank God she wasn't in the car.* Reminding himself that she remained in a safe place brought him momentary comfort, but his own safety became a worry. His fear turned to Alexander and Timothy. *Do they know I'm here?*

Nicholas noticed the identification bracelet secured to his right wrist. Lifting his arm, he gazed at the plastic band. His heart beat faster when he read the name printed on the tag: JOHN DOE.

Movement caught his eye and he noticed the door open. A young woman carrying an armful of books backed into his room then eased the door shut. She approached an ancient recliner the color of pea soup in the corner, then looked up at him.

She let out a surprised gasp, then she smiled. "You're awake. This is so great." Tossing her belongings onto the sagging chair cushion, she went to him. "I should get the doctor."

"Who are you?"

"Jessica. Jessica Taft. What's your name?"

He raised his arm and extended his wrist to her. "John Doe, apparently."

She leaned close to read the tag and gave him a look of concern.

"How long have I been here?"

Jessica glanced at her watch and her green eyes, the shade of emeralds, grew wide. "Hours. I've lost track of time, too."

Nicholas tried to lift himself and gave up, exhausted.

"Are you in much pain?"

He nodded.

"I'll go get the nurse."

"Wait. Just wait. I don't . . ." Nicholas fell silent. He thrashed at the blanket and struggled to lift himself.

"Let me raise the bed for you." She reached for a plastic box that dangled off the edge of the mattress. Testing one button then another she found the correct one. The back of the bed rose with a whirr.

"Better?"

Nicholas nodded again. "I'm so thirsty," he said in a far-away voice.

"I don't know if you're supposed to drink anything . . ."

He gave her a desperate look and she halted her words. She shook a small pink pitcher from the rolling cart next to the bed and entered what he thought must be a bathroom.

Thirst intensifying at the sound of running water, he ran his swollen tongue across parched, cracked lips. Moaning, he adjusted into a more comfortable position.

When she returned to his bedside, his anticipation peaked as he watched her pour water into a plastic cup. She bent the straw to meet his lips and he gulped with relish. When he drained the cup, he motioned for more.

She brushed off a small puddle of spilled water pooling on his chest. "Try to sip it."

After downing another cupful, he fell back against the pillow to catch his breath. "Do you work here?" he whispered.

"No. I found you and brought you here. You don't remember?"

A nurse came into the room, nearly bursting from her wildly colored smock. Her shining black face seemed kind to Nicholas. Carrying an aluminum clipboard, she met them with a blinding smile. "Well, look who's awake. I'm your nurse, Connie."

Jessica stepped away from the bed. "I'll go now," she said, crossing the room to her bag in the chair.

"You're coming back though, aren't you?" Nicholas asked, panic tapping his chest.

"Okay. Sure."

"I'll only be a minute. You can wait outside." Connie waved Jessica through the doorway. "Good to see you're back with us. Dr. Everett will be so pleased." Taking his bandaged left wrist in her chubby hand, eyeing her watch, she asked, "Much pain?"

"My head," Nicholas slurred, "and my hands."

"You're pretty banged up. What's your name, darlin?" She waited for his response. When he didn't answer, she continued, "I need to know how to contact your family. I'm sure they're out of their minds lookin' for you." Connie busied herself, adjusting bed covers, checking his IV and the bag's contents. She felt the tightness of his head bandage and halted at his vacant look.

"I . . . I'm not sure who I am," Nicholas said.

The statement caused Connie to stop. "You don't know?" Nicholas did not answer.

Connie tisked and shook her head. Actions precise, she made a notation on his chart. With a penlight, she checked each pupil, then she went to the foot of his bed and folded back the blanket, uncovering his feet to the ankles.

"What happened to me?" Nicholas asked, trying not to sound alarmed.

She ran a capped pen along the arch of his foot, causing him to suppress a giggle as he wriggled his toes. "Doctor Everett believes you've been exposed to the elements for a couple days."

Nicholas flinched, astonished by how much time had blurred past. *Days. Surely Alexander would have found me by now if he was looking.* An involuntary shudder coursed through him.

"You cold, sugar?" Connie asked, tucking the blanket along his body.

"I may never be warm again."

"They say that, you know. Once the body's gotten too cold. Cold to the core, they say. I'll get you another blanket, and don't you worry. You'll be fine, now. We're gonna take real good care of you."

"And find out who I am," Nicholas said, more than asked.

"You lie still. When I come back I'll have something for your pain." Connie winked at him and left the room.

When Jessica peeked from behind the door, Nicholas waved her back in.

"She left in a hurry."

"Off to find the doctor." He touched his right temple and winced. "And some drugs, I hope."

Silence fell between them. Finally, Jessica said, "I probably should go and let you get some sleep."

"Will you come back tomorrow?" he asked, already regretting being left alone.

"Sure. I don't have classes until the afternoon."

"You're a student?"

"Uh huh, at Western Carolina University."

Same as Elaine.

She slung the strap to her bag along her shoulder and went to the door. "See you tomorrow. Get some rest."

After she left, he puzzled over what the nurse had said about people missing him. *Wouldn't Alexander wonder? Come looking for me? Should I call him? Aranka, maybe?* Nicholas looked at the phone on the bedside table. *What am I thinking? I can't call anyone.*

His last vision of Elaine, slumped deep within the armoire, filled his already troubled mind. He squeezed his eyes shut to obliterate the horrific scene, quickly replaced by his car accident that replayed in flashes. Fury filled him and he struggled to settle down, but he clearly saw the winding road, a car in his rearview mirror coming up on him too fast, the other car heading in the opposite direction right for him. Swerving not to crash. The car from behind now close enough to kiss his bumper, then pulling up next to him, racing side-by-side for a moment before speeding past. The dark sedan seemed so familiar. He concentrated on minute details of the memory. An emblem on the hood. Round. A peace symbol. His eyes shot open with recognition.

A black Mercedes-Benz.

The same type of car Sampte always drove.

Pain and panic throughout his body seized him, taking his breath away. He remembered Timothy waiting for him at the Wilhoit Theatre. *Timothy left Elaine in my car. Did Sampte speed ahead, then turn around and run me off the road? Are they working together in this madness?* At that moment, he swore everyone involved would suffer, even if he had to die seeking revenge for Elaine.

His first impulse to pretend he suffered from amnesia reinforced, he told himself, *Be careful. Don't divulge a thing. Be patient. Wait for the next movement to reveal itself. Don't rush the timing.*

30

By late afternoon, Deputy Hawk felt certain no one had been hiding out at Alexander's country house. He had checked for residue in all the bathtubs and sink basins, even sniffed the towels for moisture. Musty sheets were folded in the linen closet. He found no trash, empty food containers, or dirty dishes anywhere. With the exception of the broken window, apparently caused by the raccoon, nothing appeared disturbed.

He intended to keep Alexander and Timothy with him on the ride back to Alexander's mansion. Maybe he could urge them to talk with the hopes one of them would reveal some pertinent information, but Alexander had insisted he and the kid ride home with Sampte.

"Can we expect you back at my house?" Alexander asked.

"No, I've taken enough of your time," Hawk replied.

"Nonsense. I'm as anxious to find my niece and nephew as you are. Needless to say I'm quite concerned."

Hawk eyed him steadily then watched Timothy slide into the back seat of the Mercedes and slam the car door shut. Hawk noted the thick tension between the young man and Alexander. Again, he regretted not being privy to the conversation they would surely have.

"I'll notify your sister. Let her know we haven't found anything yet," Hawk told Alexander.

"Yes. Best it comes from you."

Alexander waved a limp goodbye as Sampte pulled away.

Hawk pretended a gracious smile, glad to be rid of the pompous man. He went to his cruiser to make notations regarding everything he didn't find for the Kalman file.

Figuring he should check in, he reached for his cell phone, but read NO SERVICE on its display. Taking the car radio's mouthpiece from its cradle, he spoke into the mic. "Dispatch, SCD Fifteen."

After a moment, a voice came over the speaker. "Go ahead, Fifteen."

"Leaving location, Parson's Trail. Heading to one twenty-nine Vargo Canyon, Aranka Kalman's personal address."

"Roger that, Fifteen."

I only wish there was something encouraging to tell her.

As he pulled from the drive, he glanced in his rear-view mirror to see a pickup truck emerge from behind the house. Manuel Esteva sat slumped behind the wheel. He turned to look at Hawk so he stopped the cruiser. Esteva watched him for a long time.

"What the hell?" Hawk got out of his car and walked toward the truck.

Esteva suddenly accelerated and sped away, leaving Hawk in the wake of billowing dust.

"Dammit all. No tellin' what that man knows," Hawk mumbled. "Maybe I *should* check with immigration. Shake him up a bit."

31

That night, Manuel Esteva trembled in the same work clothes he had worn since dawn, stiff from sweat, wrinkled and dusty, pant cuffs stained by red clay.

Unable to sleep, he had ambled around the modest double-wide trailer his Regina always proudly stated to be, "As good as any house." She kept their home as immaculate as the grounds he tended for *Señor* Kalman.

He tumbled into his recliner and waited for dawn. Fingering a loose piece of flowered fabric, he replayed the disastrous day.

At first Manuel had prayed the deputy would not remember his name, even though he saw the lawman write it down. He worried over this small piece of cloth and his circumstances, and seriously considered calling the lawman now.

After his employer and the others drove away from the country house, Manuel used the mobile phone Sampte had provided for emergencies to reserve a U-Haul truck for the next morning. Then he tossed the handset deep into the woods.

The first step of his plan completed, he sped from the property for what he promised to be the last time.

Tomorrow, he would take Mama, Regina, and their three children away from a life they had known for five years. Loyalty to *Señor* Kalman now held too many consequences.

By the time Manuel arrived home that evening, he felt confident in his decision. Though full of regret at the prospect of uprooting his family, he convinced himself there were no other choices. To be safe, they must move on.

His mama had always warned him that shortcuts would not be favorable in the eyes of God. She had cried when he'd accepted the job from Alexander Kalman. She knew of no honest labor worth the wage her boy was offered—a fortune compared to Cuban wages. How could she have been so right? Even though she had no book knowledge, her wisdom had always frightened him, as if the Madonna spoke to her in hushed song.

She did not say a word of criticism to her son that night; only clucked to her grieving grandchildren, "Listen to your *papi*. He knows what is best. All will be well."

Fearing this very day, Manuel had stashed a good deal of his earnings in four, one-pound coffee tins and buried them behind the trailer beyond the tool shed. He had never shown anyone the tightly bound rolls of cash he had grown shamefully proud of, but he suspected his mama knew of the stashed money.

Now, as he sneaked another glance at the zippered canvas bag holding the cans, on the floor at his feet, he thought back over the events that led him to his decision to leave. The overwhelming need to flee had forced him to direct his attention to what he must do next.

He recalled the urgent phone call from Sampte ordering him to search the country house. Before Sampte and Timothy arrived, although he had no idea what he should be searching for, Manuel had walked all around the property. After finding nothing outside, he entered the house and began looking there.

Manuel checked the upstairs rooms one after the other, finally finding himself at the last bedroom down the long hall. Something about the room bothered him the moment he entered. Immediately, he noticed the broken window, scattered glass, the dead raccoon, and the smell of death. A warning of dread stopped the breath in his chest and his body shook.

The last time he had stepped inside the vacant house had been to help shut it down for winter and he was sure a blanket covered the bed in that room.

When he turned to leave the bedroom, a flash of color caught his attention. He noticed something sticking out from between the wooden cabinet's shut doors. He tugged at a piece of floral cloth. Pulling at the small handles mounted on the doors, he found them locked. Withdrawing his pocketknife, he cut the swatch enough for him to tear free. He knew Sampte demanded that everything always be kept neat, so he stuffed the frayed strings into the tight crack between the doors with the sharp blade. He considered the lock a moment, then stuck the knife's tip into the opening. As the blade scratched in the keyhole, he heard a car pull up in the drive. Feeling like a guilty child, he snapped the blade shut and ran downstairs to meet his employer.

Manuel didn't know why he did not tell Sampte or Alexander of his discovery, but he did recognize the colorful pattern. Ever since the day *Señor* Kalman's young niece stumbled into him on the mansion's front path, she had haunted him. The frantic look on her face still filled him with fright.

"Miss, are you okay?" he had asked, taking her arms in his hands.

"Don't get involved in this, Manuel," she told him in a firm voice.

He felt the heat from her trembling body and immediately let her go. When she looked upward, her face turned so hard and cold it scared Manuel. He followed her gaze to the third story window and saw Alexander looking down at them.

She ran to her car and sped away so fast he had to jump aside so that he wouldn't be sprayed with the gravel spinning from under the wheels.

When the deputy came to Alexander's mansion asking questions about her disappearance, Manuel felt it his duty to inform the lawman of her agitation. He had overheard Sampte tell Zardos that Elaine would never be back and warned the young servant not to mention her name ever again in front of Alexander.

After much consideration, and a battle with his nerves, he decided to gather the courage to face the lawman. Standing behind Timothy at the music room, hoping to speak with the deputy, Manuel was certain the look Alexander leveled at him would stop his heart. The warnings Alexander spoke in Spanish not to say a word to the deputy, left Manuel trembling in the doorway. It took all of his strength not to run away from the big house, never to return.

He wished he had. If he had only followed his intuition, he wouldn't be faced with the sense of foreboding that troubled his head and heart.

As he cleaned up the broken glass, then taped cardboard over the window, the others rambled throughout the house. Later, Manuel accomplished the task of burying the raccoon in the forest, digging scoops of red clay, thoughts of protecting his family tormenting him.

Memories of past dealings with Master Kalman came to his mind. Over the years, after he and his charges left from their visits to the country house, Manuel often had to drive off coyotes that roamed the forest around the property, searching for fresh kill. Manuel's shotgun blasts exploded the forest's calm, scaring away any living creatures for hours afterward. Manuel shook his head, pitying the number of dead rotting carcasses of night creatures he would find scattered throughout the acres of property—*Señor* Kalman, Timothy, and Sampte's abandoned kills. The stench of skunk and death permeated the calm forest air for days after the hunters abandoned the killing grounds.

Now, as he fingered the swatch of cloth, he thought about going back to the country house and breaking into the cabinet to see what could be hidden inside. But fear overtook any spark of courage.

The sound of soft footsteps rescued him from his troubles. At the tender touch of his wife's fingers in his hair, remorse filled his chest.

Regina slipped onto the arm of his recliner and tucked her head in the crook of his neck. "You must get some sleep, *amorcito*."

He kissed her forehead and they lulled each other in quiet Spanish tones.

"Are they okay?"

"Lucia cried herself to sleep. She will miss her friends."

"She'll make more."

Quiet fell over them, then Regina asked, "The policeman.

Does he worry you?"

"Not so much," Manuel lied.

"Then why are we leaving?"

Manuel softened at the sound of fresh tears in her voice. "I'll make it up to you. We'll be all right."

"You've always provided for us. I am proud to be yours."

Her sweetness caused such emotion in Manuel, a sob caught in his chest. "I am yours too, you know?"

Regina answered with a nod. "Where will we go?"

"Miami."

"Like everyone else," she said in a resigned, faraway voice. "We will be like everyone else."

"That's best for now."

"Tell me the rest of what happened," she said. "I want to know everything."

He pulled Regina into his lap and whispered in her ear. "There was something in the country house. I don't know what. A feeling. A darkness."

Knowing Regina to be a superstitious woman, Manuel sensed her fear when she tensed in his arms.

"They were there a long time, looking."

"For what?"

Manuel didn't speak English well, but he understood every urgent word his employer and the others spoke. He knew it was Elaine they all searched for.

He didn't want to alarm his already spooked wife, so he faked his own concern. "I don't know. I was afraid to ask. Sampte was watchful. *Señor* Kalman showed little worry, but Timothy . . . full of nerves. Never more than three steps behind *el maestro*."

"I never liked that boy."

Manuel chuckled, knowing Regina, only eight years older than Timothy, had never even met him.

"But *Señor* Kalman has been nothing but good to us," she scolded.

"Yes. He paid me well. That is what worries me. I've seen things I can never speak of."

They held each other in silence and soon he felt the

steady rhythm of her sleeping breaths. At ease for the first time in hours, Manuel closed his eyes and thought of their wedding day.

He heard the faint rumble of what sounded like a large truck. Their trailer stood last on the lane and he wondered who could be on the road that serviced only three other residences so late at night. But exhausted from the day's events, he couldn't seem to open his eyes, let alone get up to investigate. A moment later, the remembered vision of his new bride coaxing him to tango cancelled his puzzlement.

32

Zardos could not believe what this night had brought. Instructions from Sampte were, as always, vague and ominous. All he offered were the words to be ready at midnight dressed in dark clothing and work boots.

Half an hour early for the appointment, Zardos neared the spot where Sampte's directions indicated. Bouncing in the truck's cab along a rutted dirt road, he used only running lights to find his way as he recalled his conversation with Sampte a few hours ago.

"When you arrive, park off the road, and if anyone sees you call me right away," Sampte had said, handing Zardos a cell phone and a sheet of paper with a map sketched on the back.

"Why midnight?" Zardos asked.

"Why must you always ask questions? You have your assignment, it's the only detail you need to know."

"Is the request from Master Kalman?"

Sampte whirled to face Zardos's challenge. "Everything we do is for Master Kalman. He's why we are here. Have you forgotten that?"

Zardos lowered his head and shook it.

"Do you remember what you came from? The poverty? Relying on the generosity of strangers and only what the land provided?"

"I remember playing in the mountains as any boy would. I was only thirteen when Master Kalman sent for me with promises of comfort for my family and a life of bliss for me. This is not a carefree life, Sampte. Do you think what he asks of us is natural?"

"It's not my place to ask. It certainly isn't yours."

"For years now, all I've done is meet his demands. And what are his thanks? The lashings from his cane. I have no other life. No woman, or home of my own. He doesn't even allow us to speak Hungarian. My one friend is Nicholas and only God knows where he is. No one's telling me."

Sampte's hand upon his shoulder did not calm Zardos. His body heat rose from inside his collar. "I need to know if he's all right."

"I'm told they are looking for him. For now, you must concentrate. What is to come will not be a pleasant task. The worst so far."

"Then why do it?" Zardos asked, brushing away Sampte's touch.

Sampte raised his arm and struck Zardos across the face with the back of his hand. The sharp sound surprised Zardos as much as the attack.

Zardos held firm, not daring to place a shaking hand on his blazing cheek. He fought down hot tears and tried to hide his terror. Sampte had been like a father to him. The harsh words and look of disgust in the older man's eyes hurt far worse than the strike.

Making the final curve noted on the map, Zardos recalled the pain, holding his palm to his bruising face. He pulled off the road, backed between two huge pines, and waited for Sampte. A bit farther down the road he noticed the outline of a trailer home hidden in the stand of trees.

Not more than ten minutes later Sampte's Mercedes rolled past. When Zardos recognized Sampte's passenger, a sense of doom filled him. *Timothy.* Zardos knew only the worst assignments were issued when Timothy was involved.

Reluctantly Zardos slipped out of the truck, careful not to slam the door. By the time he reached the front drive, Sampte and Timothy had vanished. He stepped close enough to see that the curtains were open and the trailer was dark except for a glow at the back of the house.

Zardos saw a burst of light from the front room window, reminding him of a camera's flash, but the sound immediately following was unmistakable.

Gunshots.

Resonating cracks split the night as two more quick

blazes came from another window, then two more from the farthest glass.

Before Zardos could react, Sampte emerged out the front door and stopped. He ran his hands through his hair before he walked down the steps and hurried toward Zardos.

"Get the truck and back it up to the front porch," Sampte said, re-buttoning his overcoat. Trails of sweat ran down the sides of his face. His eyes darted, wild with adrenaline. He surveyed Zardos head to toe then reached out to close the top button on Zardos's jacket. "Put on your gloves," he ordered, then returned to the house.

"This is going to be bad," Zardos mumbled, running back to the truck. He pulled up as close to the steps as possible, exited the vehicle and found three large cardboard boxes on the porch waiting to be loaded.

"Stack these in the back," Sampte said. "There's more inside."

Zardos nodded as he rolled open the door of the empty truck. When Timothy emerged on the porch, he called Sampte over to him. Zardos watched them trade a few words and he trembled, seeing Timothy's eerie elation. Hair askew, his eyes danced and he bounced from one foot to the other.

After loading box after box, Zardos stood next to the truck and waited for more. Right as he decided to go into the house, Sampte backed out of the front door. He struggled with a load of something draped in plastic garbage bags. Timothy held the other end. They teetered down the steps then slid the bundle into the truck.

"Place them side by side," Sampte said, running back into the house.

Mouth agape, Zardos stared at the object, unwilling to join it inside the truck.

The procession continued, one black bundle after another, each growing smaller in size until Sampte emerged with the sixth, cradled in one arm, a canvas bag in the other. He placed the little bundle gently atop one of the larger ones.

"One more thing," Sampte said in a breathless voice.

Timothy and Sampte struggled with a bulky recliner, then

slid it alongside the wrapped bundles in the truck. Zardos noticed an uneven dark stain on the chair's back cushion.

Pulling on the strap to close the truck door, Sampte said, "Park behind the house and wait for us. You are not to go inside. Understand?"

Too stunned to reply, Zardos stumbled in a haze into the truck's cab and pulled from the drive, careful not to knock over the mailbox he hadn't noticed when he had backed in. Turning to look, he swore his heart stopped when he read the name stenciled on the side of the receptacle: ESTEVA.

33

Sampte worried about Zardos during the drive to their next stop. Their relationship had become strained over the past few months. He prayed Alexander had not noticed, fearing what his master would command. Nicholas's disappearance over the last few days heightened their battles. Zardos had become a friend to Nicholas who referred to him as his personal assistant—not merely a butler. Sampte knew his young charge felt at a loss and without purpose.

Sampte had grown to love Zardos as his own son. Often, they shared conversations remembering the Hungary Sampte had been forced to leave when he was too young to realize he'd never experience his homeland again.

Alexander's father had brought Sampte from Hungary to serve as his ten-year-old son's personal valet. After searching much of the region for the ideal servant, the elder Kalman found Sampte's family only three villages away from his own. Assured by a number of reputable citizens that the Sampte lineage was noted to be reliable and trustworthy, Alexander's father offered the farmer a sum he could not refuse for his only son.

"We'll lose the farm if you don't go," his father had said with weepy eyes. "I've taken the money. It won't be for long. Once the boy becomes a man, he won't be needing you. The old man assured me of this."

Reluctantly, Sampte agreed, and with passage to America promptly secured, Sampte found himself on a boat to the United States, assuming one day he would return to his home and family.

The Sampte generational reputation was renowned in a region far in the hills of Hungary, where they bred Kuvasz dogs. Though the Kuvasz were considered mongrels by much of the more refined society whose preferences leaned toward regal Pinschers or Danes, the local farmers cherished the fearless, one hundred pound, solid white working dogs. The Sampte's held a legacy of breeding the majestic creatures beginning with his great-grandfather.

Sampte would be the first to break the tradition.

Alexander's father's decision to employ Sampte proved to be brilliant. An unequaled servant, Sampte often accompanied the young pianist across the globe.

Sampte, six years older than Alexander, soon learned his station. It was clear who was the master. Who would always be the master. Sampte never challenged Alexander's orders. *It is not your place to judge*, Sampte often reminded himself. Nevertheless, he also felt, over the years, Alexander's games had gone too far. When Timothy and then Nicholas entered their lives, Sampte became concerned for their wellbeing. He wondered how they would turn out. He had seen firsthand how the psyche could be crushed by the pressures of performing. Alexander's teachings had reached far beyond piano tutelage.

He thought of the times Alexander had brandished his cane on Zardos. The younger servant was Sampte's responsibility, but the boy often irritated their master with interruptions and senseless questions. Sampte often lashed Zardos with harsh words, but had never raised a hand to his cherished companion. Until tonight.

Sampte anguished Zardos's second-guessing his orders. When he struck Zardos, a piece of Sampte died inside. He knew of Zardos's humiliation whenever Alexander had the occasion to hit him. And now, merely due to weakness and fear of the younger man's insubordination toward their master, Sampte had become yet another assailant. He was now afraid Zardos would run away and take his chances on his own, leaving Sampte behind, heartbroken.

He glanced at Timothy, sitting erect in his seat, still appearing pumped from the mission. *He enjoys this far too much.*

Sampte checked his mirror to make sure Zardos still followed in the delivery truck. Grateful for the dark desolation of Henri Thibodeaux's property, he pulled behind the house and parked, and then waved for Zardos to go in front of the cement building.

Sampte followed the path to the morgue's door. He fumbled to find the key he knew would be stuffed into the rotting doorjamb. Releasing the lock, he stepped inside and flipped on the lights.

By the time Sampte returned to the truck, Timothy and Zardos had already started unloading the cargo. Timothy grabbed one of the smaller bundles and waited for Zardos to do the same.

"Come on, come on! We need to do this," Timothy said, breezing past.

Zardos remained where he stood, appearing wary to move closer to the dead bodies.

Sampte scooped up the smallest plastic-clad figure weighing no more than ten pounds. He gently held the bundle out. Zardos took the body in his hands, his bottom lip quavering.

Sampte lifted a different bundle into his own arms. "Take it inside."

Zardos flinched at Sampte's insistent command. Reluctantly, he walked toward the building, never taking his eyes from his tiny burden.

The men rushed to unload the truck until no more bundles remained in the back. Sampte noticed Zardos trembling as the younger man looked around the cold, uninviting room, with its unpainted cinder block walls, the area stinking of harsh chemicals.

The bodies were laid out on two aluminum tables and the floor next to the far wall. Sampte left Zardos alone to stare at them in disbelief.

After a moment Sampte returned, carrying the canvas bag. He placed it on one of the tables and moved to the door.

Zardos lifted his ashen face. "How could you do this?"

Sampte pointed to the row of bodies. "Perhaps you prefer to join them."

The remaining color fell from Zardos's face and Sampte

knew the young man's fate was sealed. Alexander would never accept such weakness.

Returning to the black Mercedes, Sampte shook away his apprehension as he sped away from Thibodeaux's property.

It had been Sampte who delivered Nicholas's father, Charles Hunt, to Henri ten years earlier. He did so per his master's instruction, without question or remorse. There had been many other deliveries made, a few accompanied by Timothy. This would be the first time he had been joined by Zardos—and the last, he knew. He wished he hadn't involved the boy, but there were so many of them. So young. The baby . . . No, he wouldn't allow himself to go there. Alexander had issued his order and who was he to disobey? Where would he go? With Elaine gone, and no sign of Nicholas, he had no one but his master. Sampte feared for Zardos.

He feared for them all.

*   *   *

The moment Henri Thibodeaux heard the vehicles drive away, he moved from the window of his house where he had been watching the activity. He had recognized the big black car, but puzzled over the delivery truck. Anxious to find what was left for him this time, he dressed in the dark. Sliding on his boots, he fought back the intense thirst that could only be quenched by massive amounts of moonshine.

No, he scolded himself. *You've got work to do.*

Once inside the morgue, he wedged a straight-back chair under the knob. He flipped on the light switch and the fluorescents hummed and flickered, then bathed the room in its flat, blue light. Henri's mouth dropped open. He froze, gaping in disbelief. Six, black plastic-covered bundles seemed to swallow the light.

"Good God, have mercy."

The room spun. In a fog, he shuffled to one of the stainless steel cabinets and withdrew a glass gallon jug, three-quarters full of clear liquid. He pulled the cork and chugged down three gulps. Eyes watering and gasping for air, he rammed a trembling fist to his gut.

"I'll never be rid of this damned curse," he mumbled.

Henri noticed the canvas bag tucked between two of the bodies. Curious, he unzipped it and stared at four dirty coffee tins. When he unsnapped the top from one, the smell of rich earth and ground coffee filled his nose. Henri's eyes bulged at the sight of wads of cash, folded in neat halves, bound with rubber bands. Holding his breath in anticipation, he put the can aside and reached for another, finding the same contents. He emptied all the cans into the bag, removed the bands, then plunged his hands in. Twenties, tens, ones, even an occasional fifty dollar bill spilled onto the table and littered the floor at his feet.

He fanned out a handful of money. "There's thousands here. Thousands upon thousands."

Henri's legs and hands trembled, this time not from the DTs. A crooked grin spread across his whisker-stubbled face.

Then he noticed the smallest of the bundles lying on top one of the larger ones. *Less than one year old*, the experienced mortician told himself.

Staring at the money, his father's voice inside his head warned: "*At what price, my son?*"

34

Steven Hawk had stayed several hours with Aranka Kalman the previous night, and morning had come too soon for him. Certain he had set his alarm only minutes earlier, he jolted awake, shocked that the clock read six hours later. After a quick shower and shave, he pulled on a fresh uniform and rushed to work.

Hawk stood at his locker in the basement of the sheriff's department performing his daily equipment check. Adjusting the thick black gun belt around his waist, he fingered the clasped pockets containing pepper spray, handcuffs, and two clips stacked with fifteen rounds of .40 caliber ammunition. Next, he checked the chambered round in his Glock 23 semi-automatic, then re-holstered the handgun. He pulled a metal baton from the locker's shelf and with a flick of his wrist snapped the wand to its full three-foot length. Satisfied with its action, he telescoped the weapon shut and secured it into a leather sheath attached to his utility belt.

Pinning the brass nameplate above his left breast pocket, he remembered his mama's proud face at his swearing-in ceremony five years ago. As he mounted the steps to the squad room, saliva beaded his tongue, already hungering for the pork chops and mashed potatoes she had promised him for dinner that night.

"Sheriff's lookin' for you," Stiles said, his eyes on the computer screen.

"What's up? Did he say?"

"Nope. Fix your tie," Stiles said, without looking at him.

"I just did," Hawk said, his fingers on the knot.

Stiles chuckled.

"Quit messin' with me." Hawk suppressed a smile as he crossed the room to the coffeemaker.

"I know how you like to look pretty."

"Professional," Hawk shot back, pouring a cup of steaming brew.

"Pretty," Stiles countered.

Hawk waited at Sands's doorway until the sheriff waved him into his office. Taking the seat across from him, Hawk sipped hot, sweet coffee as his boss made notes on a document within a folder. Hawk sat up straighter when he read the name on the file tab: KALMAN, ELAINE C.

"Everything seems to be in order," Sands said, closing the cover.

Hawk blew into his cup. "I met with Mrs. Kalman last night after taking a look around Alexander Kalman's other property. I told her we haven't discovered anything out of the ordinary, but not to worry, we're not giving up. She's not too happy, but frankly, I don't know what else to do until a body shows up." Hawk took another sip. "You think she's gonna threaten bringing in the Bureau?"

"No cause for that. There's no indication of a kidnapping. Or any foul play."

"I want to finish checking out the B&Bs in the area. See if anyone matching their description has registered over the last three days."

"It ain't about what *you* want, Hawk. The uncle—what's your take on him?"

"He doesn't think it's as much a disappearance as an unscheduled vacation." Hawk shook his head. "I'm beginning to believe these kids never even existed."

Sands waited a long time before he spoke. "Hawk, there's no case here. Like you said, until there's a body, we've got nothin'."

"We can't let it go," Hawk said, dismay in his tone.

"You've already wasted how many hours? We've got other cases to focus on. Ones we can solve."

"But this is big. You said so, yourself. Mrs. Kalman's not gonna allow us to walk away."

"Actually, I just heard from Mrs. Kalman. She's dropped the inquiry."

Hawk's shoulders sunk. "She didn't."

"Afraid so. Says she spoke with her brother and he convinced her that going on with it's a waste of law enforcement time."

"But I saw her last night. When I left, she was adamant that we keep looking for her daughter."

"Well, now she's sure the two have run off together."

"What about the car? Surely, you don't believe running it off the road into the river was meant as a device to throw us off their tracks."

"It appears that's exactly what it is."

Hawk sat stunned in his chair, staring into his coffee. "I don't believe this."

"I'm puttin' the case on hold until somethin', or someone turns up."

"Did I blow it, Sheriff?" Hawk asked in a low voice.

"Nothin' to blow. Looks to me like you've done everything you could. Sometimes a case never gets solved. Unfortunately, I've had more than a few turn out that way."

"Something doesn't feel right. The crash. No body, or bodies. Is it a setup? There's too many unanswered questions."

"It's over for now." Sands handed Hawk the folder. "Have Shelly in records file the paperwork and your notes. Stiles's got another assignment, give him a hand."

"Come on, Sheriff. Can't I have a couple more days? I'd like to follow up on a few things to be sure."

Sands held his gaze so long Hawk thought he would refuse him.

Finally, Sands nodded. "All right. Phone calls. That's it. Don't stir up any hornet's nests, got it?"

"Absolutely," Hawk said. He rushed out of Sands's office before his boss had a chance to decide otherwise.

At his desk, Hawk blew out a long breath.

"Didn't go well, huh?" Stiles asked.

"He's put a hold on the investigation." Hawk waved the Kalman file. "In fact, he came damned close to telling me to take this to Shelly and have her file everything away as a cold case. My investigation's been downgraded to making a few phone calls."

"Did he say you did anything wrong?"

Hawk shrugged. "No. He told me some cases never get solved."

"He's right about that. Me and him, we've seen our share. Lots of secrets hangin' in these mountains, heavy as the fog. Best to let it go now, don't go doubtin' yourself. Believe me, he wouldn't have let you run with the case this long if he didn't think you'd be able to handle it."

Hawk nodded, settling into his chair. "Yeah, you're right."

"He'd have given it to someone else."

Hawk looked up at Stiles and met his playful grin. "Always messing with me, aren't you."

"I've got a juicy vandalism to clear up. You can tag along with me for a change," Stiles said, reaching for their raincoats.

Hawk's eyes fell on the Kalman file. He still stung from his meeting with the sheriff. He must be missing something—some element probably right in front of him—he just needed a little more time. Resigned to let it go for now, he tossed the Kalman dossier onto his desk and took the slicker from Stiles. Shrugging on the coat, he found himself unable to rip his eyes off the folder. He picked it up again.

Stiles glanced toward Sands's office, then turned back and nodded at the file. "What're you doing?"

"Let's make a stop first."

"A little diversion?" Stiles asked, arching an eyebrow.

"I need to check something out. You up for it?"

Stiles frowned. "Defy a direct order?" He put on his own raincoat and said, "Lead the way."

35

Jessica sat on the edge of the recliner and studied John Doe as he looked at his reflection in a hand-held mirror. Now that he wore a smaller bandage than the night before, Jessica could see more of his face. Although his eyes appeared sunken, and their whites streaked with thin blood veins, they were the color of emeralds. She took note of his exquisite Roman nose, lips perfectly shaped and wondered what he looked like in better condition. Even more handsome, she guessed.

The man surveyed his recently shaven face. The IV remained attached to his arm, and both hands were still wrapped in gauze to the wrists.

"Better without the beard?"

"Much."

Jessica went to his bedside. "Are you comfortable?"

"Yeah." He lowered the mirror and turned his hands front to back.

"Do they hurt?"

"Pins and needles when I try to squeeze them shut. About an hour before the pills wear off everything starts to ache. Right now I'm kind of on a sleepy cloud."

"That's good, sleep is the best thing for you."

"Thanks for coming back. Every time they woke me last night, I looked for you. I've lost all sense of time."

Jessica leaned closer to him. "I thought about you, too. Worried that you weren't doing okay."

"That's sweet."

Embarrassed by his words, Jessica felt her face flush.

Pointing to her stack of books next to the recliner, he asked, "What year are you at the university?"

"I graduate next semester."

His expression changed and his eyes dropped to his lap.

"What is it?"

"Nothing." He motioned for her to continue.

"I'm majoring in theatrical scenic design. My thesis is on Josef Svoboda, the famous Czech scenographer. At least this one is." She chuckled. "I've changed my mind a few times." He closed his eyes and she said, "I'll let you sleep."

"No, no. I'm listening. Your voice soothes me. Keep going."

"I've drawn up all the blueprints. Now I'm working on the text for the paper. I'm starting to regret choosing such an eclectic subject. There's so little published about him. If I'd have realized it would take this much research, I would never—"

Jessica stopped at the sound of a light knock. Dr. Everett entered the room, holding an aluminum clipboard in one hand, a bulging, clear bag in the other. Jessica nodded to him in greeting and laid a hand on the patient's shoulder. "Your doctor's here."

She watched him open his eyes and blink rapidly as he looked at Dr. Everett, then scan down the doctor's body to lock on the bag in his hand.

"Good morning," Everett said. Pulling the rolling table bedside, he set the bag on it, then opened the chart.

Jessica noticed that John Doe stared at the bag for a long time.

"Things are looking good for you. Your chest has cleared, and your stats are normalizing. The plastic surgeon did a great job on your face. You'll hardly have a scar. Just enough to make you appear dangerous to the ladies. He winked at Jessica and gave Nicholas a playful smile. "I'll take another look later when Connie changes your bandage later." He took a small flashlight from his breast pocket and checked the patient's pupils. "Pain manageable?"

The patient answered with a nod.

"And how's your memory? Anything coming back? Do you remember any details? Your name perhaps?"

John Doe shook his head.

Taking a step closer, Jessica rested her arms on the side

rail of the bed.

"Unfortunately, there was no identification found on you." Everett pointed to the bag. "But, maybe something in there will jog your memory."

John Doe's attention bounced from the doctor, to Jessica, to the bag.

"How about if we give him a minute," Everett said to her.

She patted John Doe's arm. "Be back in a bit."

"I'll be here," he answered in a soft voice.

Nicholas's heartbeat raced in his chest. The entire time Jessica and the doctor were in the room he had warned himself, *Don't let them know you recognize anything in that bag.* He did his best to look indifferent while the meager remnants of his life screamed for his attention.

Alone, Nicholas tore open the bag's seal and removed each item one at a time. The Breitling watch, though fogged, still kept time. Gold pen he used to sign autographs. Money clip wrapped around a few bills. The powder blue envelope caught his attention. Hands shaking, he pulled out the letter. Reading Alexander's bold printing drew thoughts of Elaine and the night of the crash to his mind. His anger flashed again as he stuffed the note back into the bag.

He reached for his father's journal. Caressing the cover, he took in a ragged breath. Although each page had been committed to memory, he flipped through a few and began to read.

I miss the piano. The sound of notes strung together. Creating magic. Not even the pieces you would think. No Bartók or Debussy.

A simple Brahms is what I dream of. His F Minor Sonata rings clearly in my mind. I can even smell the yellowing pages of sheet music I learned the piece from. The mere act of playing now haunts me.

There are times when I've found myself standing in front of the local music store, peering in the window at the Steinways and Baldwins, smelling the varnish and wood from memory. Knowing what the keys would feel like under my fingertips. The action of a Bösendorfer compared to a Mason & Hamlin. I'm certain I could sell a dozen grands if they would only let me play a few compositions for them.

I stand at the front window and consider asking, but know I'd be turned away. Banished because of my appearance. A raggedy bum stinking of booze, scaring off patrons from their exquisite showroom. They glare at me from inside until I shuffle away.

It hurts beyond measure to know the two things in life I've been put here on earth to do—father and pianist—elude my grasp.

Tragic, the things you learn too late.

Nicholas lifted his bandaged hands and placed them in a keyboard position. Attempting to move his fingers, only two on the left hand and three on the right presented much dexterity. Frustrated and angry, Nicholas slowly squeezed his throbbing hands shut for a moment. Clenching his stomach muscles until they twitched. He squinted his watering eyes and pushed aside the feel of razor blades slashing at his injuries until his discomfort diminished.

He thought back to a performance last month where he sat at a regal Steinway grand piano, dressed for performance in a black tuxedo, accessorized with a blood red rose. That night his hands danced over the keys. He had never played Schumann's Kinderszenen Opus 15 with such confidence.

When the piece came to an end, Nicholas stood and bowed, gracing the audience with his gratitude. The theatre thundered with the patrons' applause, cheers, and bravos.

Nicholas, charged by the response, played three encores. After the last note, rising to stand with shaking knees, he bowed again, kissed his hands, and opened them to his cheering crowd. He strode off the stage and into Elaine's arms.

Pain coursed through his hands and ankle. The memory made his present agony more intense as his ribs and head throbbed. He fumbled for the nurse's buzzer. Medication had proven a sure way out of his physical suffering. And the haze the drugs provided blurred his aching soul.

While Nicholas waited for the nurse, he fished the armoire key from the bag. Turning it in his bandaged hands, he thought of his love. His heart ached for Elaine. Grief swept over him. He yearned to gaze at the picture of her in his wallet, but he did not find the leather billfold in the bag. Then he remembered the doctor's words of not having any identification on him. The memory of putting the leather billfold inside the duffel that night flashed in Nicholas's mind. He had tucked the satchel behind the driver's seat of the Porsche. *Have they even found my car yet?* Nicholas had so many questions.

Reaching for the blue note again, he wondered if someone had read it, deciphered its ominous message and found the location. Would they go looking for this Henri Thibodeaux? Has anyone found Elaine? *Should I tell?* He wondered how long he would he have to wait before they came looking for him. Who would it be? Timothy or Sampte? Alexander would send one of them.

A terrifying thought came to him. *Or will Alexander come himself?*

36

Jessica stood with Doctor Everett outside Nicholas's hospital room. "How is he really doing, Doctor?"

"He's suffered dehydration and lost a good deal of blood from his head injury. He didn't have any breaks, but his ankle is sprained and quite swollen. He's in good general health. He'll heal quickly."

"But why do you suppose he doesn't have any memory?"

"Head injuries are always dicey."

"Will it come back?"

"His form of amnesia is brought on by a blow to the head, accompanied by a traumatic incident. When we figure out what the troubling event was, and once the patient is willing to face their ordeal, the outcome is usually positive."

"I feel awful for him."

"I'm sure he appreciates your spending time with him until we can find his family."

"Is it okay that I stay with him?"

"Of course. He'll benefit from any sense of security."

"I won't get in the way, and if he wants me to leave—" Jessica stopped speaking when she noticed a woman approach them.

"Excuse me, Dr. Everett?" She appeared apprehensive, yet barely able to conceal her excitement. "I'm sorry to interrupt, but I've got urgent news."

"Well, tell us before you burst, Ellie," Everett said.

"It's about the John Doe."

"Jessica and our patient are great friends by now. What is it?"

Ellie seemed reluctant to continue. "Turns out a state trooper called here the other night looking for a man meeting his description."

"What night?" Jessica asked.

"The night before you brought the John Doe in."

"And no one told me?" Everett asked.

Ellie's shoulders dropped. "I think the information was, well . . . overlooked."

"You mean someone forgot," Everett snapped.

"Ummm, yes," the woman said, avoiding the doctor's glower. "I have the details and he matches the description."

"Who took the info?"

"Nurse Cabrillo in admissions. She's not on until six o'clock."

"I need to speak to that trooper."

"I have the number somewhere," Ellie said, flipping through the pages of her portfolio.

"We'll figure this out. I'll keep in touch." Everett told Jessica, then hurried away, Ellie trailing close behind.

Dread about possibly being involved in a police matter cautioned Jessica to be wary, but she knew it was too late. The John Doe had no one. He needed her. She wasn't going anywhere.

37

Still unable to grasp his desperate situation, Nicholas stared at his belongings. His only consolation was that he still had his father's leather journal he cradled in his stinging hands. Although the words filled him with trepidation, the revelations allowed Nicholas to finally know the man he had been too young to remember. The regret of not having Elaine to share the words with left Nicholas hollow inside.

Nicholas blamed Alexander for the losses in his life. He now had no doubt that the man who commandeered everything had taken his father, his mother, and now the woman he loved. He rubbed the worn leather cover. Even after reading the journal, his parents' deaths or disappearances remained a mystery to him. Sampte would do anything for Alexander, as would Timothy. Could they have elevated their hobby of killing small game to a higher level?

He had no one to ask the question. At twenty, he would be forced start all over. This time without the only person he had ever allowed completely into his world.

Not knowing what would come next tied his stomach in knots. The past ten years had been a rigorous task of endurance; every waking hour scheduled, regimented, always focused around music. These few days had been the only time he'd been away from a piano since he could walk on his own. He raised his battered, bandaged fingers that had been manicured every five days by Zardos whether they needed grooming or not.

What would his future be? Always on the run from Alexander's wrath? Constantly on the lookout for Sampte's black car? Awaiting Timothy's revenge for defying their mentor?

His heartbeat raced, his breathing became rapid and shallow. A light knock pulled Nicholas from the worries that threatened to escalate to terror.

The door opened to reveal Jessica. "Okay to come back in?"

"Yeah." He cleared his throat and attempted a feeble smile.

She pointed to the belongings spread out on the cart in front of him. "Did anything in there help you remember?"

He shrugged.

"It'll come, don't worry. Doctor Everett told me with your head injury—"

"I know who I am."

Jessica froze at the door a moment. Then, grasping his meaning, she beamed and hurried to his side. "That's great!"

Nicholas let out a deep breath, preparing for what he would tell her—even more, for her reaction to his words.

"You don't seem too happy about it," she said, frowning. "Are you all right?"

He fingered his father's journal. "I may never be all right again."

She laid a tender hand on his arm. "Should I get the doctor?"

Nicholas shook his head.

"What is it?" she whispered.

Staring at the journal for confidence he suddenly lacked, he said, "My name is Nicholas Kalman. I'm twenty years old." A single tear trickled down his cheek as he lifted his gaze to meet Jessica's worried expression. "And I think I'm in danger."

"What's going on? You can tell me. Anything."

How much should I say? "I'm really scared."

A nervous laugh came from her. "You're scaring me, now." Taking his hand, she leaned closer. "Tell me."

"What happened to me was no accident. I was forced off the road. He did it on purpose."

"Who? Are you saying you know who did this to you?"

"Yes. I mean, I think I do." Nicholas settled in the bed, tucking the sheet to his chin. "I'm a concert pianist. I live not far from here with my uncle. I had a performance the other night." *Careful*. "Going home, somewhere on that winding road, a car came right for me and I lost control of my car and went down the embankment. I guess I blacked out because I can't remember some of the details, but obviously I was thrown from my vehicle and it must have gone down the river. Eventually I dragged myself to where you found me."

Jessica stared at him, eyes wide. "You said he did this on purpose. Who did?"

"Someone else lives with us. Timothy Sagan. We're kind of professional rivals. He's Alexander's other pupil. But I'm afraid my uncle may be involved, too."

"Why?"

Nicholas shook his head, avoiding her question. "I've got to get out of here as soon as I can."

"What are you going to do?"

"Try to figure out what's going on."

They sat in silence for a while before Nicholas spoke again. "Will you help me?"

Jessica frowned. "Help you what?"

"Find out why they did it."

"What makes you think I can help?"

"You're the only person I can trust."

Jessica reared back and crossed her arms across her chest. "You don't even know me."

"I think I do. Most people would have driven past. Either not have noticed me lying in the road, or not given a damn. You stopped. I can't chance anyone finding out about who I really am. There's no point going through every detail right now, but my life depends upon everyone believing I don't remember anything about my past. At least for now."

Jessica fell quiet again before she left his side to retrieve her things.

Nicholas worried he'd frightened her away, along with any hope of reassembling his life. Most of all, he was afraid he would never find out the truth about who killed Elaine. He needed this woman. "I'll understand if you don't come back. It's a lot to take in. And you owe me nothing."

"It's not that I *want* to leave," she said, in a tender voice.

"I have to go or I'll be late for class."

When a reassuring smile settled on her lips, he let out a relieved sigh.

"Nicholas Kalman, I'll see you in the morning."

"Don't tell anyone you know my name, okay?"

She hesitated at the door a moment before she said, "I don't know why this is some big secret, but you must have a reason. Don't worry, you can trust me." Then she slipped out of the room.

Left alone again, Nicholas relaxed having shed a bit of his burden. By not telling her everything, he believed she would help him. He closed his eyes and drifted off to memories of Elaine wrapped in his arms, warming his soul.

"I'm coming for you, baby. I haven't forgotten."

38

Hawk and Stiles bounced along the rutted dirt road in the cruiser, searching for Manuel Esteva's trailer in a secluded area twelve miles from Alexander Kalman's estate. The hairpin curves of the two-lane highway, followed by a treacherous, rutted, unpaved road made their journey slow going. Hawk glanced at his watch; because they had gotten themselves lost a couple times, it had taken them an hour to reach their destination.

"Shelly said the number's twelve fifty-four," Stiles said, reading from a slip of paper. "Gotta be gettin' close."

Hawk craned his neck to see through the dense trees. "Haven't seen another house for nearly a mile."

"That must be it. Up ahead on the right."

Hawk parked near the front of a doublewide trailer. As he got out of the vehicle a set of tire tracks caught his attention. He followed their grooved indentations in the mud all the way to the front porch.

"Definitely fresh," he said, squatting to study the marks. "Good size truck. Bigger than a pickup."

Stiles mounted the steps and knocked on the front door. "No answer. Should I try it?" Stiles asked, hand on the doorknob.

Hawk joined Stiles on the porch as he turned the doorknob and nudged. The door creaked open. "We've got no probable cause. You sure you want to do this?"

They looked at each other a moment, then Hawk nodded. "Thought I heard something."

"Sounded like a scream, didn't it?"

"That's what my report's gonna say."

They entered a silent room.

The stench of bleach hit Hawk so hard his eyes watered. He turned to Stiles and touched his nose. Stiles nodded. Both slid the Glocks from their holsters.

"*Señor* Esteva?" Hawk called out. "It's Deputy Hawk."

Only large pieces of furniture were scattered around the room. An overturned child's high chair lay on its side. A few collapsed boxes and empty tape rolls were strewn on the floor in the front room.

"Nothin' feels right about this," Stiles said, easing down the hall.

"You check the bedrooms, I'll hit the kitchen."

There, Hawk found the cupboards fully stocked. The refrigerator motor kicked on and he discovered fresh food inside. He returned to the front room and squatted to inspect four equidistant indentations in the thick-pile carpet.

"Three bedrooms, all clear," Stiles said, holstering his weapon. "Stinks like bleach pretty strong in there, too. Clothes are missin' from the drawers, but the furniture's still here. Beds are stripped, and the pillows are gone. Seems like they would have taken the mattresses, too."

"Look at this. Must have been a big chair here," Hawk said, pointing out the small square impressions.

"They'd take a recliner but not the high chair?"

"Esteva must have figured I'd come looking for him. No tellin' where he's gone."

"We'd better clear outta here, Hawk," Stiles warned. "Got no authority without a warrant."

Something near the baseboard caught Hawk's attention. He picked up a crumpled wad and fingered it open. A brightly colored swatch of floral-patterned cloth bloomed in the palm of his hand.

Hawk puzzled over the fabric and realized that with one less person to question, the already cold Elaine Kalman case now turned virtually artic.

39

Timothy sat at the Steinway, staring at the keyboard. When he did not begin to play, Alexander turned to him. "I was under the impression you were here to work," Alexander scolded. "You've only two more evenings until your performance."

"I am working," Timothy said. "In my head."

"I cannot hear the notes in your head. Play."

Rising from the bench, Timothy sat on a chair across from Alexander. He noticed the older man bristle at his insubordination. Timothy had never dared to challenge him before, but things were different now. "I've been wondering what that deputy is up to. Isn't it strange that they haven't found Nicholas's body by now?"

Alexander looked beyond him, refusing Timothy his eyes. "I would feel much better if the matter were resolved."

Timothy got up and walked to the marble table where a tea set waited. Pouring a cup, he took several deep breaths before he approached his maestro. Throughout the morning Timothy had worked over the plan he had been formulating in his mind until he felt confident enough to present it to Alexander, but he had yet to gather courage enough to speak the words out loud.

Timothy knew Nicholas was dead, and that soon someone would find his body, but with still no sign of Elaine, he would need solid proof that her body would never be found. He had no idea how to rectify that particular situation for Alexander. Sampte had warned him not to return to the country house, that surely the police would be watching. Timothy thought the risk of getting caught was worth it, but if Nicholas had really hidden Elaine's body there and Timothy found it . . . then, what would he do? Repulsed by the thought of touching her dead body, he supposed he could set the house on fire to destroy her corpse. But didn't the cops have a way to find even a charred body?

He had so many questions for Alexander. The pressure of the deputy's investigation, with no sign of Nicholas or Elaine, seemed to occupy his mentor's full attention. Timothy felt cheated yet again.

Bending to hand Alexander the cup of tea, he said, "Sampte and I have been up and down that stretch of highway. We only found burnt-out flares. Probably where Nicholas's car went over." Without offering a response, Alexander took the cup from Timothy. "I found a place where—"

"Why do you find it necessary for me to hear this?" Alexander gave Timothy his eyes for the first time that morning. "Take care of it."

Timothy flinched, taken aback by Alexander's coldness. His gaze so unemotional, so hateful; the look made Timothy shudder. He crouched beside Alexander's chair and bowed his head. "All I want is to please you," he said in a low, apologetic voice. His stomach fluttered when he felt Alexander's hand on his shoulder.

After a moment Alexander said, "And all I want is for you to be more."

Timothy settled his hand atop Alexander's. "More like Nicholas, you mean."

Alexander yanked his hand away from Timothy's touch. "I will not tolerate your disparagement."

Standing, then stumbling back, Timothy felt his face flush. "I'm sorry. I'm so frustrated." Timothy paced a tight circle and raked fingers through his hair. "I'm not Nicholas. You know that. I would never dream of disrespecting you, or of missing performances, or choosing music other than what you have approved right before curtain." His stride became more rapid with each declaration. "Messing with . . . her. I know the importance of focus, and Nicholas hasn't in a long time." He stopped and extended his arms in a plea. "Unlike Nicholas, it matters to me what you think. You matter to me.

More than the music. More than anything."

Alexander lifted the cup with trembling fingers, rattling the saucer.

Elated by the possibility of getting through to his mentor's emotions, Timothy mounted the two steps to sit at the piano. "I'll play the Eleventh, flawlessly." Then Timothy said in a confident voice: "Uncle."

The first time having spoken the word out loud, Timothy loved how it felt on his lips.

40

Parked off the highway, Hawk made notations in his logbook. Heavy mist enveloped the cruiser. His cell phone rang and when he lifted his head he noticed the dew had turned to a drizzle. He flipped on the windshield wipers and connected the call.

"Get to the county hospital," Sheriff Sands ordered over the crackle of the connection. "Looks like they've got someone matching Nicholas Kalman's description listed as a John Doe up there."

Hawk reared back in his seat. "You're sure?"

"Hell no. Get up there and find out."

Hawk reached for the folder that never left his possession. "Mr. Kalman provided a photo of Nicholas. I'm on my way."

Hawk clicked off his phone, switched on the blue flashers and screeched the cruiser onto the slick blacktop, siren blaring.

*　*　*

After speaking to admissions at the hospital, Hawk couldn't find Dr. Everett, so he decided to meet the John Doe on his own.

Hawk emerged from the elevator and scanned room numbers as he passed them. Finding room 209, he stood at the closed door and flipped through the Elaine Kalman file until he located the performance program featuring the photograph of Nicholas Kalman. Committing the picture to memory, he straightened his hat, mashed the knot in his tie, gave the door a light knock and entered.

The young man lying in bed turned in his direction. Hawk needed only one look to be convinced of who greeted him with an easy smile.

My God, it's him. Hawk's heartbeat accelerated.

The young man scanned Hawk head to toe. He didn't appear shocked or scared to see an officer in uniform. He attempted to straighten himself in the bed and his face lost what little color it had.

"I'm Deputy Steven Hawk. I believe you're the man I've been looking for."

The man blinked three times. "Why would you be looking for me?"

"I've been investigating the disappearance of a couple people."

"I'm sorry, but I don't remember anything since . . ." He cleared his throat, touched the bandage on his forehead. "Whatever happened to me."

"Excuse me?"

"Have you spoken to Dr. Everett?"

"No."

"He can explain. I'll buzz for him." The man fumbled for the call switch.

"I'd rather talk with you for now."

"But he can tell you about my . . . condition."

Hawk set his jaw and took on his most professional tone. "A black Porsche Targa was pulled from the Nantahala River." He approached the bed to get a closer read of the patient. "Now, I'm no doctor, but with that head injury and the way you struggled to sit up just now, I'd guess you've got a mess-load of bruises, maybe even a few broken ribs. The same kind of injuries you get from bein' thrown from a vehicle."

Hawk watched the rise and fall of the man's chest become more rapid as beads of sweat glistened on his forehead. "The car is registered to Alexander Kalman. He claims his nephew drives it."

The man did not respond.

Hawk withdrew the program from his folder and held it out. "You're Nicholas Renfrew Kalman."

The man stared at the photograph, his expression

revealing nothing.

Hawk shook the playbill. "You can't deny that's not you."

The man shrugged.

Holding down his anger, Hawk tossed the program atop the bed covers. "Maybe if I brought this Alexander Kalman to meet with you?"

The man frowned and said, "Who is this man you're talking about?"

Hawk studied the John Doe he now knew to be Nicholas Kalman. "Sir, where is Elaine Kalman?"

The young man's breathing now seemed to stop. In a steady voice, he said, "I really think you need to speak to my doctor."

"I'll do that." Hawk withdrew a business card from his breast pocket and laid it on the rolling cart beside the bed. "When you're ready to straighten this matter out, give me a call."

The man handed Hawk the program.

"No, you keep that. I know where to find more." Hawk worried that if the man didn't breathe soon, he'd have to buzz for the doctor himself. "I'll be talking to you again. Count on it." He issued the man a sharp nod, turned, and exited the room.

Hawk grew more impatient with every word Dr. Everett spoke as they stood at the nurses station, not far from Nicholas Kalman's hospital room.

"Deputy, the man you claim to be Nicholas Kalman has experienced head trauma. The medical term is retrograde amnesia. It may take some time before he regains his memory."

"I don't claim it's him. It *is* him." Hawk looked away from Everett and calmed himself before he continued in a less harsh voice. "How long does it normally take?"

"Unfortunately, there's no way to determine that. Results from his MRI and blood work have ruled out any metabolic causes or chemical imbalances. We're forced to wait and see how he recovers."

Hawk thought a moment before he asked his next question. "Can you fake amnesia?"

A frown creased the doctor's forehead. "Are you suspicious of that?"

Hawk waved the file folder at Everett. "This case has been nothin' but trouble, Doc. No one is cooperating. Witnesses are disappearing. The uncle's giving half-truths. Hell, the case was closed until an hour ago when you called the sheriff."

Hawk took in a weary breath. "Only one fact remains. There's a missing woman out there somewhere and your patient is our best shot at finding her. She could be hurt. She may be lost wandering around the forest down by the river. She could be dead." He hitched his thumb toward Nicholas's room. "Until that man lying in that bed starts talkin', there's nothing we can do for her."

"Very unfortunate, I agree. I'm sorry I can't give you anything more concrete, Deputy."

Hawk slumped his shoulders and glanced back at the patient's door, wanting nothing more than to storm in and beat the answers from the kid. "Will you let me know if anything out of the ordinary happens?"

"Such as?"

"If he says anything that might make you think he knows more than he's letting on. That sort of thing. Also, if any visitors come around claiming to know him, I really need to hear from you."

Everett met Hawk's stern gaze. "I don't know how ethical that would be, Deputy."

"This has turned into a possible murder investigation, Doctor Everett. I know the sheriff would appreciate your cooperation."

"You think he's got something to do with this missing woman?"

"At this point, anything's possible. And everyone's under investigation."

41

Nicholas sat in his bed trembling. The deputy's visit had unnerved him to the point of near-paralyzed fear. Thoughts, worries, evasions spun in his mind. Hawk had obviously spoken with Alexander to find out who drove the car. He wondered if the deputy had notified Alexander that he had found his missing nephew.

Is Alexander coming? The deputy doesn't seem to know anything about Elaine. Or does he? Is he trying to trick me?

A knock at the door threw him into a panic.

"You up to a visit?" Jessica asked, closing the door after her.

Nicholas let out a relieved breath at the sight of her instead of the cop with more questions, maybe even a closed fist.

"How are you doing?"

"I had a visitor."

Her eyes grew wide. "Is that good, or bad?"

He pulled the program from under the sheet and handed it to her.

"Where did you get this?" Opening the cover, she began to read. "Nicholas Renfrew Kalman, celebrated classical pianist. World-renowned. Finalist, Tchaikovsky International Competition in Moscow. Junior and Intermediate Winner of the Vladimir Horowitz Award. Winner of the Franz Liszt International Piano Competitions in Budapest and Germany." She looked up from the program and arched an eyebrow. "You must be very good."

Nicholas covered his face with the crook of his arm, avoiding her impressed fawning. A trickle of sweat pooled at the crease in his stomach and traced an aching rib. Every muscle in his body tensed, his stomach flipped and threatened to unleash the tasteless mashed potatoes and chicken he had choked down for lunch.

When she handed him the program, he pushed it aside.

"Take it away." He nodded at Hawk's business card. "That too."

She ran her thumb along the raised county seal. "A Deputy? He came here?"

"That's who brought the program."

"What did you tell him?"

"Nothing."

"You sure that's a good idea?"

The doubt in her voice agitated him.

"I mean, it's his job to find out who tried to kill you, right?"

She had said it. The very thing he had been avoiding— what scared him most. Someone had tried to kill him. The same person who probably killed Elaine.

He took a deep breath and spoke again. "There's something else."

Alarm parked in Jessica's sparkling eyes.

"Someone I know is missing. My aunt's daughter, Elaine. The deputy asked me if I knew where she was."

"Do you?"

Nicholas avoided her pointed question. "I've got to get out of here." Sweeping the sheet off his body, he slid from the bed, wincing as his foot hit the floor.

"And go where?"

"I don't know. I just want this nightmare to be over."

She urged him back to the bed. "You're too weak and beat up to be going anywhere. Get back under the covers."

Doing as instructed, Nicholas slouched with exhaustion. He rested his pounding head in his hand and squeezed his eyes tight.

"I'll ask Nurse Connie to give you something to help you sleep."

After Jessica left, dread filled Nicholas. Although he felt certain she had not told anyone about him faking his amnesia, he needed to be cautious about what more he revealed to her. He regretted the possibility of taking advantage of her kindness, but he needed her and had no choice but to trust her. *Should I tell her about Elaine*? There was danger in that. Tears stung his eyes, his loss a misery that would not subside. Guilt for abandoning Elaine at the country house shamed him. He would have to tell someone soon, before the disgrace of leaving her there sent him over the edge.

42

Hawk called Alexander Kalman to inform him that his nephew had been found. Of course Alexander insisted they meet *immediately*. Hawk regretted another encounter with the irritating Hungarian, but he knew Sheriff Sands would only reopen the investigation if he could convince either Alexander Kalman or Aranka that enough evidence had presented itself to proceed further.

As he wound the cruiser into the drive, he saw Alexander waiting on his front porch. Before Hawk even slid from his vehicle the man hurled his first demands. "Tell me what you've discovered."

"Your nephew is at the county hospital. A John Doe meeting his description was admitted two days ago—"

"Two days ago? Why was I not notified earlier?"

"Sir, I don't have any details, yet. I wanted to let you know in case I need a visual ID. Will you be around?"

Alexander did not answer Hawk's question. Instead, he asked, "How are his hands?"

"His injuries aren't critical. He's conscious, although not very mobile."

Alexander smacked the tip of his cane onto the porch. "Tell me of his *hands*."

"They're covered in bandages."

Head lowered, shoulders slumped, Alexander's body swayed.

"I've spoken to his doctor and he doesn't appear to remember the accident. In fact, he doesn't remember much of anything at all."

Alexander cocked his head. "I don't follow."

"Looks like he was thrown from his vehicle when it crashed. He's suffered a head injury. As soon as we get the okay from his doctor, we're going to proceed with questioning him about Elaine's whereabouts."

In a quavering voice, Alexander asked, "What is the condition of his face?"

"Like I said, he has a head wound. There's another bandage covering the left side of his face."

"God," Alexander whispered. "He's ruined."

"At least he's alive," Hawk spat, amazed by Alexander's dismissive attitude.

Alexander turned away and limped heavily toward the door.

"Would you like me to take you to your nephew, sir?"

"Not necessary," Alexander said, the words trailing behind him.

Hawk shook his head with contempt at the man creeping up the steps. Returning to his cruiser, he noticed an unfamiliar man dressed in khakis trimming spent roses from Alexander's impressive bushes.

"New gardener, I see," Hawk called to Alexander. "By the way, I went by Manuel Esteva's house. He doesn't seem to live there anymore."

Alexander turned to him. An unemotional expression matched his voice when he said, "Manuel has found other employment."

"I'll need his new address."

"Why would he possibly matter?"

"Well, sir, although your nephew has been located, your niece is still considered a missing person. Anyone I've made contact with who might be able to answer questions regarding her case needs to be available to us."

"I have no idea where Mr. Esteva could be. I'm sure he has family in Miami. Most of those people do. Other than that, I'd be of no help."

"Maybe Mr. Sampte would know? Or your other employee?"

"Zardos?"

"Yes."

A stiff smile crossed Alexander's lips. "Doubtful. But I'll be sure to inquire. May I ask why?"

"I'm sure the sheriff will be reopening this case. We're going to need to speak with everyone who's ever even met Elaine Kalman."

Alexander issued Hawk a terse nod, but no objections as he resumed his steps toward his front entrance.

Before the Hungarian could disappear behind the door, Hawk asked, "Don't you find it odd that so many people in your life just up and disappear?"

Alexander stopped. After a long moment he turned back to Hawk. "I've never given it a bit of thought." Then he pivoted on his cane, and went into his house.

Hawk muttered under his breath, "Well, I sure as hell have."

43

Timothy and Sampte sat in the idling Mercedes, parked at the far edge of a dirt lot next to the Smoky Pines Lodge and Cabin Resort. Hidden deep in the forest, the two-story resort loomed against a backdrop of dense tall pines. Apart from the main structure rustic cabins dotted the secluded area, nearly hidden by lush overgrowth.

Notes of Prokofiev's 7th Sonata ran through Timothy's mind as he played the chords on his thighs. *Two more nights until my unveiling*, he reminded himself, already terrified he would be unable to perform. He shuddered every time he imagined his upcoming unveiling.

"What is it we're waiting for?" Sampte asked, impatience in his tone as he tapped the steering wheel over and over with his long finger.

After a moment a young blonde woman burst through the trees and into a clearing. She pierced the quiet with her squeals.

Timothy pointed to her and smiled.

"God. She looks like Elaine," Sampte said.

Then a young, dark-haired man ran to catch up to the woman.

"Nicholas," Sampte exclaimed, reaching for the door handle.

Timothy grabbed his arm. "No. It's not him. They look a lot alike though, don't they? That's why we're here."

They watched the two tussle and fall to the ground. The man pinned the woman down and covered her face in kisses.

"How did you find them?"

"The lodge's website caters to honeymooners. I hoped I'd be lucky." Timothy's eyes glowed with devious delight.

"Do you think Alexander would approve of your stalking innocent people instead of spending your time practicing for your concert?"

"Well, it's a good thing I did," Timothy snapped. "Otherwise I wouldn't have found them, would I?" He pointed at the couple who raced toward a dock that led to the water. "As soon as the owner locks up the lodge tonight, I want you to break in and take care of the paperwork trail. I'll take their car. I know a place where I can ditch it not far from here. Meet me where I showed you five miles back."

Sampte nodded his understanding. "What are your plans?"

Timothy reached into his jacket pocket and withdrew a matchbook. He thumbed the cover open.

Sampte stared at Timothy.

"They'll be mistaken for Nicholas and Elaine."

"You're quite sure you're capable of this?"

A wicked laugh rumbled in Timothy's chest. "I know exactly what to do."

44

Nicholas replayed his conversation with deputy Hawk over and over in his mind. He knew it would be only a matter of time before he'd have to confess his identity to the authorities. His biggest fear left him in constant turmoil: Alexander would come through the door next.

Earlier, after delivering a pain pill to Nicholas, Nurse Connie had redressed the wound on his face with a smaller bandage. Jessica stayed at his bedside, his hand clutched in her own, supportive, a reassuring smile on her lips.

Relieved not to have his vision covered, he focused and found his sight and senses intensified. His mood lifted, and he felt optimistic and slightly more in control. He opened and closed his mouth and the tautness from the line of stitches running down the length of his face tugged his skin. He refused the mirror Nurse Connie offered for fear of what horror he would see, so had no idea of the damage beneath the gauze.

"It really didn't look that bad," Jessica said. "Remember, Doctor Everett said you'll hardly notice the scar after it heals."

Nicholas looked straight ahead without saying a word.

"I almost forgot." She pulled a portable CD player and a pair of headphones from her bag. "I thought you might like to listen to some music. This thing is ancient, but I put fresh batteries in it." She dug in her tote again and plucked out a CD. "I'm sure this is a cheesy recording, but it's the only classical music they had in the used bin at school."

Nicholas caressed the cracked CD cover to *Beethoven's 25 Favorite Hits*.

"I haven't listened to Beethoven in years," he mumbled.

"It's okay if you don't want—"

"No, no. This is great. Thank you."

"I thought it might be a good idea to get your mind off of . . . everything."

Nicholas laid the player and CD on the bed beside him and gazed up at the ceiling.

Jessica crossed the room to sit on the recliner. "That deputy really upset you, didn't he?"

He nodded. "When do you think I can get out of here?"

"I don't know. Have you tried to walk?"

Nausea and head spins had made him reluctant to leave his bed unassisted, but now that those effects had subsided he ramped up his movements, anxious to discover how much mobility he had. He raised his ankle and began to unwind the bandage.

"What are you doing?" she asked, rushing to his side.

"I want to see how far I can walk."

"You're sure?"

Nicholas nodded.

Jessica pushed his hands aside, pulled the covering tight again and re-fastened the clasps. "Well, keep your foot wrapped, you need the support."

"Feels like the swelling has gone down quite a bit since yesterday." He slid to the edge of the mattress. "Doesn't hurt nearly as much." Putting weight on his right foot, he grimaced as hot searing pain shot from his toes to his hip.

Hand to her mouth, she cringed. "Maybe you should stay off it."

"No. I think it's okay. I'm going to walk a little."

"Careful now."

He took a few tentative steps around the limited space.

She held her arms out, ready to catch him. "Why are you doing this?"

"I told you. I have to leave." He stopped before he said too much. "I need to talk to my uncle."

"Well, I'll call him for you."

"No!" He spun to face her so fast he nearly tumbled into her. "He can't see me like this. Weak and vulnerable. I won't have that."

Jessica put up her hands as if in resignation. "Okay. It's

up to you."

"There's not enough room in here. Would you check and see if anyone's outside?"

Jessica stuck her head out the door and searched the corridor. "All clear. No one's even at the nurses station."

He limped after her. "I'm curious to see how far I can go."

"Maybe we could get you some crutches."

He winced as he laid a gentle hand to his side. "Not with these ribs."

She draped his arm over her shoulder. "What about a cane?"

Nicholas shook his head, thinking of his uncle and the ironic predicament they now shared.

45

Mr. and Mrs. Joseph and Angelina Barelli sat on the small pier in front of their private cabin at the Smoky Pines Resort. Arms wrapped around each other, they watched the water lick at the pilings. After a long embrace, Joey's roving hands turned into tickling fingers. Angie's laughter bounced off the river's surface. She jumped up and raced along the planks, then up a hill. Joey trailed behind, relishing the opportunity to watch her shapely body and flowing golden hair.

When he had checked in, Joey requested an isolated cabin with a view of the water for their honeymoon. They hoped their plan to disappear for two weeks with no phones or television would be the perfect ending to their storybook wedding.

At the woodpile, Angie stacked another log onto Joey's outstretched arms. "Just a couple more."

"That's enough," he said, groaning from the weight.

Angie leaned in for a kiss. "You don't want to come back out in a few hours, do you? I have other plans for your time." She plopped two more logs on his stack and pushed him toward the porch.

The front room of the rustic cabin included a cramped kitchen and a counter where several empty champagne bottles stood. A picnic basket rested on the hand-hewn table, a bounty of partially unwrapped packages scattered upon it.

Joey teetered up the steps and once inside, dumped the heap of wood onto the hearth. Then he stood, hands on his hips, looking back and forth from the wood to the opening of the empty fireplace.

Angie watched, amused. "Are you going to start a fire for me, or what?" Joey scratched his head and shifted one foot to the other. She laughed. "Don't tell me you don't know how to build a fire?"

"Hey, I'm a city kid. First no sopressata *or* cannoli anywhere in Hicksville, and now I'm expected to make fire?"

"Make *a* fire. You're not a caveman. You make *a* fire."

He wrapped his arms around her waist and cooed, "Maybe we won't need one."

They pulled apart when a man appeared at the open doorway.

He held a handful of kindling and wore a wide smile. "Need any help?"

Joey eased Angie behind him. He did not recognize the red-haired, freckle-faced man from when he checked in. "Who are you?"

"I'm from the lodge. Thought I'd give you a hand." Breezing past the couple, he entered the cabin and stacked the sticks inside the fireplace, then added a few logs.

"Listen, we appreciate it, but I think we'll wait a while."

"You sure?"

Joey pulled a wad of bills from his jeans and selected a few singles.

Disdain crossed the other man's face as he waved the money away.

"Maybe we'll give you a call later," Joey said. A forced smile on his lips, he ushered the intruder to the door.

The man shrugged, and backed out of the cabin.

Joey closed the door and went to the window to watch him disappear down the path. "That was creepy."

"You are so suspicious. They call it 'Southern Hospitality,'" she drawled.

"Oh, you know all about it, do you?" Joey kidded, pulling her to his chest.

"I did my research."

"You and your research. How many hours online did it take you to find this place?"

"Lots. But it was worth it, right?" She spun away from him and swept her arms outward. "I love it here. No traffic noise."

"Birds screaming everywhere," Joey countered.

"Clean air."

"No ESPN."

"No family calling every fifteen minutes."

"Yours or mine?"

"Yours." Angie taunted in a playful voice, "Baby of the family."

Joey bolted after Angie and chased her into the bedroom, her giggles filling the cabin.

Hours after dark, Joey and Angie lay snuggled together. A knock at the front door interrupted the stillness. He opened his eyes and listened, unsure if he had heard a noise. It had taken what seemed like hours after their last lovemaking for him to fall asleep. At first, he heard crickets, leaves rustling, night birds, and then, suddenly it all became quiet. *Like a tomb*, he thought, right before drifting off.

Another knock split the silence, more insistent this time.

"Dammit," Joey mumbled. He glanced at his sleeping bride, slid out of bed, felt for his robe, and draped it around his naked body. Shutting the bedroom door behind him, he ran blind hands across walls as he stumbled into the dark room and fumbled to turn on a table lamp. Another knock propelled him to front window. He eased the curtain open a few inches and tried to make out the identity of someone standing in shadows on the porch. He flipped the switch at the door, but the porch did not light up.

"What do you want?"

"Sorry, but you're going to have to move your car . . ."

Joey struggled to hear the rest of the man's words. "Did you say, move the car?"

"Yeah, sorry. If you give me your keys I'll take care of it for you. Don't mean to bother you. It'll just take a minute."

Joey watched the man a moment. Muttering a few obscenities in Italian, he scooped up the keys from a table next to the door. Tightening the knot on the robe's belt, he looked back at the bedroom, then flung the front door open.

The redhead Joey recognized from earlier stood on the

front porch, a big smile on his face.

"What the fuck, man? Can't it wait—"

Before Joey could finish speaking, or even react, the man took a step forward, raised his arm, and hit Joey's left temple with what he thought looked like the butt of a pearl-handled gun. Stunned, Joey hit the ground. The car keys fell from his hand and skittered on the porch. *ANGELINA*, he tried to scream, but the word was trapped in his numb mind. He struggled to stay conscious. His eyelids drooped shut.

Timothy snatched the keys from the porch and listened to the man's raspy breaths. He looked around, and satisfied no one had witnessed the assault he knelt down and took hold of his victim's ankles. A track of blood smeared the porch as he dragged the limp body into the cabin.

He dropped the robed man and flipped off the light switch. He went back onto the porch and gave the light bulb one full turn, screwing it back into the fixture. He picked up the one-gallon container he had tucked under the windowsill, the contents sloshing as he hurried back into the front room.

Bending to take hold of the man again, he pulled him the length of the room and dropped him near a closed door Timothy assumed led to the bedroom. He ran a glove-covered hand across his brow and noticed a sweating champagne bottle on the bar. More thirsty than he'd ever felt before, he took the bottle to his lips and gulped down the remaining contents. He banged the empty bottle atop the counter.

"Joey?" a woman's muffled voice called out.

Timothy turned toward the closed door. Then he unscrewed the gas cap, tugged the spout out of its lip, and sloshed some of the liquid onto the motionless man. The thick pile robe sucked up the gas within seconds.

"Joey, honey, come back to bed."

Angie sat up and leaned against the headboard, straining to listen. She thought she had heard voices, but she didn't know how long ago. Too much champagne had clouded her mind.

The door creaked open and a silhouette stood in the bedroom doorway. "Joey? What's going on, babe?" Taking quick sniffs of the air, she said. "Do you smell gasoline?"

Joey stepped toward her. Light from the front room illuminated him enough for her to realize it wasn't Joey at all.

Angie swept up the sheet to cover her bare breasts. "My God! What's going on? Who are you?"

The man flicked something he held in his hand at her. Wetness drenched her body. She batted at the liquid, the stench of gasoline made her gag. "Where is Joey?" she shouted.

The intruder's lips turned upward in a menacing grin. He held up a long wooden match she recognized from a container on the fireplace.

Angie screamed, then she begged. "Stop. Please, I'll do whatever you want."

She heard a scratch.

Flipping the covers aside, she bolted off the bed. Trapped in the farthest corner of the small room, Angie backed up against the wall and slid down its length. She knelt on her knees, tapped the sign of the cross on her chest, clasped her hands together, and pleaded for her life.

The red-haired man held up the burning match, taunting her with it.

Mesmerized, her eyes locked to the fire.

The man stepped closer. He tossed the match at her.

Angie heard a ghastly whoosh as a flame ignited and engulfed her in a ball of fire.

46

Sleep eluded Hawk. He struggled to get Manuel Esteva and the hastily abandoned mobile home out of his thoughts. Although he had been re-assigned to other duties, the Elaine Kalman case stayed constantly on Hawk's mind, and in his opinion remained far from closed.

He attempted to conjure Inola Walela's silky hair, high cheekbones, the curve of her long neck, but her vision morphed into the headshot of the college student instead. Turning to glance at the digital clock beside his bed, it glowed 11:17. Fed up with thrashing the sheets, he went to the kitchen and prepared a pot of coffee.

The first phone ring caught him by surprise—the next filled him with worry. *This can't be good.* Anxious that it could be bad news from his mother, he snatched the handset.

"Hawk, it's Sands," the sheriff shouted, sirens blaring in the background.

"Sheriff? Where are you?"

"Place called the Smoky Pines Resort. You familiar with the location?"

"Yeah. I went there a couple of days ago for the Kalman case."

"We've got two dead bodies in a cabin out here. Manager says a young couple was checked in."

Hawk's heart slammed in his chest. "Who are they?"

"Just get down here. Better if you see for yourself. Pick up Stiles on your way."

"We'll be right there." Hawk clicked off the phone, then dialed Stiles's number.

"Ken, it's Steven. Get dressed. Sheriff's got a couple fatalities. I'll be there in twenty."

Hawk hung up without waiting for Stiles to respond.

At 12:30 A.M. Hawk and Stiles arrived to chaos at the Smoky Pines Lodge. State trooper vehicles, sheriff's cruisers, and three fire trucks were parked in the dirt lot in front of the main structure. Flashing red and blue lights reflected in a stream of water that trailed from somewhere Hawk couldn't yet see. The stench of smoke and smoldering plastic permeated the still night air.

"All this excitement looks familiar doesn't it?" Hawk told Stiles as he reached for the Kalman file and exited the car. He moved toward a group of uniformed officers, then stopped in his tracks.

"What?" Stiles asked.

Hawk pointed to a paneled van, its satellite dish high in the air. "Press got here fast."

"Damned police scanners," Stiles said. "They should be outlawed."

They walked up a path toward the sound of voices that grew louder as they approached. A lump formed in Hawk's throat as they sidled up next to a coroner's van parked not far from what remained of the charred-out shell of a cabin. Trails of white smoke floated from the smoldering structure. He stepped out of the way for two men in white jumpsuits carrying a black body bag to pass. He didn't take his eyes off the vinyl shroud until Stiles nudged him.

Spotting the Sheriff, they wove their way between uniformed officers and firemen to reach him.

"What's the story, Sheriff?" Hawk asked.

"Two dead inside," Sands said, running a hand across his whiskered chin. "What's left of 'em is burnt to a crisp. They'll gather DNA and dental on both victims then send them to Charlotte to expedite. We'll need a sample from Elaine Kalman's mother. Best if the request came from you, Hawk."

"You believe it's her?"

"Likely, based on the description."

"Damn," Hawk muttered.

"So here's the story. Manager of this place claims a couple in their twenties registered at two o'clock in the afternoon, day before yesterday. Says someone made an on-line reservation, paid by credit card when the man checked in. Never heard any problems or complaints about them from the other guests. Stayed to themselves. Bought food at the market up the road—cabin had a kitchen set-up. None of the staff say they saw them except at a distance, requested not to be disturbed. Claimed to be on their honeymoon."

Hawk waited for more details, but received nothing more. "That's it?" he asked.

"Gets complicated. The lodge has been burglarized. Computer's missin'. Credit card receipts are gone. Even the registration log. Manager can't even remember their names."

"They can get a credit card number trace through the resorts' on-line service," Hawk offered.

"Could, if they operated that way. Hard copy receipts are run and tallied on a weekly basis. They kept them in a lock box under the counter."

"Don't tell me," Hawk moaned.

"Also stolen," Sands confirmed.

"You're kiddin', right?" Stiles said after letting out an exasperated breath.

Sands motioned with his head toward the folder stuffed under Hawk's arm. "I see you still got the Kalman file."

"Well, sir, I—I know you said—"

"Show him your pictures. Maybe he'll recognize one of 'em."

Relieved his boss hadn't reprimanded him for not following through on the order to send the case to records, Hawk rifled through the paperwork. He placed the photograph of Elaine and Nicholas's program to the front of the file. "It can't be Nicholas Kalman. He's still at the hospital, far as I know."

Sands glared at Hawk. "What do you mean, 'far as you know?'"

Hawk spread his arms wide. "You took me off the case. I haven't looked in on him since."

"Better check it out." Sands hitched his head toward the path. "Manager's the fidgety fella' at the office. Can't miss him." Sands returned to the somber officers who meandered around the scene.

Hawk and Stiles sidestepped the fire hoses snaked in the path that led to the main structure. Every window lit in the two-story log lodge reflected in the pools of standing water. The deputies followed the gravel lane lined with manicured azalea bushes in silence. Hawk didn't know what Stiles could be thinking, but Hawk thought of Aranka Kalman and how he would possibly be able to tell the woman her only daughter was dead. He would want to be the one to deliver the news. He cautioned himself not to get too far ahead of himself, not to give up hope, the victim could be a different woman.

Dread tapped Hawk on the shoulder as he caught sight of a business suit-clad woman holding a microphone. She nudged a man with a video camera perched on his shoulder and they headed toward the deputies. Stiles dropped his hand to the butt of his gun and issued the reporter a taut scowl. She immediately lowered the microphone and retreated a few steps.

Hawk repressed a laugh and geared back into professsional mode as they reached a balding man draped in a robe. He shook his head over and over, hot-boxing an unfiltered cigarette as he paced a tight circle in front of the bottom step to the lodge.

Hawk had spoken to an elderly lady when he had stopped by a few days earlier. He had seen this man cutting the grass, but didn't interrupt his chore. Now he wished he had already established a rapport with the clearly distraught man.

"Sir, I'm Deputy Hawk, this is Deputy Stiles."

"Turner. Eugene Turner. I own that mess over there. This is awful! Just awful. Those poor kids. I can't believe this has happened."

Hawk glanced back. Hidden by a profusion of pine trees, the cabin couldn't be seen from where they stood, but white smoke that trailed into the sky between the branches indicated its exact location.

"We need you to calm down, Mr. Turner," Stiles said,

angling his body to stand directly in front of the man.

"Can you answer a few questions?" Hawk asked.

Turner nodded, and took a deep breath.

"Are you the manager, sir?"

"Manager and owner. Me and my wife."

"Where is she, sir?" Stiles asked.

"We've got a cabin like that one . . . was. Around back, behind the lodge. Ladies from the church are with her. She's a mess. Couldn't bear seeing any more. Thinking about those kids has . . ." Tears beaded in Turner's wild eyes. "Wiring's good. I told the fire chief. And stove's electric, not gas. I insisted on that, for safety sake. I can't imagine what went wrong in there."

"So you didn't hear anything?"

"No. Just the sirens. One of the guests called nine-one-one. By the time the firemen got here it was too late," Turner said in a faraway voice.

"I understand you met the male victim when he checked in," Hawk said.

"Yeah, but like I told the sheriff, I don't remember his name and somebody stole all my records."

"Were his hands bandaged?" Hawk asked.

"No."

"How about his face? Did he have a wound on the left side?" Hawk drew a line from his eyebrow, down his cheek with his index finger.

"No. The kid was fine."

Hawk turned to Stiles. "Couldn't have been Nicholas, then."

"Do you have customers stayin' inside the lodge?" Stiles asked.

"Three couples. They didn't see or hear anything. I listened in when they talked to the sheriff."

"All right. I'd like to show you a photograph if you don't mind." Hawk angled toward the light from the wraparound porch that bathed the area and held up Elaine's headshot for the man to look at.

Turner removed his horn-rim glasses with a shaking hand

and leaned close to the picture. He studied the photograph top to bottom. "I reckon it could be her. Didn't see the lady up close, though. She seemed tall, but like I said, only saw her from a distance. Dealt with the fella." He pointed to the photo. "I know she was blond like that gal. Real pretty, like her, too."

"What did he look like?" Hawk asked.

"Dark hair. Young, probably twenty-two, three. Good-looking kid. Italian name, as I recall now." Turner snapped his fingers. "He asked if there was an I-talian restaurant nearby. Told him Rosie's up the road makes pretty good spaghetti." Turner flicked his cigarette butt and slid his glasses back on. "That's all I remember."

"What about a vehicle? They must have driven here, right?"

"Yeah. Little white four-door. Looked new. Not sure what make though, they all look alike nowadays."

"Could you point it out to us?" Hawk asked with a glimmer of hope, knowing they could run the license plate to find out the owner, or who had rented it.

"Sure. There's no parking in front of the cabins, everybody's gotta park in the lodge lot. Turner looked and pointed across the area full of nothing but official vehicles. "Huh, I don't see it. Thought for sure it was parked over where that fire truck is." He scanned the entire parcel and shrugged. "I do remember seeing it before dark. I was making sure lids on the trash containers were closed. Got a bear problem lately. Anyway, it was there, I'm sure of it."

"Did you notice anyone unfamiliar hanging around yesterday or last night?" Stiles asked.

Turner lowered his head and stared at his soggy slippers a while. "Saw a car that kinda stuck out late this afternoon. Big black sedan. Didn't think much of it, though. Lots of tourists come by here lookin' for the trout farm. It's the next turnoff down the way."

"What about the driver? Did you see him?"

"Naw. Windows were tinted dark. Drove around real slow and stopped at the far end for a while. Whoever was driving didn't stay long, then he drove on. Haven't seen that car since." Turner slid a weary hand across his smooth crown. "Look, I gotta get back to my wife."

Hawk took a business card from his breast pocket and handed it to Turner. "If anyone contacts you looking for anybody, or if there's anything else you remember, anything at all, would you give me a call?"

Turner removed his glasses again and squinted at the card. "You bet." He sighed, and returned to shaking his head. "No more sleep tonight."

"They're gonna be here a while," Stiles said.

"Well. Okay then. I gotta get back to my wife," Turner said again. He turned from the deputies then stopped. "Come to think of it," he said, walking back to them. "I thought I did hear a door slam coming from that black car. But I didn't see anyone get out."

"All right, thank you, sir. If there's anything else—"

"Yeah, I'll call."

The deputies left Turner who reached into his robe pocket and fished a cigarette from a crumpled pack, as if to gather enough courage to walk away and face his wife.

"He's tore up," Hawk said.

"It's a tragedy, no doubt about it," Stiles agreed.

Turner had taken only a few strides before the reporter and her cameraman swooped. She barraged the man with questions as she rushed after him. Turner shielded his eyes from the glaring light clipped to the camera and adamantly shook his head. A trooper stepped into the fray and mercifully ushered Turner away.

"This is gonna be all over the TV by mornin'," Stiles grumbled. "No tellin' what story they'll come up with."

"Yeah. The sheriff's been careful about anyone leakin' anything about Elaine Kalman."

"Not much chance of that now."

"I know the first thing they're gonna ask once they figure everything out," Stiles said as they approached their cruiser.

"What's that?"

"If it really was Elaine Kalman in there . . .?"

"Yeah?" Hawk asked, taking one last look at the cloud of smoke through the trees.

"Who was the guy?"

Hawk shook his head. "Haven't got a clue. But I sure as hell have a lot more questions for Nicholas Kalman."

47

Nicholas awoke at 3:00 A.M. to pins-and-needle pain in his hands. A light at the head of the bed he had yet to figure out how to extinguish bathed the room in a faint glow. Staring at his fingers, he worried about the inability to function at even menial tasks. Whenever he attempted a keyboard position, the tightness frightened him. *Will I ever be able to play again*? Then he thought of Elaine. Grief squeezed his chest and he found it difficult to breathe. *I'll never hold her again.*

His heart pounded every time the door to his hospital room opened. *Alexander must know where I am by now. And Timothy. Even Sampte. It's only a matter of time before at least one of them comes for me.*

Remembering Elaine's fate, he feared for his own life. Anxiety turned to anger as he contemplated the punishment he would dispense when the chance presented itself. Robbed of sleep, he remained restless and on edge throughout the night.

Nicholas replayed the visit from the deputy in a constant loop. At the time, he felt confident the deputy believed Dr. Everett's explanation about the amnesia and the effects of a head wound. But when Hawk returned less than an hour later to ask a few more questions, Nicholas recognized doubt written all over the lawman's face. He didn't know if he would survive another round of questioning. He knew he should tell the deputy everything, but the need to hear the truth about Elaine from the person responsible for her death far outweighed any rational thought.

First would be to find out why he—whoever it is—killed her. Fate would determine what he would do to whoever confessed to taking her from him.

He had to get out of this comfortable, although vulnerable

place. He couldn't risk facing Alexander under these circumstances. It helped that he felt stronger, and that his wounds were healing well, but he realized any appearance of apprehension or weakness to Alexander held tragic circumstances. Nicholas knew he needed to be the one in control—that their face-to-face meeting must be on his terms, not his mentor's.

He had to be as alert and coherent as possible, so refused the last offer of pain medication that put his mind in a fog.

Tchaikovsky's piano concerto *Symphony Pathetique* came into his mind. The crashing chords instilled him with confidence. He unwound the bandages to reveal red fingers covered in abrasions turning to scabs, chipped nails, ragged cuticles. Doing his best to ignore the sickening sight, he began devising a plan for his escape. Jessica would be key. They had forged a bond together, and she was the only person he trusted.

The need to stop his racing mind urged him to take the Walkman she had brought him from the bedside table. He slid on the headphones and pushed the play button. The CD whirred to life and notes filled his ears. He closed his eyes and took deep breaths. Beethoven's *Egmont Overture* swept over him as he waited for morning, and Jessica to return.

48

The sun's first light hit the windshield of Hawk's cruiser as he drove up the private gravel drive to Aranka Kalman's sprawling, single-level ranch-style house. It had been night-time when he visited her the only other time and he hadn't noticed the postcard vision of the barn painted the same stark white, and dark green trim of the house. Bereft of horses or livestock, the arena and paddock areas looked newly raked. Stable doors stood wide open, ready to wel-come the thoroughbreds, as if they were to arrive any time.

Clear-cut of pines, the grounds were surrounded by a groomed lawn on rolling hills. Magnolia trees studded the yard. Hydrangeas and azalea bushes lined the front of the house. The scene reminded him of a comfortable oasis dropped in the middle of the forest.

Standing at the front door, dreading the visit, he twirled the brim of his hat in his hands and tried to steady the pulse that rocketed in his neck. He expected hired help to answer the door; instead, Aranka Kalman greeted him with an unsteady smile. She held a cell phone and he wondered if she had yet to put it down since her daughter vanished. Still dressed in a robe, her surprise to see him verified she had not read the morning paper.

"I'm sorry to bother you this early, ma'am."

"Oh, God. Did you find her?" Aranka asked in a rushed voice, her apprehension evident by the way she clutched her robe tight against her neck.

"No ma'am, not yet. Should we sit?" He motioned to the bench on the porch where they sat the last time they met.

"Why don't you come inside?"

She ushered him into the modestly decorated house where she clearly lived contrary to Alexander Kalman's opulence. Once again he noted the differences between the siblings, admiring her even more. Walking through the front room, he took mental note of everything. His attention settled on an impressive black feathered, Native American ceremonial headdress. Encased in Plexiglas five feet in length, the treasure hung in reverence over a fireplace. His boot heels clicked on the dark hardwood floors, interspersed by what looked to be hand-woven rugs like the ones sold at the nearby Cherokee reservation.

Entering the kitchen, he took in modern stainless steel and dark granite. All of the appliances, countertops and sinks sparkled.

Hawk followed Aranka as she pushed through a door to the rear of the kitchen. They stepped into a greenhouse covered with dark mesh.

"This is the only place I feel sane. Everything in the house reminds me of Elaine," she said, plunging a hand into a mound of cubed bark and what looked like pieces of hairy coconut shells piled on a nearby planting stand.

Struck by the humidity, the cloying atmosphere reminded Hawk of the summer to come. Surrounded by beauty everywhere he looked, he saw orchids in various stages of bloom, color and variety. They were planted in plain clay pots atop ten-foot long tables. Some hung in baskets, their curled exposed roots woven like nests of snakes. Others had tiny rust-colored, dragon-faced blooms that seemed to grow directly out of snarled pieces of driftwood. *Her sanctuary.* Hawk thought of his mother; how amazed she would be at Aranka Kalman's paradise.

"Please, go ahead," she said, in an apprehensive voice.

"I have something to tell you."

Hawk watched hope fill her eyes.

"There's been a fire at a resort not far from here." Hawk fell silent, reluctant to continue.

"Oh, God." Her body gave a shudder. "Go on."

"Two bodies were found inside."

Hawk watched her hope fade to despair. "Bodies?" she asked. Traces of soil stuck to her hand as she reached to clutch the robe against her neck again.

"A man and a woman. We need to verify whether one of them is your daughter."

"Elaine?"

"Yes, ma'am."

"You're sure?"

"No, ma'am. Not at all. We're hoping it's not her. It doesn't appear that the male victim is Nicholas, so there's still hope."

"My brother tells me Nicholas is at the county hospital."

"Yes." Hawk watched her eyes glaze over, knowing she must merely be going through the motions of living right now.

"Alexander ordered that under no circumstances am I to visit Nicholas."

"Well, ma'am, I—"

"I plan to visit him this morning."

Hawk gave her a slight smile, impressed by her readiness to defy her brother. "We need to know for sure if this woman is your daughter or not. Soon as you can, we'd like you to provide a DNA sample."

"Sample?"

"They swab of the inside of your mouth. It doesn't hurt and won't take but a minute. And could you contact Elaine's dentist and have him provide her records? It would be most helpful and might speed up the process."

"I fear they'll be of no help."

"Why is that?" Hawk asked.

"Elaine never so much as suffered a cavity. Even her wisdom teeth remain."

Hawk thought about Aranka's comment for a moment. "Actually, that information might work in our favor."

"How so?"

"If the woman at the cabin *did* have dental work, we'll know sooner that she isn't Elaine."

Although not seeming to take comfort in Hawk's explanation, Aranka nodded her head. "When will you be certain?"

Hawk knew if they had to rely on DNA alone it would

take months to receive verification. He didn't have the heart to disappoint her further, so instead he said, "I can't say, ma'am. We'll be sending the DNA samples to Charlotte to expedite."

Aranka's wild, flashing eyes made Hawk wonder whether she could make it through another day, let alone months.

"Would it be possible for me to see her?"

"Do you mean the woman from the fire?" He looked away from her probing stare. "No, ma'am. There's no need for that."

She let out a relieved-sounding sigh and seemed to draw into herself, getting smaller before his eyes.

He wanted to take her hand, do something, anything to comfort her, but all he could offer were his words. "Ms. Kalman, your daughter's case is our top priority. And finding out what's happened to Elaine is the only thing I'm working on."

"I don't know what I will do if . . .," she whispered.

"Maybe you shouldn't be alone. Would you like me to take you to your brother's house?"

"That won't be necessary. It's very kind of you, but I'm quite sure you have other duties. And my brother is the last person I would ask to accompany me."

She straightened her posture, raised her head, stuck out her chin and Hawk knew she would be all right.

"Where do I need to go for the DNA test?"

"The county hospital. Anytime. They're waiting on you."

"I believe Alexander mentioned that's where Nicholas is."

"Yes, ma'am. Are you aware of his condition?"

"Alexander tells me Nicholas remembers nothing."

"Or anyone."

"Not even Elaine?"

"I'm afraid not. Nicholas's doctor thinks maybe by seeing his uncle—well, it may trigger his memory. And that might help us find Elaine."

"Because the woman from the fire might not be her."

Hawk nodded, repressing a shudder at the memory of the

body bag being carried from the ruins of the cabin.

"I'll get dressed." She brushed the debris from her hands and moved to the door.

"There's one more thing. If you run across the local paper? Well, ma'am, I'd avoid it."

The phone in her hand peeled high-pitched notes and her body jerked.

Hawk guessed her nightmare must feel never-ending.

49

Timothy straightened his body to reach its full height as he always did before he subjected himself to Alexander. Entering the music room, he hoped his mentor would finally see that he truly belonged at the Steinway, deserving of the maestro's complete attention. A master of ability instead of a charity case. The local newspaper tucked under his arm brought him a sense of confidence. He knew Alexander would be pleased.

At the sight of his mentor's stern stare, Timothy's optimism wavered. He shut the door and crossed the room to pour himself a shot of whiskey at the wet bar, then slosh brandy into a crystal snifter.

A bit of the amber liquid spilled from the decanter's lip. Timothy checked over his shoulder to make sure Alexander didn't notice, knowing he would be reprimanded for his carelessness. He quickly sopped up the puddle with a linen napkin then tossed the soaked cloth in the sink.

He took a pull from his glass, set it down, then approached Alexander. "I know it's early, but I thought we should celebrate . . ."

Alexander rose from his chair. Cheeks flushed, he limped to meet Timothy face to face. When Timothy held out the glass, Alexander batted the snifter from his hand. The glass exploded into shards against the fireplace. Timothy leapt back out of range of Alexander's cane, aware firsthand of the damage the man could wield with the stick.

Alexander smoothed the lapel of his smoking jacket and rasped in controlled tones, "Tell me. Have you found Elaine?"

Timothy raised his empty palm. "There's nothing to be concerned with anymore." The moment Timothy spoke he realized he'd made a serious mistake.

Alexander quickened his pace, raised his cane and swiped it in a wide arc. The staff whistled through the air and struck the top of Timothy's shoulder. Timothy flinched, one arm flying up to cover his head, the other grasping his throbbing clavicle.

"This is destroying me, do you not understand?" Alexander roared. "Where is she?" The cane rose in the air again and shattered a two-foot tall crystal vase atop a nearby table. Glass, calla lilies, and water erupted into the air.

Timothy scrambled to safety.

Alexander fell into his chair and massaged his temples.

Hoping the storm had passed, Timothy emerged from behind the piano and reached for the newspaper he'd dropped. With shaking hands, he unfolded the pages and cautiously approached Alexander who snatched the news-print from him.

"See? I told you I'd handle it," Timothy said.

Alexander's eyes fell on the headline.

BANKER'S DAUGHTER AND CELEBRATED PIANIST FOUND DEAD IN HIDEAWAY BLAZE

Alexander's face turned ashen. Shaking his head he said, "The deputy has told me Nicholas is in the hospital, so it can't be him." He looked at the headline again. "Is it her?"

"Does it matter? As long as the authorities think it is, there's nothing to worry about."

Tears filled Alexander's eyes. He crushed the paper in his fist and dropped the ball at his feet. A moan rose in his throat as he lowered his head into his hands.

It had never occurred to Timothy that Alexander could feel grief. Feel anything at all for that matter, except passion for the music.

"You loved her," Timothy whispered, shocked that he had never considered the notion.

Alexander lifted his head to reveal his anguished face.

Shame filled Timothy. *If only I had known. I wouldn't have been so careless to leave Elaine's disposal to Nicholas.*

The pursuit of the couple and their subsequent fiery death had only intended to be a ruse to pull attention away from Alexander. Now Timothy realized this error could very well prove fatal for him. He thought about all the bodies abandoned at Henri Thibodeaux's and of the times he had accompanied Sampte with plastic-covered, lifeless forms. Whenever any hint of indiscretion or liability to Alexander arose, another delivery would be made.

The list started when Timothy was a boy, not long after Nicholas had moved into Alexander's mansion. The first body he knew of had been Nicholas's father, Charles. Then Nicholas's mother, though Timothy couldn't remember her name. Sampte had told him that even Elaine's father had met a similar fate after Alexander had discovered his sister's peril caused by her husband's indiscretions. Other workers had attended to their various jobs at the mansion, never to return, so Timothy figured there must have been others delivered to Thibodeaux. He didn't know for sure, nor did he care. Alexander convinced Timothy that they had been inconsequential; no one would miss them. Manuel Esteva and his family also came to mind. They were gone now, too. All for Alexander.

Timothy watched the older man, knowing he would continue to do anything for his mentor. Not merely out of fear, but because the life Alexander had chosen for Timothy was the only life he knew.

He returned to the glass he had abandoned and downed the whiskey in one gulp. He climbed the three steps to the Steinway, lifted the lid, and sat at the bench. "I've mastered the Prokofiev," he said in a soft yet confident tone. "I know you'll be pleased."

* * *

Alexander pushed his grief aside, left alone after Timothy had presented the Prokofiev to perfection. He doubted even Nicholas could have performed the piece with more passion. On his peaceful terrace, sipping a cup of tea, he tried to enjoy the unseasonably warm morning and wondered if winter would ever arrive. Each year his favorite season became less severe in temperature. Snowfall in the mountains had diminished to nearly immeasurable amounts. He loved to watch the snow: cleansing and refreshing in its whiteness. For the first time since he had acquired the property and built his mansion, he began to think about relocating. He let out a sigh, resigned to the fact that everything he called home could now be a closed chapter.

Perhaps it is time to move on, start fresh. Find some snow.

At first he seethed with anger over Timothy's behavior, but then realized his student's attitude was a learned one. That he alone had awakened the beast in the young man.

Alexander thought of what he needed to accomplish. He would place Timothy at Nicholas's seat in the performing arena. Confident that Timothy's skills were in order, Alexander actually looked forward to his new protégé's upcoming concert. More than that, he felt assured of Timothy's loyalty—the boy would do whatever Alexander deemed necessary.

For the first time in months, he felt proud that his teachings were not in vain, as it appeared they had been with Nicholas. Timothy had become an exemplary pupil. At that moment, Alexander decided to take him wherever he would eventually go. He would focus his efforts undividedly on creating a Timothy that would surpass Nicholas's talents.

Before anything could be set in motion, Alexander knew he must face Nicholas. He had been wary to do so. Based on Deputy Hawk's description of his injuries, he was terrified of what his once stunning pupil now looked like. A twisted monster scarred for life. Long suppressed memories played in his mind of how as a boy he had been taunted for his own imperfections. The unnerving thoughts filled him with sorrow.

He batted away a tear, knowing how life would now be for Nicholas. Damaged goods. Of no use to anyone.

50

The news hit Dr. Everett the moment he arrived at the hospital. Unfolding that morning's *Smoky Mountain Times* he had purchased from the gift shop, he stopped in the atrium, stunned by the headline. Tucking the paper under his arm, he pulled out his wallet and searched for Deputy Hawk's business card as he hurried to his office.

Ellie greeted him, looking worried, clutching her own newspaper. "Have you read this?"

Everett waved his copy. "Has he seen it?"

"I don't know. Why are they saying it's him?"

"I have no idea." He handed her Hawk's card. "Call the deputy. When you reach him, page me right away," he said, sliding on his lab coat. "I'm going to see if Jessica Taft is here."

"I passed her in the corridor. She said she was going to the cafeteria until visiting hours started."

"I'll go speak to her. Make the call," Everett said, rushing out the doorway.

Everett took the turn into the cafeteria and searched for Jessica among visitors of patients in the hospital and the assorted personnel dressed in lab coats and colorful scrubs. At times, he felt like an intruder in this sacred space. He knew that for some, the cafeteria with its smells of steam tables and hours-old cuisine seemed more important than the chapel on the first floor. Food in the South brought comfort.

He found Jessica sitting alone at a table near the cash register. He stuffed the newspaper into the pocket of his lab coat and wove his way to her.

"Excuse me, Ms. Taft?"

Jessica looked up from her textbook. "Hello, Dr. Everett."

"May I join you?"

Clearing books from the chair next to her, she motioned for him to sit.

Everett sat on the edge of the seat and leaned close to her. "I have something to show you." He unfolded the newspaper and smoothed the creases. "It's rather disturbing." He watched as she read.

Then she glanced up. "This obviously isn't true. What's going on?"

He shrugged. "Right, it's not him. I've got a call in to the deputy who stopped by yesterday. Perhaps he can give us some answers."

"I don't understand. I mean, they're writing about Nicholas, but he's here, and who is this woman?"

"I don't know."

Jessica sank deep in the chair. "Unbelievable."

"This could all be a misunderstanding, but I'm afraid, soon it will be all over the hospital."

"Has Nicholas seen this?"

"Not to my knowledge. I hope you'll help me with that. He trusts you and I think he would take the news better coming from you rather than the deputy, or even me."

Jessica folded over the paper, hiding the unsettling photographs of the charred remains of a unidentifiable structure, and two white-suited men carrying a body bag.

"Maybe we shouldn't tell him."

Everett pointed to a table where six people were huddled over an identical newspaper, talking over each other in excited voices. "I don't think that's a good idea."

51

Newly shaven and dressed in a pair of sky blue surgical scrubs, Nicholas sat in the recliner, his father's journal open on his lap. He remembered an incident the morning of his twentieth birthday. It had been the beginning of his rebellion against Alexander.

His mentor, leaning heavily on his cane, paced a tight circle in the music room.

Nicholas sat watching, growing more and more amused by Alexander's lack of emotional control over the latest request.

"I'd like to buy a car for my birthday," Nicholas had said.

"Nonsense. It would be a waste of your earnings."

"It's my money, I should be able to spend it any way I like."

"Legally, the funds are not yours for another year."

"I know, I know," Nicholas said. "When are you planning to tell me more about the Nicholas Kalman trust? And tell me again, why are you my trustee? You never did explain that to me."

"Because I have your best interests in mind at all times."

"Right. Well, I'd like Elaine to look over the portfolio."

Alexander chuckled. "What makes you think she's qualified?"

"One more semester and she'll be living the world of finance. She's already received three job offers, one in Brussels. She's more than qualified."

Alexander dismissed the information with a wave of his hand.

"Come on, Uncle, it's just a car," Nicholas said. "I know it's a lot of money, but look at it as an investment."

"It's not about the money," Alexander snapped. "Don't you understand? You must keep up appearances, not only for the public, but to impress your rivals as well. Holding your ranking in these performances is not an easy task. It's all about ticket sales, young man. Your opponents will use anything against us to taint our good name. Riding around in an expensive sports car when your time would be better served at the keyboard would be seen as an advantage to those less competent."

Alexander brushed lint from Nicholas's shoulder. "If you want to appear a class above your competitors, I will rent you a car and driver. I assure you, give your competitors any excuse and they will play their little mind games to make you doubt your ability."

And you know all about mind games, don't you, Uncle? Nicholas thought, but instead he said, "I don't give a damn what my competitors think of me."

"This is a serious matter. It is not merely your rivals I speak of. Consider the promoters and booking agents as well. You must hold your ego at bay until you've secured a stellar performance status. We've yet to play in a few of the most elite performance halls in Europe. The Flaiano in Pescara, Italy. Theatre De Vevey in Switzerland—"

"Since when did you start playing beside me?"

"Whatever do you mean?" Alexander asked.

"You said they'll use anything against *us*, and where *we've* yet to play. Believe me, when *I'm* playing, the *last* thing I have on my mind, is *you*."

The next instant, Alexander stormed to Nicholas, grabbing his throat in a vice-like grip. "You ungrateful prig. How do you think you've achieved all that you have? It is as much due to my efforts as your own. You should have realized by now it takes a hell of a lot more than talent to become successful. Quit frothing over your assets and senseless vehicles and devote more time to practice."

Nicholas gasped for air, heat rose to his face. He wrenched away from Alexander's grasp. Heartbeat throbbing in his neck, he rubbed his larynx. Deciding not to give Alexander the satisfaction of knowing he had rattled him, Nicholas swept back his tousled hair and straightened his collar.

"I'm not a child anymore. I can't live only to compete or perform. I need a life aside from the keyboard."

Alexander spoke in a steady, cold voice. "You take and never give. That is a concern of mine, Nicholas. This behavior is a distasteful flaw you must challenge and conquer."

How could Alexander's perception of the situation be so twisted? Nicholas had always been the one to give and never take. He never expected anything from Alexander except the necessities of everyday life. Alexander had insisted Nicholas live in the luxury he had grown accustomed to.

Nicholas responded by slowly shaking his head. Debating with Alexander had always been futile.

A week later, after winning rave reviews from his exhibition at Carnegie Hall, Alexander relented with a peace offering. Upon Nicholas's return, the sleek black Porsche Targa he had wanted sat shining in the circular drive.

Nicholas found great escape from Alexander's manipulations by racing along the mountainous roads surrounding his uncle's property. Elaine, seat-belted securely in the zooming vehicle, urging him to go faster, Paganini bursting from the speakers, brought the first taste of real freedom he had ever encountered.

Now Nicholas looked around the hospital room at his stark surroundings. He compared the clean but worn white sheets on the single hospital bed to the champagne-colored Egyptian cotton percales that dressed his king-sized bed in Alexander's mansion. And here, flimsy aluminum blinds covered a small window instead of ten-foot-tall openings adorned with thick burgundy velour, plush as any stage drapery.

Yet, Nicholas felt a sense of comfort and safety in the hospital room, smaller than his private bath at home. In this place, a nurse checked on him every couple hours, wounds were tended to, and his doctor assured him the injuries would not be permanent with the exception of the scar on his face. He even believed his hands would be fully functional after extended physical therapy.

Feeling stronger by the hour, Nicholas found himself able to bear most of his weight on the bad ankle and the pain in his ribs had abated. He rubbed his irritated fingers, then lifted his father's journal to read.

> *Within the mansion, terror reigns. His hair is like the sun, but his eyes are dead as coal. No sparkle, no light. Teeth pearly and enticing.*
>
> *Lips holding an easy smile. Clothes flawless and crisp, shoes polished like mirrors, cufflinks gleaming in tailored shirts. The cane tapping.*
>
> *Tap. Tap. Tap. You hear it approaching, but you can't escape. His power will drain your own until you cannot run any longer. The moment you realize how much power he wields you will try to flee. Too late, you will realize you've been running from evil so long the exhaustion overpowers you. Sorrow will come to rest. After your bones are too weary and your mind too spent, he will find you, haunt you, envelop you—*

Nicholas flinched at a knock on the door. He slammed the journal shut, his pulse throbbing within every injured area of his body. He wiped a trail of sweat from his temple and attempted a calm voice. "Come in."

Jessica slipped into the room. "You're out of bed. Look at you, actually dressed."

"Yeah, Nurse Connie found me something more presentable."

"And your bandages are off."

"I couldn't stand them any longer," Nicholas said, picking a soft scab on his middle finger.

"So they feel better?"

"Much."

"Then this will come in handy." She pulled a palm-size, red ball from her jacket pocket. "It's supposed to help strengthen your fingers."

Nicholas took the supple rubber ball in his right hand and mashed it gingerly. "This is perfect. Thanks."

"Has the doctor been in today?"

Nicholas nodded toward the bedside table. "I'm supposed to put ointment on every once in a while."

Jessica reached for the silver tube on the table and uncapped the lid. "I'll help you."

She squeezed out a bit of cloudy gel and dabbed it on his finger pads and cuticles. Her warm fingers melted the medication. He leaned his head back, relishing the sensation of her gentle touch on his damaged hands.

Watching her clean her hand on a tissue, he suspected something bothered her. "Is everything all right?"

She paused a moment before she spoke. "I have something you need to see. It's terrible, but Doctor Everett thinks you should know about it." She took a newspaper from her bag, but didn't give it to him. "I don't know whether to show you or not."

"Now you have to," he said, holding his hand out.

She knelt in front of the chair and gave him the paper.

He looked at the photographs and started to read. A rush of queasiness swept over him. He dropped the front page onto his lap and leaned his head back against the cushion. "They're saying it's me."

"The woman has your last name."

Nicholas nodded, his ears ringing at a deafening level. "Elaine," he whispered.

"Look, someone must have screwed up. It's a mistake. They obviously don't know who that man really is." She poured a cup of water from a pitcher on the rolling cart and handed it to him. "Doctor Everett's calling the deputy you met yesterday. He'll let us know what's going on."

Ignoring the cup, Nicholas raised the newspaper again. "I have no idea who the woman in the fire is, but it's not Elaine Kalman. Unless . . . Oh, God."

A terrifying thought came to him. He sat up straight in the chair. *Is it possible Timothy found Elaine in the country home? Put her in that cabin? That he started the fire?*

"What?" Jessica laid an urgent hand on his arm. "Nicholas, what's the matter?"

He regretted the alarm in her eyes. He gently clasped his knees to keep his hands from trembling. Rocking his body lightly, he struggled to keep the imagined vision of Elaine's burnt body from taking over his sanity.

Jessica knelt to face him and placed a tender hand on his cheek. Finding it difficult to hold in his emotion any longer, he stifled a sob and lowered his head to avoid her worried look.

"I might be able to help if you tell me what's going on," she said.

"I will. I promise." He searched her eyes for the trust he craved. Taking her shoulders in his hands he focused his gaze on her. "But first, you've got to get me out of here."

52

As Dr. Everett exited the hospital staff break room, he noticed an older man who propelled himself down the corridor with his cane. Although dressed impeccably, the man's hair looked tousled and the wild-looking glint in his wide-open eyes cued Everett that trouble brewed.

As the man reached the nurses station, he rapped the head of his cane on the counter. "Nicholas Kalman's room. Where is it," he commanded more than asked.

Several nurses and attendants immersed in charting notations turned to the disturbance.

"Who is in charge here?" the man roared.

One of the nurses reached for the phone and dialed as another asked, "What can I do for you?"

"What will it take to make you understand?" He shoved a hand into his front pocket and withdrew a gold money clip that clasped a thick wad of bills. Waving it above his head, he announced, "I'm certain this is more than any of you earn in a month. Whose will it be?"

Everett hurried to the belligerent man. "I'm Dr. Calbert Everett. What's going on here?"

"None of these imbeciles will tell me where my nephew is."

"Who might that be?"

The man turned away and muttered, "Another idiot."

"Sir, I need you to calm down."

"Where is my nephew?" he shouted.

"Calm down or I'll call security," Everett said, through clenched teeth.

The man held Everett's gaze, took a deep breath, then smoothed his jacket. "Nicholas Renfrew Kalman. Where is he? I am Alexander Kalman, his uncle. You can't deny my visit."

"I have no intention of doing that. If you'll come with me, I'll take you to him." Everett backed down the corridor and motioned for Alexander to follow him.

As they reached Nicholas's room, Nurse Connie emerged through the door. "I think he's gone," she said.

"What do you mean, gone?" Alexander barked.

"He's not in his room, and his belongings aren't there."

"You're sure?" Everett shouldered past Connie and entered the hospital room. He pulled open the bedside table drawers. Yesterday he had watched Nicholas pull out the top drawer and set a leather-bound book atop the plastic bag containing his few personal items. Now, nothing remained.

Alexander tapped his cane impatiently on the floor. "What is going on here? Where is he?"

"Connie, call down to the cafeteria, see if he's there."

The nurse and Alexander shared glares as she bustled past.

"I'm sorry, Mr. Kalman. He hasn't been released as a patient, but he is ambulatory. He must have left of his own accord."

"He isn't at my home. Where else could he possibly be?" Alexander scowled. "You're keeping him from me."

"Why would I do that?"

"I will find him. You can be certain of that. And if I don't, I will sue you and this hospital for every dime you will ever see." Turning on his heel, Alexander limped down the corridor, cane tip and polished shoes clicking on the tiles.

No telling what that lunatic will do if he finds Nicholas. Hurrying to his office to see if Ellie had been able to reach Deputy Hawk, he remembered what the lawman had asked him about the possibility of Nicholas faking his amnesia.

Coming face to face with who—and what—the young man lived with, Everett wondered if Nicholas had been deceiving everyone all along.

53

Still clad in hospital scrubs, Nicholas followed Jessica from the parking space in front of her nondescript apartment complex. He carried the plastic bag in one hand, his father's journal in the other. He felt liberated and safe knowing Alexander would never find him here.

With every step his heartbeat pulsated in his temples, but at least his ankle didn't bother him much. Although his ribs were sore to the touch, as long as he took small breaths he no longer felt piercing pain. His fingers itched—another sign of healing, according to Nurse Connie. He regretted pulling the bandage off his face. Although he'd brushed the hair low over his forehead to cover some of the injury, the chill air burned his incision and the stitches stung and pulled the skin. He felt self-conscious, thinking every stranger's eyes locked to his wound.

They walked along a sidewalk and passed two identical three-story structures and soon arrived at an atrium devoid of plant life. Jessica waved to a woman climbing onto a mountain bike. "Here we are."

Nicholas heard the muted sound of rock music heavy with bass, thumping from her next-door neighbor's identical dwelling.

"It's not much, but it's comfortable," Jessica said, unlocking the door.

Nicholas entered the cramped front room stuffed with mismatched furniture. He scanned the room and searched for the one item he wanted to see most. He sighed, feeling sad for her, thinking what was a home without a piano?

"Sorry," she said, closing the door after her. "No piano."

He whirled toward her. "How did you know I—?"

She shrugged. "I figured you probably miss playing."

He raised his hands and glared at his unsightly wounds.

"I'm sorry. I didn't mean to remind you."

"No, don't be. I'll be back to playing soon," he said, unsure if he convinced her . . . or himself. He breathed deep and recognized the faint scent of cinnamon. "This is great. It smells nice."

"What do you mean?"

"Clean. Sweet. Hey, I've been smelling disinfectant and crappy hospital food for days."

"True. That place was kind of freaking me out, too." She swept an arm to the nearby couch. "You should take it easy."

"I really appreciate your letting me stay here. I won't get in your way."

"Don't worry about it." Jessica's words grew fainter as she went into another room. "Be right back."

He walked a few steps to a drafting table angled near the window and ran a finger along the precise pencil lines on the blueprint of a theatrical set. A description written in a box at the bottom right of the drawing stated: INTERPRETATION OF JOSEF SVOBODA'S 1968 PRODUCTION: "THE ANABAPTISTS"—NATIONAL THEATRE, PRAGUE.

Elaine loved Prague. He had taken her with him when he performed at St. George's Basilica a few months ago. The trip filled his senses again as he recalled their drinking Pilsner Urquell at Tretter's in Old Town. He had experienced the best meal of his life as they dined on milk-fed veal and risotto at the Allegro Restaurant inside the Four Seasons Hotel where they stayed. Nicholas closed his eyes, remembering the sound of the river Vltava running under the Charles Bridge. Smiling, he recalled Elaine as she teetered on stiletto heels, attempting to maneuver the cobblestone streets of the square. When he whisked her into his arms, her squeals of surprise bounced off the ancient stone buildings.

Jessica's muffled voice brought him back to reality. Fresh tears beaded his eyes, he brushed them away with the back of his hand.

"I don't want to get in the way of your studies," he said, looking around at the modest surroundings of Jessica's apartment.

"Don't worry about it. I'm ahead of schedule. The only thing left is to get my notes into the computer."

Nicholas lowered himself onto a lumpy couch covered with a peach-colored slipcover. Noticing a framed picture on the table beside him, he took it in his hands and studied the laughing face of an embarrassed-looking older woman standing on the shore.

"Actually, I'll welcome the company," she said, barely audible. "You probably should eat. I haven't been to the market in days, but we could go out. Then we can get you some clothes. There's a Kmart down the road."

"I've never even been inside a Kmart." He smiled hearing her laughter coming from the other room.

He thought of his finely tailored slacks and handmade silk shirts hanging on cedar hangers in his closet at Alexander's mansion, the Italian leather Tanino Crisci, Nosler shoes lined up in a precise row, his collection of Maui Jim sunglasses tucked in his top dresser drawer.

Possessions now meant nothing without Elaine. He wondered if he would enjoy anything ever again. A wave of sadness swept over him. All that mattered was making Alexander and Timothy pay for taking Elaine from him. He had vowed vengeance when he left her at the country home, and he would not betray her memory with thoughts of his own comfort.

By the time Jessica reappeared, Nicholas had fallen into a blue funk. He sunk deeper in the couch, the frame nestled on his chest.

She took the picture from him and rubbed the corner of its frame. "That's my Aunt Sarah. She raised me."

"She looks like a nice lady. What about your parents? Any pictures of them?"

"No." Her voice turned somber as she set the picture on the table. "They left when I was a kid. Couldn't handle the responsibility. It's just the two of us."

"Is your aunt still alive?"

Jessica nodded. "She's got a little house in Spartanburg. I

get down to see her every couple months or so. She'd love you. I can hear her now. 'He's handsome to the bone.'"

"Do you think I'm handsome?" He grinned when her cheeks flush.

She turned from him and straightened a stack of CDs in a cheap veneer cabinet next to the ancient RCA television set.

"I noticed your drawing over there. You're very talented. Why did you decide to go to the university here?"

"I'd love to have gone to Asheville or even Clemson in South Carolina. The local college was all Aunt Sarah could swing. I'm grateful, though. I'm kind of top dog at the theatre. The designer and I practically build and paint the sets on our own."

"Sounds challenging."

She answered with a shrug, then said, "Anyway . . ."

"You don't like to talk about yourself do you?"

"I'm pretty boring."

"Far from it."

"You don't have to be so nice, you know?"

Nicholas lifted himself from the couch and stood inches away from her. "You have no idea how much your kindness means to me."

"Okay. So, we should go." Easing away from him, she fumbled for the keys in her pocket. "What would you like to eat?"

"Anything. As long as it's not spongy, runny, or gray."

"I promise, nothing even resembling hospital food. In fact, I know exactly what you need," she said, going to the door.

Nicholas knew she was the one person who cared enough to help him create some semblance of normalcy. He hated keeping things from her, but didn't everyone have secrets? Still, he would have to tell Jessica about Elaine, and soon.

He felt his life reaching a crescendo. His pacing would be crucial, timing essential. A new composition evolving note-by-note, driven by circumstance, and as his father often cautioned in his writings: Fate.

54

Timothy ached not to have gone with Alexander to the hospital. He wanted to revel in Nicholas's expression when his mentor confronted him, but Alexander had insisted Timothy remain at the mansion to prepare for that night's concert.

When Alexander stormed into the music room after returning from the hospital, Timothy knew at once the visit did not go well.

Timothy took pleasure in Alexander's fury. *One more step into the fire, Nicholas. Bad for you. Very good for me.*

Now Timothy cowered as Alexander stripped books out of their shelves, and crashed yet another crystal vase. He issued commands in Hungarian: "Out! Go. Get out!"

Timothy backed from the room without a word. He heard the tantrum continue as he fled down the stairs. Doing his best to settle his nerves, he decided he would practice at the Baldwin on the first floor. He wondered what had caused the meltdown.

Reaching the bottom step, the metronome ticking of the grandfather clock near the front door reminded him of the dwindling hours until his performance. His nerves had seemed in check, despite Alexander's combustible emotion. But now, Timothy felt a rumble in his bowels.

Sitting at the Baldwin, Timothy thought about Nicholas and how he always seemed so calm before a concert, self-assured and nearly Zen-like in his concentration. Timothy conjured an image of his nemesis. He mimicked Nicholas's posture: erect at the edge of the bench, one foot atop the treble pedal, the other, resting on the floor, precisely four inches from its companion's heel.

Timothy squared his shoulders and raised his freckled

fingers above the keys. Taking three deep breaths, he began to play Prokofiev's Concerto Number. 3 with reverence and focus certain to have made Alexander weep.

55

After a light snack of cucumber sandwiches followed by three brandies, Alexander's nerves began to settle. Books, broken glass and mementos were strewn about the music room. He shook his head and bent to retrieve volume three of his treasured first edition Proust. Smoothing the pages, he re-shelved the novel and then hobbled around the rubble to the serenity of his terrace.

Instead of seething over Nicholas's abandonment, he stood on his third story balcony and surveyed the preparations for Timothy's after-concert party to be held on the grounds of his mansion later that night. Sampte had informed him that ninety people had confirmed their attendance. A rush of exhilaration surged in Alexander's chest. Although Timothy would be the one performing on stage, this would also be Alexander's first presentation in several years. He had allowed Nicholas's talents to be the center of attention for so long Alexander had forgotten what a rush being in the spotlight bestowed.

He stood on the veranda and silently practiced the introduction speech he would give for Timothy. He realized the need to placate Nicholas's adoring fans, assure them that he had not met death as reported in the newspaper. He would tell them Nicholas had merely been slightly injured, however he would be unable to make an appearance. Alexander would, of course, pass on their best wishes for Nicholas's full recovery, and then remind them this night was for Timothy.

The first trucks had arrived hours earlier, delivering tables and chairs now arranged in inviting clusters on the back lawn. Salmon-hued satin tablecloths fluttered in the light breeze. Portable propane heaters to ward off the night chill were being tested. A generator chugged in the background, which would provide power for the bank of lights interspersed around the party site.

Alexander watched a crew set the tables with the finest china and cutlery Sampte had brought out from storage for the festivities. He noticed his servant enter the music room and limped back inside.

Sampte looked around at the chaos, then at Alexander with a questioning gaze. Without a word, glass crunching under his feet, Sampte picked up a few books, cleared broken shards from a tabletop and stacked them there.

"Leave it," Alexander said in a weary voice. "Just leave it."

Sampte handed him a copy of the program for Timothy's performance at the Wilhoit Theatre. *Mere hours from now*, Alexander thought, fingering the slick paper. The pungent chemical odor of fresh ink stung his nostrils. He scanned the composition playing order, then gazed at the photograph on the cover that featured Timothy sitting on Alexander's veranda, the vista of the Great Smoky Mountains in the background.

"The photograph turned out well," Sampte said.

"He's not nearly as handsome as Nicholas." Alexander let out a heavy sigh. "Ah well, we must work with what we are bestowed. Are we on schedule?"

"Everything is in order."

"Fine. And Timothy? Have you checked on him lately?"

"We're keeping the whiskey away from him."

Alexander turned to Sampte and chuckled. "Have Zardos dress him in the charcoal tuxedo."

"Not the black tails?"

"No. I want him to convey a less traditional aura. We must be careful how he is presented. I want no comparisons between Nicholas and Timothy."

"I understand."

"And make certain he's manicured. I heard his left index nail clicking the keys this morning."

Sampte nodded in understanding. "What will you wear?"

Tossing the program atop the piano, Alexander clasped

his hands behind his back. "The black tails, of course," he said, already relishing the feel of the fine Italian cloth on his body.

56

The expanse of the bustling, product-laden big-box store had taken Nicholas by surprise, overloaded his senses, and left him exhausted. He was amazed that in less than an hour he and Jessica had been able to pick out and purchase a full change of clothes, jacket, boots and even toiletries. Far different from his shopping excursions with Alexander in New York City and Beverly Hills, which would often take days.

When they returned to Jessica's apartment, Nicholas held a bulging plastic bag to his chest, his stomach rumbling with chilidogs from the snack bar. "Do you mind if I lie down for a while?"

"No. You must be wiped out." She ushered him down the hall and into the only bedroom.

"The couch is fine."

"No, no. I've got work to do, take the bed," she said, turning down a patchwork quilt on the twin-size bed.

"You're sure?"

"I'll wash your new clothes while you rest."

"You don't need to do that."

"They're all stiff and smell like dye. Really. I don't mind." Reluctantly, Nicholas handed her the bag. "Holler if you need anything," she said, leaving the door slightly ajar.

Settling on the bed, he became embarrassed as he recalled the two of them at the checkout line. Jessica had watched each item being scanned to make sure the prices rang up correctly, then questioned the clerk about the white briefs that should have been seventy cents less. *This must be what it's like to be poor*, he had thought. She swiped her credit card, crossed her fingers, and mumbled, "Please go through."

Right before falling into a deep sleep, Nicholas made a

promise that as soon as he figured out how to get his hands on his own money, he would lavish Jessica with riches in return for her kindness, and as an apology for what he would subject her to next.

*   *   *

Dr. Everett replayed Alexander's disturbing confrontation repeatedly all morning, growing more unsettled each time Alexander invaded his thoughts. He finally phoned admissions and discovered that Jessica had provided only her address on Nicholas's admittance form. And when Ellie had tried to track her down, Jessica's phone number was unlisted. At his first opportunity, Everett decided he would visit her at home.

He knew he could not bear it if any harm came to either of them. Risking the consequences, he left the hospital and sought the two out. Skirting liability sent his nerves on edge. Such actions would have been unthinkable had he still been practicing medicine in New York, but the need to warn the young couple overrode his wisdom to be prudent.

Standing at Jessica's front door, he knocked several times and received no answer. As he turned to leave, Jessica ran into him, carrying a load of folded clothes.

"I was about to give up."

"Doctor Everett." Her eyes went a little wide, darted to the door, then back to him. "What are you doing here?"

"Mind if we talk for a minute?" He followed Jessica inside the apartment and asked, "Is Nicholas here?"

"Give me a second," she said, nodding to the pile of clothes.

He watched her walk down the hall and into a room. After a moment, she closed the door and joined him again.

"Look, I know we probably weren't supposed to leave." She began to straighten a jumble of colored pencils beside a laptop computer and spoke with a nervous edge to her voice. "I'm sure there must have been paperwork—"

"Don't worry about that right now. If he's not here,

would you tell me where he is?"

"I can't."

"You can't? Or you won't?"

Jessica avoided his questions. "Please, sit down. Tell me why you're here."

"Nicholas had a visitor this morning. A man named Alexander Kalman. Nicholas's uncle."

Jessica crossed the room to sit on a folding chair at a drafting table. "Really?"

"It was fortunate Nicholas missed him."

"What do you mean?"

"He was rude to my staff, argued with me, and assumed we were hiding Nicholas from him. He demanded to see his nephew and acted with such belligerence . . . it was quite unsettling. I nearly had to call security. He would have upset Nicholas, I'm sure."

Everett realized Jessica wasn't certain whether or not to trust him so he eased into his explanation. "I hope what I say doesn't offend you in any way. Please tell me if I'm being too personal." When she looked away, he softened his tone. "Caring for someone is one thing, but are you sure what you're doing is wise? You don't really know anything about him."

"But I do know him. He's a celebrated, world-class pianist who has traveled the world. But the only thing that really matters is that he's hurt and needs someone to help him."

"Do you know his circumstances?"

"He's been in a car accident. What's so mysterious about that?"

"If you'd have met his uncle, I think you would be more apprehensive," Everett said, his voice catching in his throat. "Think about it. He has family. Why wouldn't he want to go home?"

"Nicholas has told you over and over he doesn't remember any family."

"Yes, he has." He realized she had made her choice. There would be no swaying her. "I didn't come here to upset you. I came to warn you. I know it would be an awkward situation if this man claiming to be Nicholas's uncle showed up here."

A nervous laugh came from Jessica. "Why would he?"

"To find Nicholas."

"I told you, he's not here," she said, avoiding his eyes.

"Right. But if he, I don't know, happened to show up, and this man found out? He'd insist on seeing him."

"You're really worried about this guy."

"I still consider Nicholas to be a patient of mine. I wouldn't want any unfortunate circumstances to jeopardize his recovery. I can't force him back in the hospital as he's healing quite well. But frankly, I'm not sure I believe his memory loss."

"There's nothing devious going on," she said in a quavering voice.

"I'm telling you his uncle was enraged. I got the feeling he would stop at nothing to find Nicholas." Everett took a step closer. "I don't want you to get hurt."

Jessica brushed past him to the front door and opened it wide. "I don't mean to be rude, Doctor Everett, but I wasn't expecting you and I really need to get back to my studies."

As he approached her, Everett glanced at the closed door at the end of the hall. "I contacted Deputy Hawk and made him aware of Nicholas's uncle's behavior at the hospital."

He took a business card from his shirt pocket and extended it to her. "If there are any problems, or unwanted visitors? Promise me you'll call him?"

Jessica nodded, taking the card. "I appreciate your concern. And I know Nicholas is thankful for all you've done. Please don't worry about me. I'm sure I'm safe. This Alexander Kalman doesn't even know where I live."

Everett held her gaze before he said, "Yes, but I found you, didn't I?"

57

Nicholas had awakened when Jessica laid his clothes on the bed. He recognized Dr. Everett's voice from behind the shut door. Although he could not hear much of their conversation, he realized Jessica hadn't told Everett he was there. He put on a white T-shirt, tucked a long-sleeved denim shirt into the new jeans, then pulled cheap hiking boots over thick athletic socks. When he tugged the laces tight, the extra support on his ankle felt reassuring.

Reaching for the bag containing his belongings from the hospital, he removed Jessica's Walkman, headphones and CD and placed the items on the bedside table. Then he fished out the armoire key and fingered the cool brass as he sat on the bed and waited for the doctor to leave.

As the muffled voices continued from behind the door, the newspaper reporting Elaine's and his death caught his attention. He took out the paper, flattened the page on his knee and began to read the article. Nicholas found the story to be as terrifying as the first time he read it. He worried about what Aranka must be going through and vowed to comfort her when this torment had come to an end, as he should have from the beginning.

Turning the paper over, he read an announcement he hadn't noticed before. He stared at the tiny newsprint and stopped breathing. The brief article announced a piano concert featuring Timothy Sagan.

"Tonight," Nicholas muttered.

Hearing the front door close, he refolded the newspaper, tucked it in his back pocket, then joined Jessica in the front room. "Hey," he said.

She eyed him head to toe. "You look nice."

He did his best to meet her grin, but knew his downcast eyes must have revealed his apprehensive mood.

"Doctor Everett just left. I told him you weren't here, but I don't think he bought it."

"Yeah, I heard."

"Your uncle tried to visit you. The doctor was pretty upset about how he acted."

"Alexander is accustomed to getting his way. I can only imagine the show he performed."

She snapped a business card with her forefinger. "He wanted me to promise I'd call Deputy Hawk if he shows up here."

Nicholas nodded. "Listen, I need to tell you something." His eyes dropped to the armoire key in his hand. He took a deep breath before he lifted his head to speak. He handed her the brass key and said, "There are things Deputy Hawk will find out . . . eventually. Unpleasant things he will piece together."

Jessica's brow furrowed. "What do you mean?"

"He'll want to find out about my involvement in Elaine's disappearance."

She did not move, only met his gaze, the key settled in her palm. "Involvement? What are you talking about?"

"Doctor Everett's right, you know. We're not safe here. My uncle will come looking for me."

Her lips parted a bit and her chest rose and fell at a faster rate.

"He'll find me. He won't stop until he does. And the next time, he won't fail."

Jessica raised a hand in front of her, looking to Nicholas like she warded off a bad spell. "This isn't happening."

"Yeah. It is. And I'm real sorry." He shook his head. "You should have left me on the road. Then you wouldn't have to deal with something you'll never be able to comprehend."

Jessica paused before she said in a precise delivery, "That is so much crap. You think I don't know what it's like to be abandoned? Well, I do. More than you realize." She thinned her lips, crossed her arms tight against her chest, then turned from him and went to sit on the sofa. "So let's have it. And I think you should know by now that you can tell me anything."

Her stern look warned him to be careful. He sat beside her and angled to face her. "I never intended for you to get messed up in this. I wanted to take care of this mess myself. I never thought I would become so attached to you. And I never meant for you to have feelings for me."

She sighed. "But I do."

"And I need you, now more than ever." He tucked an errant lock of hair behind her ear. "I care about you, Jessica. You're the one person who has kept me going during all this." He remembered what she had said about her parents leaving when she was a child. "Although you don't know me, you seem to understand what I'm going through."

"No. I was wrong. I don't understand anything," she said, slowly shaking her head.

"I will always be grateful," he whispered.

She waved the key. "And what about this? No more lies," she cautioned.

After a long silence, he said, "That's the key to where Elaine is."

"You know where she is?"

"Yes."

She let out a relieved sigh and reached out for his bicep. "Well, that's great. Let's call Deputy Hawk and let him know her disappearance is a misunderstanding. That she's not missing after all."

"I can't do that, yet."

"Why?"

"There are things I need to do first. Will you take me somewhere?"

"Of course, but first tell me what you mean about Elaine."

Nicholas sat silent for a long time. "This key goes to the cabinet where I've hidden her body."

Jessica's mouth dropped open. She jumped from the couch and waited a full beat before she shouted, "Body?"

Nicholas looked up to meet her shocked, unblinking

expression of disgust.

She let out a slight chuckle. "You must be joking."

Heart pounding in his chest, he did not respond.

"Body. As in dead?"

His tears answered her question.

"God." The blood drained from her face before she turned her back on him. "Did you kill her?"

"Of course not." Rising from the couch, he batted at the wetness on his cheek. "I had nothing to do with it. Please, believe me."

He tried to reach out to her, but she sidestepped him and crossed the room. Hand sweeping into her back pocket, she pulled out the business card, and grabbed the phone.

"What are you doing?"

"Calling the deputy."

He rushed to her and clasped his hands over her own holding the phone, wincing from the jolting pain in his fingers. "You can't."

"Then you do it."

"I'm telling you, I can't." He yanked the phone from her. "I won't! Not before I figure a few things out. I need to talk to my uncle. *Then* we'll go to the police."

"What do you think he's going to say?"

"I don't know. He'll probably tell me he didn't kill Elaine and that I'm delusional. Then he'll blame everything on someone else."

"Then why do it?"

"I'll know if he's lying."

"If he's the threat you're afraid of, why would you risk the danger of it?"

"It'll be on my terms. Not in the dead of night, or when I least expect it." A sob caught in his chest. "Like it must have been for Elaine."

She gasped. "So you fully expect to be killed?"

Nicholas paced in front of her. "I don't see any other way out for him."

"This is insane." She grabbed the sleeve of his shirt, forcing him to stay put.

Gazing into her frantic eyes, he cupped her face in his hand and drew her to him. Wrapping his arms around her, he smelled a mixture of what he now knew as her scent. A fragrance so familiar a breath caught in his chest: *Gardenias and rosewater*.

"Will you take me to her?" he whispered.

She returned his tight hug, and said, "You know I will."

58

Deputy Hawk hung up the phone and shook his head. He picked up the Elaine Kalman file from atop the stack on his desk.

"What's up?" Stiles asked.

"That was Aranka Kalman. The lab took a buccal swab for the DNA analysis. I didn't have it in me to tell her it would take months to know if the victim is Elaine or not."

"No sense in doin' so."

"That's what I figured." Hawk flipped through the folder, now well-worn from his thumbing. "She said she'd foot the bill to expedite the procedure. Said no amount would be too much, but I doubt that's gonna fly with the ME in Charlotte. Sheriff says they're so backed up they can't even verify the victim's dental findings for a while. Could take months to get that report, too."

"Maybe you should try the governor," Stiles said. "He's taken a liking to you."

Hawk smiled and held up his legal pad. "He's on my list to call."

"Don't doubt it, partner." Stiles scribbled on a report without looking at Hawk. "How many times have you studied that file?"

"Too many, probably"

"What are you lookin' for? Case is closed until we hear from the ME."

Hawk set the folder aside and leaned toward Stiles. "I'm damned sure that female body at the lodge wasn't Elaine Kalman."

"Why's that?"

"It wasn't Nicholas that burned up. I know for a fact it was Nicholas Kalman lyin' in that hospital bed before he split."

"So you're thinkin' if it's not him, it's not her?"

"Exactly."

Stiles thought about Hawk's theory. "Want to check out the crash-site again?"

"No point. Trooper Wilkes's men have scoured the whole area five miles up and back."

"You think she's still missin'?"

"Or she's dead on the riverbank, carried off in pieces by wild animals," Hawk grumbled.

Stiles wrinkled his nose. "There's a pleasant thought. By the way, don't be sharin' that with the grieving family."

"Only one person grieving I can see," Hawk said.

"The mother."

Hawk nodded and raised his pad again. He showed Stiles a diagram he had sketched out of names with lines corresponding to their relationships. "I've been playing and replaying conversations in my mind since day one of this case."

Taking the tablet, Stiles began to read, "Nicholas's father. His mother. Elaine's father. Manuel Esteva and family. What is this?"

"Missing people. They're nowhere to be found."

"So, they ain't in the picture, it don't mean they met foul play," Stiles said. "Maybe Alexander drove Nicholas's family away so he could have complete control over the boy's career. Lots of money to be made from that kid's talents, don't you reckon? Could be, Kalman didn't want to share it with 'em. And, Elaine's father . . . who knows. We've seen enough MIA family men. Esteva, hell, he probably found another job somewhere. You said yourself how spooked he was about immigration comin' for him."

"True. Still can't get all these unexplained disappearances outta' my mind, though." He pointed to the notepad. "Look where all the arrows meet. Notice how they all lead to one person?"

Stiles scanned the diagram. "Alexander Kalman."

"Alexander Kalman," Hawk agreed, tipping back in his chair, hands clasped behind his head.

Stiles gave him a disinterested shrug and returned to his paperwork. Hawk wanted him to be on the same page, he needed an ally, but he sensed that his partner had lost interest. How would he be able to convince the sheriff to let him keep going with the Kalman investigation if he couldn't even sway his best friend?

"I'm tellin' you, Alexander Kalman's behind all of this," Hawk said in a voice louder than he intended. Several deputies turned their way and frowned. Hawk glared at them until they returned to their duties. "That pompous sonofabitch and his crew are hiding what they know about Elaine's disappearance. They know exactly where she is, I'm sure of it. Kalman's livin' up there in his ivory tower, thinkin' he's better than everybody else, believin' he's royalty with his fancy talk and fine clothes, like he's stepped out of a bad noir movie." Hawk tossed his pencil across the room, nearly striking a stunned officer pouring himself a cup of coffee.

"You're gettin' yourself all riled up," Stiles said.

"Damned right I am. I'm an educated man, but that asshole makes me feel like an ignorant backwoods hick." Hawk swept a hand across his tight curls and forced himself to calm down.

Stiles watched Hawk a moment before he picked up the notepad and studied the notes again. "Did you show this to the sheriff?"

"No. It's just speculation," Hawk said in a discouraged voice.

"You say no one knows where Nicholas is right now?"

"Doctor Everett told me that when Alexander went to the hospital looking for him, the kid and his belongings were gone. Apparently Kalman got pretty upset about that."

"Think Nicholas is avoiding his dear ole' Uncle?"

"Well, the kid's got a lot to answer for. One wrecked car. A missing woman he's had a relationship with. No recall of that fateful night."

"I wonder if the kid's lost all that music he must have in his head," Stiles speculated.

"Yeah, and if Alexander Kalman is wondering the same thing."

"Helluva lot's happened around here the past few days," Stiles said. "Wouldn't want nothin' bad to come down on Nicholas, would we?"

"He could be in danger."

Stiles slid from his chair and took the rain slicker from the back of his seat. A playful grin tugged at his mouth. "Good excuse to go lookin' for him, don't you think?"

Hawk glanced at the sheriff through the glass enclosure of his office. Sands barked into the phone, his face bright red, shaking a finger at no one. "Maybe I should tell the boss what's up."

"What *is* up?"

"Good point," Hawk answered, shrugging on his own raincoat. "I'll tell you, my friend, if we find out Alexander Kalman has something to do with those kids, especially if any harm has come their way . . ." He warned himself not to get worked up again, but he said in a stern voice, "I'm gonna nail his ass to the wall."

Stiles chuckled, "Don't you mean, you'll put him behind bars?"

Hawk thought about his response a mere second. "We'll see."

59

Zardos laid the suit Timothy was to wear for that evening's performance on the young master's bed. Alexander had chosen a charcoal, single-breasted Tallia Uomo tuxedo, black Perry Ellis shoes, dark gray crosswick collar shirt with matching bow tie, and black garnet studs. Regret filled Zardos when Sampte told him to retrieve the final element to complete the attire: an elegant pair of platinum Edwardian cufflinks. Zardos knew the hand-engraved, turn-of-the-century pieces had been handed down through Alexander's family from father to son, then finally to Nicholas when he began performing professionally.

Zardos entered Nicholas's room for the first time since his charge's disappearance, a sense of unease fell over him. The bed remained turned down. A royal blue Turkish cotton robe draped over the foot of the bed awaited Nicholas, as well as plush moccasin slippers.

Zardos crossed the room to the antique dresser and rummaged through the top drawer in search of the adornments. He couldn't remember the last time Nicholas had even worn them. *I haven't seen them in years. What will Alexander do to me if I can't find them?* Fearful of the blow he would receive from Alexander's cane if he failed, Zardos's pulse raced.

He scrambled through Nicholas's collection of expensive wristwatches, various tie tacks, button covers, numerous sunglass cases. At last, he found the black velvet jewelry case he had been looking for. Wiping his brow with one hand while the box trembled in the other, the case made a slight creak when he opened the lid. He released a relieved sigh when he saw the cufflinks tucked inside.

The smell of age-old silk and metal greeted him. He remembered when Alexander presented them to Nicholas eight years earlier.

Sampte and Zardos had finished dressing and grooming twelve-year-old Nicholas in preparation for his first public performance. Standing before the hot lights of the theatre's dressing room backstage, Sampte safety pinned Nicholas's waistband because the boy, terrified with stage fright, had lost four pounds in the three days since the tux had last been altered. Zardos fussed over Nicholas's pleats as Alexander burst into the room off the stage entrance. All three jumped in unison.

Alexander's voice boomed throughout the room covered with hard surfaces. "Let me see the boy." He inspected Nicholas head to toe several times, finally nodding his approval.

Without looking at Zardos, Alexander handed him a small black case. "Put these on him."

Alexander stared into Nicholas's eyes. "Hands," he commanded.

Nicholas had held a deep breath as he extended them outward, palm side up.

"Over." Alexander examined the highly buffed, precisely trimmed half-moon nails Zardos had manicured earlier that morning. Satisfied, Alexander gave one quick nod, pivoted, and said, "Twenty minutes until curtain." Black cape sweeping around him, Alexander limped away as fast as he had entered.

When Alexander opened the door, the muffled sound of an impatient crowd drifted into the room. Zardos watched the blood drain from the young boy's face.

"Not to worry," Sampte said, patting Nicholas's small padded shoulder with his huge hand. "You're ready."

Nicholas's chin dropped to his chest. "He didn't even wish me luck," he whispered.

Zardos, still on his knees, tipped the boy's face up to his own. "He knows you're up to this. Anyway, it's not about luck, it's about the music. Yes?"

Nicholas nodded and swept a trembling hand across his cheek to erase a tear.

"Let's see what he's brought you," Sampte said in an excited voice. Zardos handed him the box. When Sampte opened the velvet case, all three mouths dropped open. Platinum gleamed in the bank of makeup lights surrounding the mirrors that hung around the room.

"What are they?" Nicholas asked.

"Cufflinks," Sampte said. "This is an honor, Nicholas. They've been in the family for generations. You must be very careful with them."

Nicholas held out a wrist for Sampte to insert the first link. Zardos laughed when the weight of the heavy adornment dragged Nicholas's sleeve over his hand.

The sound of a generator sputtering to life for the party brought Zardos back to the present. His smile disappeared. Snapping the case shut, he looked around the room to be certain all was in order.

He left Nicholas's room, hoping it would not be for the last time.

60

Timothy entered his bedroom, now only hours before the concert. His confidence soared as he stared at the wardrobe laid out on the bed. Fingering the supple cloth of the jacket, he smiled at the shining shoes, then sniffed the ivory rosebud intended for his lapel. Even the silk socks which perfectly matched the fine gold threads woven throughout the shirt and tie were exquisite. He noticed an unfamiliar black velvet case and opened it.

Ancient-looking cufflinks took his breath away. He had heard the story of their existence. At last, they had come to him. Pride swelled in his chest, followed by another bout of nerves. Yet more expectations.

He clutched his stomach and stifled a retch, wondering how many more times he would feel the need to vomit. Then something else caught his attention. Atop the plush comforter, he recognized a car key remote attached to a brass ring, stamped with the initials T.S.

Puzzled, he picked up the key ring and studied the impression of the Porsche insignia pressed into a key. Timothy's eyes then locked to the window. He hurried across the room and brushed aside the thick drape. Parked in the circular driveway directly below his bedroom window sat a gleaming black Porsche Targa, the twin to Nicholas's.

Emotion welled in Timothy's chest. *The maestro approves of me.* He recalled all the years of training he had craved his mentor's attention, yet always having to settle for the meager amount that remained. So often he had relished Alexander's undivided attention when Nicholas went on tour alone.

Finally it's my time.

He tore himself from the window and fought the urge to race down the stairs, embrace the sports car's steering wheel, propel down the tight curves of the mountainside.

Peeling off his clothes, Timothy vowed to do anything in order to retain the feeling of accomplishment and acceptance Alexander had finally bestowed upon him. After the concert tonight he would go to the country house. No matter how long it took, he would find where Nicholas had hidden the body and at last deliver it to Thibodeaux. Then he would track down Nicholas and get rid of him, once and for all.

Dressed in the performance clothes, he felt renewed. Prokofiev swirled in his mind. He repeatedly visualized the problematic twelfth bar as he slid one of the platinum links into the sleeve of his shirt.

61

Nicholas felt older than his years after telling Jessica the details about the night he had found Elaine's body. He sank deep in the seat of the Taurus, a knot growing tight in his stomach as they drew closer to his uncle's secondary home.

A thick mist covered the car as the dwindling light turned the forest into an ominous enigma, muting the colors to varying shades of gray.

Jessica took the turns as fast as she dared. The car, at times, skidded on the loose rocks along the shoulder of the highway, spitting rocks from the wheels.

Nicholas thought only of Elaine. He had to be certain her body remained in the armoire. The nightmare of Timothy possibly having found Elaine, then planting her in that burning cabin, haunted Nicholas. He was certain Timothy set the fire, intending to make the authorities believe the couple had been him and Elaine. He had no doubt Timothy was capable of such depravity.

"I haven't seen a turn-off in miles."

Registering her nervousness, Nicholas said, "Just up ahead, there on the left."

As she turned off US-74, she blew out a deep breath. Majestic leafless trees bowed across both sides of the rugged road, pulling them into the darkness of the forest. Jessica leaned close to the steering wheel and guided the car along the overgrown path. The daunting road turned into a gravel drive and revealed the hulking, shuttered house. He noticed Jessica shiver.

"What is this place?" she asked in a soft voice.

"One of my uncle's houses. I hadn't been here in months." Nicholas let out a deep breath. "Not until that night."

He gathered his courage before he slid out of the car.

When he approached the front steps, he stopped and turned. Jessica didn't follow. "I'll only be a minute. You don't need to be involved any more than you already are. I think you should stay out here."

Jessica looked around at the desolate setting. "Maybe I should go with you."

The hesitance in her voice told him she really didn't want to. "No, please stay. I need to do this alone."

"Do what?" she asked.

Nicholas decided he'd better not tell her anything else. He mounted the steps that led to the front door and said a silent prayer for the key to still be there. Fishing into the ancient terra cotta urn, he found nothing. Panic coursed through him. He plunged both hands into the container, spilling crumbled potting soil onto the water-stained porch. At last, he felt a solid object.

Gratefully, he clutched the key, but dread seized his chest. *It wasn't where I left it. Someone else has been here.*

Cautious now, Nicholas opened the door wide, entered the front room, and noted that the furnishings were still covered with white sheets.

"Feels like a meat locker in here."

Nicholas started and pivoted. Jessica stood behind him, zipping up her jacket.

She stepped beyond him and sucked in a sharp intake of air. "What is that smell?" she asked, wrinkling her nose.

Nicholas ignored her question. He looked toward the staircase and said, "Promise me you'll stay down here. I need to check on something." He climbed the first steps, then turned to be certain she remained in the front room. "I'll be right back."

Jessica scanned the room three times the size of her entire apartment. She puzzled over the sheet-covered furniture and wondered why no one lived in such an extravagant place year round. The tiny house she shared growing up with her aunt came to mind. She remembered the kitchen, so cramped their elbows would knock together when they prepared their meals side by side. She imagined the kitchen in this place would be fit for a French chef.

Slits of light peeked through drawn drapes, casting discomforting shadows around the room. Hung above the fireplace, glazed glass eyes of an enormous buck with a massive rack of antlers stared down at her. Nearby, a full-size bobcat stood frozen mid-step upon a hardwood pedestal.

It seemed colder in the house than outside. So cold. Not merely due to the weather. She thrust her hands in her pockets and hunched her shoulders. *Too spooky for me.* She ran up the stairs, two at a time.

She stuck her head into one doorway after another as she searched in each room for Nicholas. Reaching the last room at the end of the hall, the first thing she noticed was the frigid air, even more bracing than on the first floor. The smell hit her again—stronger, more putrid. Her attention went to a broken window that caused the sheers to billow. A piece of cardboard with curled masking tape along its edges lay on the floor below the glass panes.

At the far end of the room, Nicholas knelt before an antique armoire, its doors open wide. His shoulders heaved with wracking sobs.

Jessica took cautious steps toward him. "Nicholas?" she said softly, one arm wrapped tightly around herself, the other hand clasping her nose and mouth.

Nicholas lifted himself wearily, and turned to her. She flinched at the sight of his colorless face and remorseful expression.

Curious, she moved closer and peered beyond his rigid body.

She gaped at the horrendous sight of a dead woman in the cabinet, a cream colored blanket tucked around her body. Blonde hair covering most of the face hid most of a garish expression, locked in an ashen mask of death.

Jessica blinked hard, hoping to erase the vision before her. Her gaze roamed to Nicholas. She wanted to scream—scream louder than she ever had, even as a child, but horror locked the voice in her throat. Whirling around, she bolted out of the room.

Nicholas turned back to the body that had once been Elaine, his love. Now that she was gone, he felt certain nothing of his past life would ever bring him comfort again. Yet, he felt relieved that at least her body was safe. Timothy had not violated her.

With regret, he tucked the coverlet tight around Elaine's body and closed the doors. He could not yet comprehend what his life would be like without her, but realization had begun to sink in. He had no choice but to go on.

The need for retribution blossomed in him as he began to create the final composition: to face Alexander and Timothy. Make them suffer for this injustice. His own life and freedom depended on it.

He plodded down the stairs and took in the once carefree surroundings. Approaching the front door, he vowed never again to visit the place he had considered his second home.

From the porch, Nicholas watched Jessica pace in front of her car. Cell phone pinned to her ear, she cussed softly at first. Then her curses rose in crescendo with each word.

He locked the front door and replaced the key in the flowerpot. "There's no service out here."

She whirled to face him. "No shit!" Face flushed, eyes darting, she moved toward the driver's side of the car. "I'm outta' here."

Nicholas hurried to block her from going to the car, then from fleeing into the nearby forest. "Wait." When she flinched, he raised his hands in a disarming manner. "Let me explain."

She jerked back. "Stay away from me. I am such an idiot. I can hear Aunt Sarah now, 'Always picking up stray dogs. All it'll get you is heartache.' I couldn't judge character if it was drawn out in front of me." Biting her bottom lip, she sat down on the hood of the car.

"I know what you must be thinking."

"Impossible," Jessica sputtered, her voice thick with tears.

"I didn't kill her. I need you to believe me." Nicholas held his hand out to her.

She slapped his forearm with the tips of her fingers. "Why should I believe you? You're not even real. You're sure as hell not human. How could you so coolly walk into this house, with a key that just so happens to fit a piece of furniture that has a dead body stuffed in it?" A shudder doubled her over. "Then you claim to have nothing to do with it?"

"Jessica, I didn't kill Elaine. I can't believe you would even think I'm capable of such a horrible thing." He stared at her in dismay. The blood drained from his head and he swayed, struggling to stay upright. Queasiness squeezed his stomach. He leaned against the warm hood of the car. "I told you at the hospital. Timothy killed her. Or Alexander, or maybe someone who works for him. I only brought her here so she would be safe until I figured out why they did it."

"Safe?" Jessica shouted. "This is your idea of safe?" She looked past him, up to the window where horror reigned. "Why are we here?"

"The newspaper made it sound like it was definitely Elaine in the cabin that burned up. I had to be sure it wasn't."

Feet on the bumper, hands stuffed into her jacket pockets, chin tucked to her chest, she said, "So, that's Elaine?"

"Yes." He slid closer to her and they fell into silence for a long time before he said, "I loved her."

"Yeah, I can tell," she snorted, looking at the cell phone again.

"You don't understand. Can't understand." He let out a deep breath. "We were lovers."

Jessica scooted away from him. "The paper said she was your sister."

"Alexander isn't my blood. Neither is Elaine. We were raised together, and over the years we fell in love." He scanned the darkening yard, his eyes stopping at the house. "We spent our summers here growing up. When I found her in my car, this was the only place I could think of to hide her until I figured out why they did it."

"You've said all along you're being framed, but all I know is, there's a dead woman in there. I've never met your uncle, or this Timothy guy, so I only have you to rely on about the threat you feel. There's no reason you would have lied to me since I've helped you this far, but I have to tell you . . ." Her eyes found his for first time since she discovered Elaine. "I don't exactly feel safe around you right now."

"I understand if you don't believe me. Why would you? I've lied to you since you found me on the road. Remember? You asked me my name and I didn't answer. But I've been straight with you ever since I revealed to you—you alone, by the way—who I really am. I don't know how to convey the desperation and terror I feel right now, except to say that time for me is running out. I may be only one step ahead of them."

Nicholas laid a hand on her shoulder, grateful she did not pull away. "You're right, we should call the deputy, and we will. But I need one more thing from you. Then I'm out of your life forever."

"What do you want?" she asked in a weary voice.

Nicholas took the sheet of newspaper from his back pocket, smoothed the folds out on the hood and pointed to the announcement.

"Is that the Timothy you've been talking about?"

Nicholas nodded.

"He's playing at the Wilhoit," she said. "That's my theatre."

"I consider it my theatre, too. I've performed there many times. I nearly did the night of . . ."

As his words trailed off, Jessica said, "We've probably passed each other backstage."

"It's possible."

"So, what now?"

"I want to go there and confront the bastard."

"Why didn't you call the cops in the first place?"

"Alexander would never confess anything to the police. He thinks he's above the law. He has contempt for everyone.

He would have come up with the most elaborate, fabricated story—and the cops would believe him. He's the most consummate performer I've ever seen. I wasn't going to risk him getting away with anything. No. Timothy's the first step to getting what I need from Alexander."

Jessica thought for a moment before she said, "We should at least tell the deputy where we're headed."

"The performance begins at eight o'clock." He glanced at his watch. "We need to hurry before the box office opens. We'll call Deputy Hawk as soon as we get cell phone service and have him meet us there."

Jessica thought much too long for Nicholas's spent nerves. "Jessica, please," he pleaded. "Take me to Timothy."

62

Nicholas sat slumped in the passenger seat of Jessica's Taurus as they rode toward the Wilhoit Theatre. Lost in deep thought, his eyes locked to the journal in his lap. In order to protect his psyche, time and time again he had told himself the book was merely a novel. A piece of fiction. Yet in the back of his mind, he knew the story was real. That the events Charles Ian Hunt had written of actually had happened. His father's words reached out to him from the grave.

Without opening the leather cover, he remembered the last entry.

> *I go on not knowing my fate, unclear of your future. Or if there is a future for you. When driven to the edge of insanity, I chose to fight it off. I'm not sure if it worked. Maybe you can tell me. Perhaps you can come visit me in this spectacle of a room. If you allow me, I'll serenade you on the Steinway with a rusty Chopin. Light a fire and pour you a Scotch. I hope it will be you who visits, Nicholas. Perhaps you'll read a book from my nemesis' impressive collection. I can only pray it will be this one.*

A vivid remembrance of Alexander's music room flashed in Nicholas's mind, the same room Charles had written about, and the one he himself had come to know so well. Nicholas now realized they both had shared the same apprehension, neither knowing the outcome.

When Nicholas was ten years old, still stinging from hurt and rejection long after his father had disappeared, his mother drove Nicholas to the house of the man named Alexander Kalman. He scanned the huge gates open-mouthed as they drove up to the mansion's front steps in their decade-old car that chugged white smoke from its tailpipe.

His mother had told him about the amazing house, but Nicholas never imagined he'd ever be allowed inside the mansion he could see from the highway many miles away.

A great big man dressed all in black opened the front door. He didn't say a word, only waved his hand for them to enter the house. Nicholas realized his mother must be nervous because she squeezed his hand too tight. Her eyes were red, and she dabbed at them with a crumpled hand-kerchief.

Nicholas had never seen so many treasures before. Smooth floors gleamed, urging him to remove his shoes and slide on the marble surface in his stocking feet. Sunlight streamed through the biggest windows he'd ever seen. He wondered how they washed the tallest ones. Pictures on the walls were so big they looked like he could walk into them.

He and his mother had often flipped through pages of magazines ogling photographs of magnificent estates. She promised him that one day, if he continued to practice hard, he would visit a mansion. Maybe even live in one. He never thought such a thing would happen. He pinched himself to see if he was dreaming.

They waited in the huge entryway and soon another man came out of nowhere. He wore a long cape and used a cane to walk. Behind the man followed a pretty woman who never took her eyes off Nicholas. He felt drawn to her kind expression and he liked the name his mother called her: Aranka. He returned her smile.

"Teresa, at last," the man had said, in a low, smooth voice. He took her hand in his free one and kissed it. Nicholas remembered that the man then placed an icy hand atop his own head. "I had begun to worry you reconsidered."

"No, no. I just needed a little more time with my son," his mother replied in a shaky voice.

"I understand. As we discussed, Teresa, you can be assured that your boy will be well taken care of. My sister is very good with children. She has a young daughter whom

I'm certain Nicholas will soon think of as his own sister. And I am genuinely looking forward to taking him on as my pupil." Alexander beamed down at Nicholas.

After his mother stared at the man for a while, she bent down in front of her boy. "Mama's leaving now, Nicky. You stay here with Aranka and Alexander. He's going to teach you how to play the piano even better than you do now." Then she whispered, "I'll come to see you whenever I can. I promise."

Over Teresa's shoulder, Nicholas saw the man named Alexander nod at the huge man who had opened the door for them. He scooped his massive hand under his mother's arm and pulled her to the door. She looked back and waved. Tears poured down her face and she looked sadder than anyone he had ever seen before. Then she and the man walked out, and the door closed.

Nicholas tried to run after her, but Alexander had a firm hand on his shoulder. "Not to worry, Nicholas. Sampte will see that she arrives home safely."

"Why doesn't she get to stay, too?" Nicholas asked.

Aranka knelt down, eye level with Nicholas. "Your mother has left you here to play the piano. Alexander is the finest teacher in all the land. Soon, you will learn to play the music you hear in your head. You'd like that, wouldn't you?"

Nicholas nodded.

The woman smiled. "Wonderful. Now don't worry about your momma, she's going to be fine, and so are you."

Taking a look at the shut door, Nicholas realized he would not be allowed to follow his mother.

After a while he turned back to the man and asked, "Where's the piano?"

A broad smile lit the older man's face. "Excellent," he said, then turned to the woman who also beamed her approval.

Alexander draped his cape across Nicholas's shoulders and he led him down the long corridor.

Then something caught Nicholas's attention. He saw a

man standing on the landing of the third floor, almost hidden by a pillar. His face was puffy and nearly as gray as his hair—even from that distance, he could see that the man didn't look well. Nicholas thought the man seemed scared. The man lifted his hand to wave, then took a step back. Dark shadows swallowed his form.

Nicholas tapped the journal's front cover, now certain the man must have been his father, Charles Hunt.

That's how this book got into Alexander's music room. He must have snuck into the mansion and left his journal in the bookcase. My father knew I would be going to live there. That I would find his journal some day.

Regretting he had never put the pieces together before now, Nicholas sighed.

"You okay?" Jessica asked.

"I just remembered something from a long time ago. If I had realized it earlier, maybe none of this would have happened."

"You mean, you think you could have stopped Elaine from being killed?"

"Maybe. I've been blind to most things since I was a kid. Studying, practicing, traveling, has been my life forever. You probably won't believe this, but I don't even know how to use the Internet. I've caught Timothy on the computer a couple times, but I haven't got a clue how to even begin learning what to do. Television is even prohibited in Alexander's house."

He scowled. Merely speaking the man's name sickened him. He thought of all the things he had missed in his life. Sure, very few people had been blessed with the opportunities his talent at the piano had bestowed. He had seen most of the world due to his travels, still, he felt empty and cheated of the knowledge youths his age took as commonplace.

"Ever since I found Elaine's body in my car that night, weird things about my past have started coming back to me."

"I can't get the vision of her out of my head," Jessica said, almost too quiet to hear.

"I have to make everything right. Force Alexander and Timothy to take responsibility for what they did." He didn't tell her, revenge was what he actually desired.

She took her eyes off the tricky road only long enough to glance at him. "You're not going to hurt anyone, are you? Because I won't have anything to do with that."

Nicholas stared ahead, his hands clutching the journal tighter.

When Nicholas did not respond, Jessica slowed the vehicle to a crawl, then stopped along the narrow shoulder. "Promise me."

"I'm not like them. Never have been. I realize that now more than ever." Eyes on his lap, he traced a finger along the journal's cover. "I just need to know why they would take the most beautiful thing in all of our lives."

She laid a tender hand on his shoulder. "You did love her."

"I only played the piano." Nicholas met Jessica's eyes. "She was my life. Now that she's gone, nothing matters. I have nothing else to lose."

63

Hawk drove the cruiser along the mountainous stretch of Highway 74 and considered whether to go back to Manuel Esteva's trailer to see if he and Stiles missed any evidence, or to check out Alexander's country house. Without probable cause he had no official right to drop in on either location.

He had decided it would be better use of their time to split up with Stiles, but now he missed his partner's carefree banter to take him out of his gloomy mood. Possibilities of what to do next whirled in his mind. His cell phone rang and he pulled it from his pocket, grateful for the diversion.

"Hawk, here."

"Deputy Hawk, you don't know me, but I'm Jessica Taft."

Hawk bolted upright in his seat. "I know who you are, Miss Taft."

"I need to let you know about something I've seen."

Hawk sensed tension, perhaps fear in her voice. "Go on."

"Nicholas probably should be telling you this instead of me . . ."

"Tell me what? What's going on?" After a long silence, Hawk thought his cell phone had cut out. "Hello? Are you there?"

"There's a body hidden at the house where Nicholas spent his summers."

Hawk clutched the phone tighter as he wheeled the cruiser to the side of the road. "Say that again?"

"He wants to know if you know where Alexander's country house is?"

"Did you say a body?"

"It's a woman. Nicholas said her name is . . ."

"Elaine Kalman," Hawk and Jessica said in unison.

"He says he didn't do it," she blurted. "Kill her I mean.

But she's definitely dead."

"Are you safe?"

"Yes. We're fine."

"We, who?"

"Me and Nicholas."

Hawk returned the cruiser to the road and raced up the highway. "He's with you now?" Blood pulsated in his ears. He flipped on the cruiser's lights and sirens.

"Yes."

"Would you be able to tell me if you weren't safe?"

"I'm fine. Really, I am. Please believe me. Everything's going to be okay."

The line crackled, and Hawk heard garbled voices.

"Deputy, this is Nicholas Kalman."

Hawk focused his attention on Nicholas's faint voice. "What's going on? Where are you?"

"Elaine is at the country house. Will you see that she's taken care of for me?"

"Let's talk about that."

"No time. We're almost there."

"Where? You're almost where?"

"You'll find the key in a flowerpot on the porch. She's upstairs, in a cabinet in the far bedroom."

Hawk listened to dead air, again wondering about the connection.

"Be careful with her," Nicholas said, his voice cracking with emotion.

Before Hawk could respond, the line buzzed, then went dead.

64

Timothy pulled his new Porsche into the empty Wilhoit Theatre parking lot and glided into the same slot where Nicholas had parked six evenings ago. The night of his rival's ruin, Timothy recalled. His wicked laugh filled the tiny compartment.

He kept the car idling while he stroked the hand-stitched, tan leather upholstery. The Killers rock song *Under the Gun* blasted through the sound system; forbidden music by Alexander's standards. The thought of defying his master thrilled Timothy. Then he regretted his betrayal and flipped the player off.

He killed the purring engine and checked the dial of his gold Omega watch. "Only two more hours," he muttered, sliding from the vehicle.

After taking another look at his shining prize, he jogged the expanse of the lot. His nerves raged and he tasted blood where he'd gnawed a gash into his right cheek. *Remember every moment*, Timothy reminded himself as he counted the eighteen steps that led to the box office. Fiddling with one of his cufflinks, he caught the attention of a blue-haired attendant behind the glass window.

"I'm here to perform," Timothy said to the woman. "Let me in," he commanded, imitating his best impression of his maestro.

She nodded her head and retreated around a corner. Timothy stood there, stunned for a moment, unsure of what he should do next. Then the woman reappeared at a bank of glass doors and opened one of them.

"I haven't unlocked the doors downstairs yet," she said. "Follow the lobby, then go through the double doors. Steps will lead you down to the stage. Have a good show, Mr. Sagan."

Timothy glowed, relishing the respect she paid him. "I intend to."

Although he had been to the Wilhoit numerous times, he felt as though this was the first. Inside the expansive lobby, his feet whisked on thick burgundy carpet as he skidded fingertips along the raised velvet wallpaper. Gilded frames bordered colorful life-sized posters paying homage to past performances. He looked up to see crystal chandeliers sparkle and dance, reflecting soft light as he passed under them.

Pulling a set of twelve-foot-tall doors open, Timothy emerged into the theatre's auditorium. His breath caught in his chest as his eyes locked on the Hamburg Steinway grand piano, far in the distance, presented slightly to the right of center stage. The highly buffed instrument glowed from the lights hung high above it.

In a daze, he descended, passing row after endless row of lush burgundy-colored seats. Walking closer, he marveled at the seamless plaster rear wall bathed in a sunset pattern, deep crimson at the bottom that gradated in shades upward to a deep blue.

As he climbed the steps onto the stage, he turned to the empty seats. He imagined the standing-room-only crowd Alexander had promised would be in attendance. Soon, the audience—meant only for Timothy—would listen to him play, cheer his excellence, revere him.

Looking back at the piano, he stared at the instrument in quiet awe. A pang of jealousy pierced him when he realized how cheated he had been of this experience for so many years, always ordered by Alexander to sit in the audience and study Nicholas's performance.

Timothy had never ventured around the theatre before. He walked offstage and looked up at the ancient-looking counterweight rigging system that enabled scenery to mysteriously float to the cavern above. He followed the direction of the three grated catwalks that lined the side wall to a vertical, caged ladder bolted to the rear wall and looked to lead all the way to the roof. Squinting, his vision blurred as he searched for where the ladder ended.

Crossing the stage to sit on the piano's bench, Timothy concentrated with all that he had learned, all that he had now become. His mentor's urgent words rang in his mind: "Be bold, *audace!* Majestic, *maestoso!* Play the piece with flourish. Your finest *virtuoso!* Do it for me."

Timothy placed trembling fingers on the keys and began to warm up with a run of scales. "I won't disappoint you, Uncle," he said, his voice resonating with the timbre of the Steinway.

65

Hawk's pulse throbbed in his temple as he sped closer to Alexander Kalman's country house. Darkness fell fast around him. He switched on the cruiser's headlights, and urged the vehicle as fast as he dared.

He took up the microphone attached to his radio unit under the dashboard. "Dispatch? SCD Fifteen. I'm approaching destination, seventeen eighty-four Parson's Trail," he announced into the handset.

The dispatcher's voice crackled through the tiny speaker, "Copy that, SCD Fifteen."

"What's the ETA on my backup?"

"Still none available, Fifteen."

"Request permission to enter the house."

"Negative, Fifteen. Wait for backup."

"What's the timeframe on that?"

"We're working on it."

The landscape became familiar to Hawk and he knew he must be close to the turnoff for the house. He flipped on the spotlight mounted to his window frame and scanned the opposite side of the road with its powerful beam, searching for the private drive. "Did I pass it?" He pulled to the shoulder and stopped, grabbing the mic again.

"Dispatch, SCD Fifteen. Need coordinates on that Parson's Trail address." Waiting for his answer, Hawk checked his rear-view mirror in time to see a large, dark vehicle pull onto the highway from a side road he had passed. The car raced in the opposite direction. "Cancel that, dispatch."

Hawk waited for the vehicle's taillights to vanish around the bend before he turned the cruiser around. As he rolled to the overgrown road, he took note of the rusted, nearly hidden sign that revealed Parson's Trail Road.

Pieces fell together in an instant. Mr. Turner at the Smoky Pines Lodge mentioned seeing an unfamiliar large black car the day of the fire. The vehicle Sampte drove for Alexander was a Mercedes-Benz. The car Hawk now followed at a distance looked like a similar model. *Sampte's behind all of this*. The realization made Hawk's heart race. *Focus*.

He lifted the handset from its cradle again. "Dispatch? SCD Fifteen."

"Go ahead, Fifteen."

"Be advised. Leaving location Parson's Trail. Following current model, black Mercedes sedan, believed registered to Alexander Kalman. Probable driver known as Sampte, last name unknown, employee of Alexander Kalman. Will keep you apprised of final destination."

"Copy, Fifteen."

Hawk followed the sedan at a prudent distance along the mountainous two-lane as it snaked through the dense forest. The taillights of the car he pursued winked through the trees and couple times he thought he had lost the only car he had yet to encounter on the road.

A few minutes later the Mercedes slowed and turned into what Hawk recognized as the Thibodeaux graveyard compound. He extinguished his headlights and pulled onto the narrow, unpaved lane after the black car and rolled to a stop. Powering down his window, he listened beyond the noise of the crickets and night birds.

A car door slammed. Hawk crawled the cruiser as close as he dared, then killed the engine behind a stand of brush. He watched the black car park in front of a nondescript cement building behind the main house. After a moment, its trunk popped open.

Hawk peered over bushes to see Sampte standing at what he figured must be the door of the mortuary. The door opened to reveal a man, shoulder-high to Sampte. Hawk had never met old man Thibodeaux's son, but the man standing there resembled the now deceased undertaker.

Sampte said a few excited words before the younger man

emphatically shook his head, then disappeared back into the building and slammed the door.

Sampte stormed to the vehicle and raised the trunk lid fully open. He looked down for a moment, then bent over and removed a bundle wrapped in fabric. A bare arm dropped to Sampte's side. Hawk shot up in his seat. Light hair flowed from the blanket and the hem of a dress skimmed the ground.

Hawk fumbled for the radio's mic and turned down the volume on the unit. "Dispatch, SCD Fifteen."

After what seemed an endless wait, a voice crackled through the tiny speaker. "Dispatch here. Go ahead, Fifteen."

"I've got suspicious activity at the Thibodeaux Mortuary off county road one-oh-eight, marker two-twenty. Request backup ASAP," Hawk said, his voice quickening.

Sampte carried the body up the path. In one fluid motion he raised his leg and kicked beside the doorknob. The door flew open, splintering its frame.

"Copy that, Fifteen."

Hawk craned his neck to see through the trees. "Request no lights or sirens on rollup."

"Be advised, wait for backup, Fifteen . . . Copy."

"Affirmative. SCD Fifteen, out."

Relieved to then hear dispatch request the assistance of Stiles's call letters, Hawk took a deep breath. After a long uncomfortable silence, a familiar voice rang out through the intercom. "What've you got, Hawk?" Sheriff Sands barked.

"Well, Sheriff, I'm pretty damned sure I found Elaine Kalman. I'm outside the Thibodeaux Mortuary. Looks like they're getting ready to dispose of her body."

"Don't approach."

"Can you give me an ETA on that backup, sir?"

"Stiles and Gibbs are on the way."

The Mercedes continued to idle, its headlights flooding grave markers that studded an expanse of land. The smell of exhaust hung in the still air.

Checking his watch, Hawk took a few deep breaths to settle his thudding heart. Senses alert, he heard the muffled sounds of an escalating argument. He slipped out of the cruiser, then crept to the open door.

Unsnapping the trigger guard of his holster, he clasped the pistol's grip. Easing closer, Hawk made out every word of the booming voice he recognized as Sampte's.

Almost to the door now, Hawk heard Sampte say, "You will do it, dammit, or I'll kill you as you cower like a child."

A shot rang out. The hollow rapport clacked off the cement walls of the morgue.

"The next one goes into your head," Sampte shouted. "Do it now!"

Hawk pulled his gun, lowered himself to a crouch and ducked his head through the opening, taking a quick look into the room. Sampte stood over a man cowering and sobbing in the corner. Sampte had a gun pointed at his head.

Hawk burst into the room, aiming directly at Sampte. "Deputy Sheriff! Raise your arms. Drop the weapon."

Sampte whirled in Hawk's direction, arms raised in the air, mouth opened in a shocked circle.

"Drop it, Sampte."

Hawk challenged Sampte's glare until the stunned man lowered his arm and the small caliber weapon slid from his hand, then dropped to the ground.

"Push it toward me with your foot."

Sampte did as commanded. The gun clattered as the blue steel bumped along the cement floor. Hawk bent to retrieve the pistol and tucked it in the waistband behind his back.

"Hands in the air," Hawk said.

Sampte kept his arms raised as he backed into a rolling cart. Surgical instruments clanged atop the aluminum tray. "What's going on, officer?" he asked in a bewildered voice.

Hawk turned to the crouched man in a corner, a clear glass gallon jug in his lap, arms crossed over his head. Then he returned his attention to the body on an aluminum table. *Elaine Kalman.*

Hawk recognized the colorful floral dress the woman wore to be the same pattern as the torn piece of cloth he had discovered in Manuel Esteva's trailer the day before.

He trained his gun back on Sampte. "Turn around, and keep your hands in sight."

Sampte followed Hawk's command and the deputy patted him down, then backed a few feet away.

"I didn't have anything to do with this," the other man said, choking back sobs.

Sampte whirled on him. "Silence!"

"Who are you?" Hawk bellowed.

"Thibodeaux. Henri Thibodeaux. This is my property."

"Sampte, keep your hands up," Hawk instructed.

Sampte smiled. "You misunderstand what's going on here, officer," he said in a voice that dripped of innocence as he took a step toward Hawk.

"Don't come any closer. I won't warn you again."

Henri found his feet and shuffled a few steps toward Hawk, the quarter-filled jug now tucked under his arm. "He always brought the bodies. I only buried them," he said, his voice stronger now. "Tell him, you bastard!" He lifted the container over his head and hurled it across the room. The jug shattered against the wall, mere feet from where Sampte stood. The liquor's pungent sweet smell, mixed with gunpowder, permeated the thick air and seemed to suck the oxygen from the room.

Sampte looked from Hawk's eyes to the barrel of his gun. "He speaks the truth." Sounding exhausted, Sampte eased onto a stool near the trembling Henri.

"And what about Alexander?"

"My master had nothing to do with any of it," Sampte snapped.

"How about Nicholas? Is he involved in this?"

Sampte let out a feeble laugh. "No. Not the boy. Never Nicholas. He is Alexander's hope for immortality. It all just went . . . badly." He turned to look at Elaine's body. "For everyone." His last words lowered an octave.

"Tell him about the other boy," Henri said.

Sampte glowered at the suddenly fearless Henri.

Hawk motioned with his head to the mortician. "What's he talking about?"

"Tell him," Henri said to Sampte.

Sampte offered only a contemptible glare.

"Don't know his name," Henri said. "Redheaded kid. I'm surprised he's not here, too. Usually is. I told him I was done with all this. Then the bastard shot at me!"

Hawk took a step closer to Sampte. "Who killed Elaine Kalman?"

Sampte sneered.

"Tell him, you prick," Henri said.

"That's enough from you," Hawk warned. "Sampte, were you involved in this woman's murder?"

After a long time, Sampte answered. "I've nothing to say."

"Fine, then." Hawk withdrew a pair of handcuffs from its leather sheath on his gunbelt. He tossed them to Sampte. "Fasten one end to your wrist, the other to his."

"No way," Henri screamed, shaking his head.

Hawk relaxed a bit at the sound of the cuff snapping locked around Sampte's wrist.

"He'll kill me with his bare hands."

"You're probably right." Hawk motioned with his head to a sturdy-looking piece of conduit fastened to the wall, two feet off the ground. "Lock the other end to that pipe."

Sampte complied, never taking his hate-filled eyes off Henri.

"I'll go back to the house," Henri said. "I won't go anywhere. I promise."

"Not nearly good enough." Hawk took his arm. "You'll ride with me."

Wide-eyed, Henri squealed, "In a cop car?"

Hawk tugged the squirming man from the building. "Get used to it."

66

Could it have been only six nights since this nightmare started? Nicholas wondered as Jessica turned into the Wilhoit Theatre parking lot.

He looked up from the journal in his lap to see a black Porsche Targa parked at the far end of the nearly empty lot. His breath tightened in his chest, a twinge of pain shot through his damaged ribs and ankle.

"Do you know whose car that is?" Jessica asked.

"Alexander's bribe for a good show from Timothy, I suspect."

Jessica wheeled her Taurus to the rear of the building.

"Where are you going?"

"The loading dock door will be open. It's still nearly two hours before curtain," she said, nose diving the car down the steep ramp. "The crew's probably still at the diner up the road."

She parked at the bottom of the incline. They hurried from the car and up the loading deck. Next to a closed, roll-up opening, another smaller door, propped open with a steel stage weight allowed entry.

Once inside the scene shop, Nicholas began to get his bearings. *If I was performing tonight, where would I be right now?* Running the floor plan of the theatre through his head, he heard the faint resonance of a piano piece he recognized as Prokofiev's 7th.

That's not a recording. He turned to Jessica and said, "It's Timothy."

Her eyes widened a bit as she took a step closer. "Are you sure?"

"He's on stage."

Jessica pulled out her cell phone. "I'll try Deputy Hawk again."

"I'm going out there."

"No." Jessica grabbed his sleeve. "Don't go alone. Please. You know what he's capable of."

"That's why I can't wait. I don't want him hurting anyone else. Stay here." He leveled a steely gaze. "I mean it this time."

Phone to her ear, Jessica watched Nicholas ease through the enormous steel fire door that protected the scene shop from the stage, then close it after him. Familiar scents of wood, solvent, and paint reassured her. She felt confident here, capable, talented. She had spent endless hours in this space, building and painting set pieces with nothing but coffee and loud music to keep her going throughout the night.

Looking down at the spattered floor, she identified each dominant color she and the designer had chosen for the past three productions. Focusing all of her efforts on the colorful flecks and splotches to calm herself, she waited as Hawk's phone rang and rang. Finally, his voice came over the line.

"Deputy Hawk, we're at the Wilhoit Theatre," she said before the officer could finish stating his name. "Nicholas found Timothy. We need you. Hurry!"

67

From side-stage Nicholas saw Timothy sitting at the piano, fingering an arrangement that sounded devoid of emotion. Nicholas knew Alexander would have insisted Timothy practice the arrangement endlessly the last few days, and yet the presentation sounded cold and passionless, one merely playing the notes.

Rage and the desire to avenge Elaine's death filled Nicholas. Squeezing his stiff hands into fists, he approached the pianist. Nicholas knew the piece well. The rhythm of the music rejuvenated him. Adrenalin coursed throughout his body the moment he moved onto the stage. The smell of rotting hemp and hot Roscolux color filters smoldering in the lighting instruments brought back memories of past concerts. He felt as if in a performance, his body merely a vehicle to what would be the outcome.

Remember what he did to Elaine, he reminded himself.

"Prokofiev," he said, now mere feet from Timothy. "How fitting."

Timothy jumped. His fingers struck the keys, sending an unnerving racket of tones from the instrument. He lifted his head to face Nicholas.

"His pieces always suited you. Cold and precise."

Their eyes locked. The piano between them, each waited for the next movement.

"Alexander is through with you," Timothy challenged. "After tonight you'll be history." He tapped his chest. "I'll be the star."

"You don't really think I'd let you perform, do you? There's no tonight for you."

"You will not take this from me!"

"You can't demand a damned thing after all you've taken from me. Why did you kill Elaine?"

All the color drained from Timothy's face, intensifying his freckles. "I don't know what you're talking about."

"You're part of it. You can't deny it."

"You're crazy. I didn't do anything to that bitch," he sputtered.

Nicholas lunged a step forward and stopped.

Timothy cowered.

"You could have walked away."

"Away from this?" Timothy swept his arms around the stage area. "It's all I dream about. All I've ever wanted."

"Enough to kill for?"

Timothy waved his hand in a dismissive manner. "I've never killed anyone."

Nicholas recognized the perfect mimic of the gesture Alexander used so often. "You put Elaine's body in my car. Then you tried to kill me by forcing me off the road."

"So, you're going to avenge *her*? Prove your love for *her*?" Timothy's face contorted, voice spitting with disdain.

"You're so full of hate and envy you can't even say her name. Elaine. Elaine. Elaine." Nicholas slapped the side of the piano with each pronouncement.

Timothy flinched with every thump. The strings reverberated in a hollow hum.

"I loved her." He inched toward Timothy. "You found out about us, didn't you? That's why you left her in my car, isn't it? That extra knife turn in my gut, right? Have me get rid of her body at Thibodeaux's in order to satisfy your precious Alexander."

Now close enough, Nicholas took Timothy's arm. "Come on. There's a deputy who wants to talk to you."

Timothy wrenched his arm free and started toward the steps that led to the theatre's seats.

"This place is probably crawling with cops by now."

Timothy halted at Nicholas's words. Squinting, he scanned the exit rows.

Nicholas crossed to stand between Timothy and the lip of the stage. "There's nowhere for you to run. Let's go."

Timothy hesitated a moment, then shot a clumsy punch at

Nicholas. The jab connected, re-opening the stitched wound along the side of Nicholas's face. Nicholas screamed out. He swept away blood that trailed into his eye and watched as Timothy bolted upstage.

He heard the sound of thumping and moved to where Timothy had disappeared into darkness. In the dim light backstage, Timothy tugged at a doorknob. He slapped the locked door, then ran upstage to the only other door along the wall. But that door forbade passage as well.

Letting out a frustrated growl, Timothy looked to his left, at the vertical ladder bolted to the rear wall of the auditorium. He glanced over his shoulder at Nicholas, now only a few paces away, and lunged himself onto the first rungs of the ladder that, Nicholas knew, led to the catwalks.

Nicholas followed him up the hazardous incline. The nightmare of scrambling up the mountain ravine sparked so vividly he felt beads of sweat gathering on his forehead.

They passed one catwalk, then another, until there were no more rungs to conquer.

Breathing hard and pushing aside the searing pain in his hands, ankle and ribs, Nicholas lifted his foot from the top of the ladder to meet the treacherous gridiron. He watched Timothy struggle to keep his balance on the small platform at the top of the ladder, then clamber onto the nearest landing.

"Timothy, there's no way out from up here," Nicholas said.

Timothy staggered his first tenuous steps to stop ten feet ahead, onto the thin rail. His path consisted of thick beams of steel that ran parallel to the stage. Every four feet, smaller three-inch strips of channeled iron ran perpendicular to the main beams.

"Come on back," Nicholas said. "You don't know where you're going. There's no exit." Now atop the grid of steel, he cradled his throbbing hands to his chest. "Alexander will get you a good lawyer."

Nicholas slowed as Timothy inched ahead toward the end of the grid-work, toward even more treacherous ground a few yards ahead. Determined to close the gap between them, Nicholas took tiny side steps along the I-beam.

Halfway across the stage's expanse, Timothy stopped. Hands on his knees, gulping air, he looked back and glared at Nicholas.

"You've never been up here, have you?" Nicholas asked. He hated Timothy, needed answers from him, wanted to hear him beg for his life, but he didn't want him to die. "I'll give you a little advice," he said. "Don't look down."

Nicholas's opponent dropped his gaze. He swayed, arms outstretched, lowered his center of gravity.

"I told you," Nicholas said, shaking his head. He braced himself against the cinderblock wall, catching his breath.

"What do you want from me?" Timothy asked, his voice crackling with fear.

Nicholas laughed. "What do I want? What do I want! I want what you took from me."

Timothy's wild eyes darted around, then down at the stage below. "I want to go home." He pulled something from his pocket, tucked it in his fist and rubbed the item with his thumb.

"Tell you what. I'll help you down." Nicholas slid closer to Timothy. "All you have to do is tell me you killed Elaine."

Timothy shuffled away a few steps, then teetered, nearly throwing himself off-balance.

"I know a way out of here. I'll help you escape from the police. Just tell me!"

"Yes. I killed her," Timothy screamed. "For him. I did it for him." He scowled at Nicholas. "I'd do it again."

Hearing the confession he so longed to hear, tears merged with blood, blurring Nicholas's vision. He followed Timothy's gaze down to the piano. On the stage, directly below Timothy, the Steinway gleamed from the coats of clear varnish over ebony paint. The keys, vibrant white, reminded Nicholas of a gapped-tooth smile.

"I can't believe the animal he's turned you into," Nicholas said.

"All I ever wanted was to please him," Timothy countered.

"There's nowhere to go, Timothy. It's just you and me. No piano. No music." Nicholas sighed, exhausted. "No Alexander."

He knew he needed to somehow get Timothy down before his opponent froze, unable to move. In an effort to force Timothy to focus, he said, "Look at you, you're trembling. How will you ever perform tonight? My guess— not well," Nicholas laughed, then turned serious. He blazed a glare at Timothy. "You shame Prokofiev."

Timothy glowered. "And you shame him."

"You must be talking about your precious Alexander, now. Don't you see how he's manipulated us? I'm his pawn and you're his assassin. He's turned us against each other."

Timothy hissed, "You've always hated me."

"Frankly, I've never given you much thought."

"Go to hell."

Nicholas took tentative steps toward Timothy, ten feet away. "I'm sorry, but it's true. I never knew what went on during your little trips with Sampte. Or the private conferences between you and Alexander. I never cared. I only wanted to perform." He lowered his head. "And to be with Elaine."

Nicholas drew to within an arm's length and reached out. Timothy cringed when Nicholas tried to snatch his sleeve. "Stay away from me!"

Timothy pinwheeled his arms one direction, then the other. The soles of his shoes slipped on the grime-covered I-beam. His body teetered, bobbed, over-compensated, canted, dropped. Timothy toppled through the opening between the gridiron's beams, his face a mask of terror, mouth opened wide.

Nicholas screamed, but his was the only voice that echoed.

After what seemed an endless ten-story free-fall, Timothy crashed face-up atop the Steinway. Portions of the lid cracked and ripped off, skidding along the stage. Plucked and snapped piano strings resounded with a cacophony of sound, thundering throughout the auditorium.

After a full a minute everything went silent except the hum from the lighting instruments that bathed the carnage in an amber glow.

68

Hawk finally caught up with Nicholas and Jessica at the Wilhoit Theatre. He heard an explosion of unidentifiable noise as he ran into the backstage shop. Drawing his Glock, he sidled up next to her.

"That didn't sound good," she said, wide-eyed, her body trembling.

"Where's Nicholas?"

She pointed at a massive steel door.

"Stay here," Hawk instructed.

She pulled the door's handle and it rolled along wheels attached to a rail on the ceiling.

Extending his weapon, he used the door to shield his body as he peered from behind it. Seeing no one, he eased backstage, tucked behind one of the black drapes, scanned the stage.

"Nicholas?" Jessica called out from the scene shop.

A sinking feeling settled in Hawk's gut as he inched from the curtain. Hearing a movement, he turned to see Jessica disobeying his instructions. He frowned at her, but she stepped even closer. Hawk lowered his gun and held up his left hand in a halting motion. Reading her shocked expression, he followed her stare.

He took in the piano's splayed legs, shorn plank of black lacquered wood on the floor. Easing onto the stage, gun trained forward, he saw a piece of black fabric draped over the side of the instrument. He rushed closer. Throat seizing, he struggled to swallow at the sight of Timothy's shattered body.

"Nicholas," Jessica said again, looking up as she ran past Hawk to the other side of the stage. "I see him."

"Where?"

She pointed again, this time straight up. Then she bolted

toward the back wall toward the tallest ladder Hawk had ever seen.

He holstered his weapon and called out, "Jessica, wait. I've got backup coming."

Ignoring him, she started pulling herself up the rungs as if she'd conquered the challenge a thousand times. Hawk felt dizzy as he watched her fade into the shadows.

A sudden movement prompted Hawk to pull his Glock again. He whirled to the motion across the stage.

Stiles stepped from the dark wings, into the light. Chuckling, empty hands raised in the air, he said, "Kinda like the Wild West, huh, Partner?"

"Where the hell you been?" Hawk let out a relieved breath as he re-holstered his weapon.

"Drivin' over half the damned county," Stiles replied, walking to Hawk. "First go here, then go there. Your locations were slick as a copperhead. You did some pretty fancy drivin' tonight." Stiles clipped him on the back. "Couldn't keep up."

"Your timing could definitely have been better. Glad you're here now, though." He hitched a thumb toward Timothy's lifeless body.

"Got a mess on your hands." Stiles approached the piano and let out a slow whistle. "Looks like I missed all the fun tonight." He placed two fingers on the boy's neck and shook his head.

Something in Timothy's partially closed hand caught Hawk's attention. He leaned closer and frowned at a toy soldier nestled in Timothy's palm.

"So what's the story?" Stiles asked.

"Not sure yet. Nicholas Kalman's still up there. Jessica went after him. Hopefully she can talk him down."

Stiles used his hand as a visor and looked up. They both scanned the gridwork above. "Gotta' be a hundred feet to the top. Maybe we should see how she does with him."

Hawk searched the darkness for Jessica. He didn't like heights. Never had. Nerves rumbling in his gut, he nodded and said, "Exactly what I was thinkin'."

After Jessica had climbed the vertical ladder beyond the third catwalk, she realized Nicholas must be at the highest position of the theatre. As far as she knew, in its history, there were only three stagehands daring enough to reach the heights of the gridiron level. She had been one of them. It had taken all her concentration and a slow, methodical pace to maneuver the narrow slats. Adding even more hazard, the space above the gridiron allowed less than six feet of headroom.

Reaching the top, Jessica stepped up the last two rungs and dropped onto the gridiron's platform. She blew out a relieved breath when she saw Nicholas sitting down a few yards ahead.

Rubbing the grime from her hands onto her thighs, she inched her way toward him. "Nicholas? Are you all right?"

"Is it over?" he asked in a soft voice.

"You're safe now." She crouched down in front of him to shield his view of the scene below, wincing at his re-injured face. "You're bleeding." With the heel of her hand, she wiped fresh blood from his check and jaw.

"Is he dead?"

She placed a tender hand on his shoulder. "Are you ready to come down?"

"To what?" he mumbled.

After a long time, she said, "He can't hurt you anymore."

Dropping his head to his arms crossed atop his knees, Nicholas began to sob.

"Deputy Hawk is here." She stroked his hair and sat down in front of him. "This wasn't your fault."

Nicholas raised his head to look at her. "How do you know?"

"Because I know you. You're good and kind. And you would never hurt anyone."

"You met me less than a week ago. For all you know, I'm a monster." He looked downward. "Like him."

"He's just a man."

Nicholas slowly shook his head.

"Nicholas Kalman," Hawk's voice echoed from below, "I need to speak to you. Now."

Jessica stood and held out her hand. "Let's go."

Nicholas took her firm grip and held it tightly. Her hand clasped firmly in his, she led him to the ladder.

When Nicholas and Jessica reached the stage floor, they joined Deputies Hawk and another deputy. Exhausted and drained of emotion, unable to wrench his eyes away, his attention locked on Timothy's lifeless body sprawled on the destroyed Steinway.

"What happened up there?" Hawk asked.

Nicholas shrugged. "He slipped."

"You're gonna have to give me more than that."

Jessica crooked her arm through Nicholas's. "It's dangerous up there, Deputy. Safe on the catwalks, but they were all the way up on the gridiron level. I've been up there before. The footing isn't more than a few inches wide in most places, and it's really slick."

Nicholas took an unsteady breath and looked at Hawk. "The more I tried to convince him to come down, the higher up, then farther out he went." He looked back at the piano. "Then he fell. He didn't scream, he didn't cry out. He just kept falling, and then landed . . ."

Nicholas's voice trailed off as the vision of Timothy's writhing body crashing onto the Steinway filled his mind again.

"Why'd you confront him on your own?" the older deputy snapped.

"I needed to talk to him about Elaine . . . To find out why . . ."

"What did you need to know, Mr. Kalman?" Hawk asked.

"Why he killed her." Nicholas replied bluntly.

"What makes you believe he killed her?"

Nicholas gave Hawk his full attention. He didn't blink or evade. He merely said, "He told me he did."

69

Although they had removed Timothy's broken body from the Steinway an hour ago, Hawk noticed that Nicholas still stared at the instrument, its legs askew, lid splintered, fresh wood spiking from its ebony finish.

The Wilhoit Theatre house lights bathed the burgundy chairs where Nicholas and Jessica sat side-by-side in the last aisle of the theatre. Hawk stood a few rows away and spoke to Stiles in a quiet voice.

"I've got Henri Thibodeaux locked up in my cruiser. Told him he should keep his mouth shut 'til he talked to a lawyer, but I couldn't get him to shut up. All those missing people I told you about are definitely tied to Alexander Kalman. Thibodeaux's been burying people for him for years. I've got his sorry-ass confession on tape."

"Does he implicate Nicholas?" Stiles asked.

"Claims he's never seen or heard of him. Talks about a red-haired kid, though. He has lots to say about him."

"Timothy Sagan," Stiles said.

Hawk nodded. "No doubt. He's been accompanying Sampte on his little deliveries since he was a boy." He ran a hand through his hair. "We've still got a lot to figure out about this case."

"Why's that?"

"Well, according to Nicholas, Timothy said he killed Elaine."

"Right. So what's the problem?" Stiles said.

"Sampte also claims to have done it."

"Interesting."

"Can you take Thibodeaux to the jail for me?"

"Sure. You okay?" Stiles asked.

"Yeah. I'm not lookin' forward to seein' Aranka Kalman."

"Think the kid's innocent?"

Hawk turned to Nicholas and nodded. "Looks like he's a victim in all this."

"What are you going to do with him?"

"I want him to go with me to pick up Sampte. Then we'll swing by and get Alexander. Maybe with all of them together, I'll get more answers."

"That'll be an interesting ride. Sure you want to do this alone?"

"I'll keep Nicholas up front with me. Sampte and Alexander can ride in the cage behind us."

"Right where they belong." Stiles unsnapped one of the leather cases on his gunbelt, pulled out his set of handcuffs and handed them to Hawk. "Don't take any chances."

Hawk approached Nicholas and Jessica. A twinge of sorrow filled him as he watched Nicholas drag his attention from the piano, his face registering loss, fear, loneliness, defeat.

"We're going to need to get a full account of everything you know," Hawk said. "I want you to come with me."

Wearily, Nicholas pushed up from the chair. He clasped his hands out in front of him.

Jessica stepped between the two men. "You aren't going to handcuff him, are you?"

"No, you're not under arrest, Mr. Kalman. Too many people have confessed that you've never been involved in anything for me to be concerned with. As it stands now, you're not in any trouble at all."

Jessica issued a relieved smile and stroked Nicholas's back.

"I do have one question for you," Hawk said. "A lot of people in your life have disappeared over the years. Weren't you ever curious about that?"

Nicholas's face revealed no emotion. "I've been asking myself that same question."

Hawk took Nicholas's arm. "One of the troopers will get you home, ma'am." He ushered Nicholas past Jessica, her eyes full of tears.

"Thank you," Hawk heard Nicholas tell her. "For everything."

70

Alexander flew into a rage after receiving a call from some law enforcement fool, insisting he remain at his home. Peering out from the music room window, he saw the police car that remained parked in the circular drive.

Hours earlier, he had ordered the workers preparing for the party to get off his property, cursing them until they scrambled to load up their equipment and leave. He craved hot tea, but Zardos couldn't be found, furthering Alexander's fury. *Probably hiding like a scared rabbit. No backbone, that boy.*

And Sampte had been gone far too long. Alexander sneered, looking around at the music room's destruction. Never had he waited so long for a servant to put a room back together.

Clearing a path with the tip of his cane, he sidestepped to the bar and reached for a tumbler. Hand trembling, he poured a shot of Scotch from the decanter, tinkling the glass rim. He downed the liquor in one gulp and sloshed more into the glass.

Timothy's concert curtain time had long since elapsed, and everyone in "authority" had refused to answer his questions as to why he was being kept from his protégé. He had even placed a call to the governor, to no avail. His fury peaked when the state trooper arrived and spoke to him like a commoner, ordering him to stay put and wait.

Soft tones of Hans Huber's Third in D Major finally lulled Alexander to some semblance of calm. His mind traveled to his last day with Elaine. He shuddered, remembering her departure from his music room the last morning he would ever see her again. Colorful dress flowing behind her, his nose filled with her fresh scent he still could not exorcise from his memory.

His hopes for a life with Elaine forever dashed, Alexander began to orchestrate the postlude of his former life so that he may compose a new future. Though grieved by Nicholas's decision not to seek him out after his accident, because of his shunning, Alexander felt free to turn his back on his once-favored pupil. He would, instead, create a new beginning, find a new residence, and even accompany young Timothy on his inevitable concert tours.

He felt full of pride over Timothy's growth the past month. The lesser student did not exhibit Nicholas's prowess and class, and Alexander resigned himself to the fact that Timothy never would achieve those qualities. Nevertheless, what Timothy lacked in passion, he mastered in self-discipline. The pieces Timothy had studied for this evening's performance were flawless. Tonight had been cancelled, but there would be many more concerts ahead.

Alexander knew Timothy would never embarrass him with indiscretions, as Nicholas had. He would share with Timothy his talents as a maestro completely. Timothy would be a faithful companion, one who would accept his master's knowledge and suggestions without question or confrontation.

It is best if we leave the country for a while. Travel to the London flat. Although much smaller, without Nicholas—and once Alexander gave Sampte instructions, without Zardos—there would be plenty of room.

Nicholas was no longer his concern. From now on, Alexander decided, he would spend his future molding his apprentice. He counted in his mind the riches hidden in three European bank accounts. Those funds, in conjunction with the money he had siphoned from Nicholas's trust fund would be more than enough to continue living as he had come to know and expect for a lifetime.

He regretted the possibility of never being permitted back into the United States once a thorough investigation ultimately revealed his past dealings, but he surged with exuberance, rejuvenated by the challenge of starting over.

The list of desired countries and their cities ran through

his mind, many without extradition policies.

All will be well.

A smile crept to his lips as he thought of the journey to come. He began to relax. Settling deep into the plush upholstery of his velvet chair, he waited for Timothy and Sampte to return to him.

71

Nicholas had no idea where Hawk could be taking him. He had hoped never to travel the mountainous highway again, but now he found himself in the front passenger seat of the deputy's cruiser, winding along the same fateful path that had started his downward spiral. He worried if his misery would ever cease.

The sound of Timothy's body thudding onto the Steinway replayed in a constant loop until he thought he would go mad.

Leaning his burning forehead against the cold glass window, he looked out at the blackness. The ominous outline of pines flashed past, hypnotizing him into his first calm in as long as he could remember. Closing his eyes, he recalled his last night with Elaine.

Her long hair had fallen to hide her face, and when she swept it back to look at him, he marveled at the look of love and passion she gave him. He could practically touch the soft lavender shirt she wore, its silver pearl buttons slipping through his fingers as he released them to expose her ivory breasts, feel the heat of her skin under his touch. He breathed deep, imagining her floral scent.

The motion of the car turning, then bumping over a cattle guard brought Nicholas back to the present. He read the ancient, paint-flecked sign that announced: THIBODEAUX MORTUARY.

Remembering Alexander's note, he muttered, "Oh, God. That's what this place is." He turned his puzzled gaze to Hawk. "Why are we here?"

"I've got Sampte locked up inside."

"Sampte? I don't understand."

Hawk maneuvered between several sheriffs and state trooper cruisers to park near a cement structure behind the main building.

Sliding from the car, weary and stiff, Nicholas followed Hawk to a cluster of uniformed officers who stood outside the entrance.

Nicholas stopped when he saw a white paneled van marked CORONER.

Hawk placed a hand on Nicholas's shoulder. "Best if you prepare yourself. Elaine is in there, too."

"Elaine?" Nicholas murmured. Fresh pain pierced his heart.

The officers parted when he and Hawk approached them. Nicholas watched a deputy lead Sampte from the building, hands cuffed behind his back, head bowed.

"Sampte, what's going on?" Nicholas asked, as Sampte brushed past.

Sampte's shoulders slumped lower. He didn't raise his head. He did not say one word.

Nicholas's gaze fixed on the open door of the cement block building.

"You don't have to do this, you know," Hawk said. "Let her identification be left to her mother."

Studying his shoes, he said to himself more than to Hawk, "No. I've caused enough pain to Aranka."

Hawk nodded, took off his hat off and clutched its brim.

Nicholas gathered his courage and stepped to the door. After a few nervous breaths he crossed the threshold. The frigid, pungent room spooked him. He shuddered, drawing his jacket tight around his body.

Fully inside the cold, uninviting space, Nicholas's eyes locked on Elaine's lifeless body, laid out on an aluminum table in the middle of the room. Taking tentative steps, he reached out. He wanted to rest his trembling fingers on her cheek, smooth the hair from her forehead, but Hawk stopped him with a shake of his head.

Nicholas clasped his hands behind his back to resist the urge to ignore the deputy. He stared at the ashen, waxy, colorless face that barely resembled his lover. "Have you ever been in love, Deputy Hawk?"

"Yeah, sure."

"I mean the sweaty palm, heart pounding, gasp at the sight of her when she enters the room, love."

Hawk shuffled from one foot to the other. "No. I'm still lookin' for that."

"That's what we had."

"I'm sorry, Nicholas," Hawk said. "I really am." Then the deputy gently pulled the coverlet over Elaine's body and head.

Nicholas straightened his posture and said, "Take me to Alexander Kalman."

Clamping his hat back on his head, Hawk led Nicholas from the morgue.

He searched the group of officers and spotted Sampte right away—a foot wider and a head taller than any of the others, even as he leaned on a police car. Nicholas ran to him, grabbed the man he once considered a friend, and swung him around.

"Why?" Nicholas shouted. "Tell me, you bastard. Why did this happen?"

Sampte kept his chin tucked to his chest, refusing to look at Nicholas.

A flash of lightning lit the area, halting all action for a moment. A deafening crack, followed by a train-like rumble, resounded through the trees.

When Sampte raised his head, Nicholas searched the man's eyes for any clues. Instead, he recognized the flat, resolved gaze, rivaling a look only Alexander could brandish.

To Nicholas, Sampte's silence seemed louder than the thunder.

72

Torrents of rain slashed at the deputy's cruiser. Nicholas sat beside Hawk while Sampte, still locked in handcuffs, rode behind the mesh cage protecting the front compartment from the rear. It felt to Nicholas as if they stood still on the highway, but pine trees whizzed past his window. Out of words and drained of emotion, he swayed with the motion of the vehicle as they made their way to Alexander's mansion.

Nicholas noticed Hawk press buttons on a mini-cassette player, then he placed it on the dashboard. Nicholas jerked when Hawk's booming voice filled the car.

"I've got a lot of questions for you, Sampte, but the one I just can't let go of is, why did you kill Manuel Esteva and his family?"

Nicholas, stared at the deputy, stunned by the revelation, unsure if he had heard right. He thought of the madness his father warned him of on the very first page of his journal. His hand went to his inside jacket pocket, feeling the outline of the cover. He withdrew the book with throbbing fingers.

Nicholas barely recognized Sampte when he finally answered in a faraway voice. "It was never intended for the entire family to perish. Unfortunately, Manuel's wife was sitting on his lap when I shot him in the back."

"But why the kids, dammit?" Hawk roared. "They weren't a threat to any of you."

"Leave them to live their lives alone?" Sampte said. "I could never do such a thing."

Nicholas and Hawk exchanged looks of dismay.

He knew what Sampte was capable of. He had witnessed the Hungarian kill a full-grown deer Alexander had shot, but had not killed, at the country house one summer. The massive man had snapped the buck's neck without so much as a groan. It took little imagination to picture Sampte taking the life of Manuel and his family.

There was no sound except the windshield wipers' squeal across the glass for a long time before Nicholas spoke. "Why did he order it?"

Sampte revealed nothing more.

"Tell me," Nicholas said, adjusting in the seat to look better at the man he had known since childhood. "Why did he tell Timothy to kill Elaine?"

Sampte held Nicholas's gaze. "Master Alexander wanted her, too."

Nicholas winced. "What do you mean, he *wanted* her?"

"She wasn't meant to be yours."

Realization hit Nicholas, an impact to his chest so hard he forgot to breathe for a moment. "But they're blood relatives. That's sick."

"For him, nothing mattered."

"You're saying I got in his way?"

"You went too far."

"I didn't know."

"You weren't meant to. She didn't even realize my master's intent until it was too late."

Nicholas shook his head. "She wouldn't have dreamed of being with him."

"That's why she had to die."

Nicholas lunged for the cage, his fingers intertwining in the mesh. "You say it so easily. Like killing her meant nothing!"

"There was no other choice." Sampte leaned forward, his face close to the barrier. "She was outraged when Timothy brought her to Alexander and you weren't at the mansion. Screaming at Timothy for tricking her, cursing Alexander until she was frantic." Sampte's words rushed out. "Her anger sparked his and the more he tried to reason with her the more furious she became. He slapped her and she slapped him back. Then he grabbed her around the neck and he wouldn't let go—"

"Stop," Nicholas shouted, then mumbled barely above a whisper, "Just stop. I don't want the details of how Timothy killed the woman I loved."

"Timothy?" Sampte's forehead wrinkled in confusion.

"Yes," Nicholas said. "He told me he killed her before he died. That's really all I need to know."

"No, you don't understand." Sampte slowly shook his head. "Alexander killed your love."

Nicholas said nothing for a long time as he tried to comprehend the terror revealed to him. He released the cage to face the windshield. "Well, now no one has her."

"You'll leave our master alone?"

Hawk spit the words, "Your *master* has a lot of explaining to do. Tell him to buy a good lawyer."

"Nicolas, you would betray Master Alexander?" Sampte asked.

"After what he's done?" Nicholas stated. "In a heartbeat."

"Think of all he's provided, sacrificed. You would take his freedom?"

Nicholas turned to Sampte again. "That's not my decision."

Sampte halted Nicholas's heart with menacing glower. Then the man simply said, "Yes, it is."

Nicholas looked at Hawk. The deputy's jaw muscle bulged and he looked ready to pull over the cruiser, pull Sampte from the car, pull out his gun, pull the trigger. Instead, Hawk turned onto the private road that led to Alexander's mansion.

Nicholas began to prepare for the confrontation with his uncle. *This could be the most important performance of my life.* Slowing his breathing until he relaxed, he trilled his fingers atop his father's journal that rested on his lap.

Following the drive, they arrived at the double gates. "This is strange," Nicholas said as they passed through. "These gates are never left open." An abandoned party set-up on the mansion's lawn added to his confusion. "What the hell's going on here?"

"Timothy's celebration party," Sampte answered.

"Of course. The unveiling. I still remember mine."

Hawk veered around a delivery truck and parked the

cruiser in front of the house. When Nicholas strode from the car, Hawk yelled to him. "Hold up. Sampte's going with us." Hawk helped the reluctant, handcuffed Sampte from the back seat. Rain pelted their bodies, immediately drenching them.

A state trooper, clad in a rain slicker to his shins, rubber boots, Stetson covered with plastic, emerged from a cruiser parked close to the steps. He touched the brim of his hat and said, "I'm Trooper Donnelly. Need a hand?"

"Yeah, Donnelly. I'm Deputy Hawk. We're here to see Alexander Kalman. Is he inside?"

The trooper chuckled. "Oh yeah. He's in there, but I doubt he'll be happy to see you."

Hawk nodded toward Sampte. "Help me keep an eye on him, will you?"

"You're all goin' in?" Donnelly hung back, looking down the driveway. "You sure you don't want to wait for backup?"

"You're my backup," Hawk said. "You up to it?"

The trooper stood a little taller. His hand settled on the grip of his holstered gun. "You bet."

Entering the foyer, their soles squeaked on the marble floor. Water fell off them, creating puddles on the pristine surface.

As Nicholas climbed the three flights of stairs and wove his way down the long hallway to the music room, he relived the once comfortable smell of old books, leather upholstery, pipe smoke, fresh-cut flowers, buffing compound that gave the Steinway its rich glow.

Could this ever be home to me again?

The mansion was where Alexander had murdered Elaine, and caused his own ruin. Fueled by anger and resentment, he recalled his vow to avenge his love from the first moment he saw her lifeless body. He prepared himself for any surprises Alexander might throw his way.

When they reached the music room's closed door, Hawk said, "Nicholas, keep your distance. I don't want you going anywhere near your uncle."

Uncle. Nicholas snorted. The term, once an endearment,

now meant nothing to him.

"Donnelly, you're a witness to whatever happens in here so pay close attention and stick with the prisoner," Hawk instructed. "Sampte, no tricks and no one gets hurt."

"Maybe we should have a plan," Donnelly said, looking pale and apprehensive.

Nicholas agreed, but knew there wasn't time. Surely, reinforcements were on the way. The deputy was doing him a favor by letting him confront Alexander before more officers showed up. Nicholas needed answers and he suspected the lawman did too. Hawk and Jessica had been the only people to believe in him. Now it was Nicholas's turn to step up.

He glanced at the gun in Hawk's holster, then to Trooper Donnelly's. He decided which pistol would be easier to take. Alexander would talk, or he would die.

73

Nicholas squared his shoulders, slicked his soaked hair straight back and took a deep breath. He turned the cold doorknob. For the first time ever, he stepped into the music room without Alexander's permission. His eyes fell long-ingly on the Steinway. For days he had yearned to sit upon the tufted leather bench, feel the precise action of the ivory keys that had provided thousands of hours of frustration as well as joy, to hear the room resonate with the perfect notes of composers he cherished. If only he could—even to play a single piece of music—perhaps that would soothe his devastated soul.

Hawk nudged Sampte into the room. Donnelly followed and closed the door behind them.

Nicholas wrenched his vision away from the piano and noticed the cyclonic disaster of the music room. Books, broken glass, and trinkets were scattered everywhere. On the floor around Alexander's chair, Nicholas recognized photographs of himself as a boy and as a man, old concert programs, folds of sheet music on yellowing paper.

Focus, Nicholas warned himself. Anticipating any prospect of surprise, cautious of every step, he pushed his fury aside and eased toward Alexander sitting in his red velvet chair. He looked old, somehow spent, eyes closed, head slumped as he dozed.

At first, Nicholas wanted to go to him, ached to hear the melodious accented words flow from his mentor say that he had done him no wrong, that everything had all been a horrible mistake. Come home, we will begin again. Cold resolution filled Nicholas, knowing that could never happen. He took a step closer and faced his betrayer.

Alexander bobbed his head and grumbled, "What is going on? Sampte!" He reared back and scowled when he noticed Nicholas standing before him. "What are you doing here?"

"Why did you kill Elaine?" Nicholas said, as devoid of emotion as he could put forth.

Alexander ignored the question. "So, you've come home. An apology would be appropriate. Leaving me to worry what's become of you has been an insult. Have you no shame?"

"No more manipulations," Nicholas snapped. "I'm here for the truth."

Alexander glowered at Nicholas, disgust clear on his face. He stared at the raw, oozing gash along Nicholas's temple. "Look at you. It is worse than I feared." Lifting wearily from the chair, he stumbled, his attention going to Hawk, the trooper, and then Sampte. "What is the meaning of this intrusion?"

Nicholas snatched a glass from the table beside Alexander's chair and hurled it across the room. Glass exploded against the wall and tinkled onto the floor to mingle with the other shards. "Answer me!"

Alexander waved his hand dismissively and turned his back on Nicholas.

"Mr. Kalman, I'm placing you under arrest," Hawk said. "You'll have to come with me to the station house."

"Whatever for?" Alexander hissed.

"For questioning, regarding your involvement in a number of missing persons. And for the murder of Elaine Kalman."

Alexander ignored Hawk and turned his attention to Sampte. "Where is Timothy?"

"Timothy's dead, you son of a bitch," Nicholas answered.

Alexander pivoted to Nicholas, a stunned expression on his face.

"He's another dead body in your sick path of destruction."

Alexander advanced on Nicholas in a rage, his cane thumping the Pakistani rug.

Sampte made a move to interject, but Hawk blocked him.

Donnelly gripped the butt of his holstered weapon and pulled the servant back.

Nicholas held his ground as Alexander moved at a surprising speed, closing the gap between them. He raised his cane in the air.

"There's no need to hit me, old man. I'm not afraid of your punishments anymore. Nothing you could possibly do can hurt me now."

At Nicholas's words, Alexander halted, his walking stick hovering above his head.

"Elaine didn't even see it coming, did she?" Nicholas asked. "You're always cut off from your emotions and precise with your actions, so she must have pissed you off. Catch you off-guard, maybe? Did you use your precious cane on her? Maybe hit her a little too hard by mistake? Or is that what you meant to do? You bastard. You killed her, didn't you? Your own flesh and blood. Your sister's daughter. Not Sampte. Not Timothy. You. She was good and kind. And, she was mine." Nicholas challenged Alexander inches from his face. "But you couldn't have that, could you? My being close to her. Sharing our bodies. Did you see our love as a betrayal to the music? To you? Tell me why, Uncle. Make me understand."

Alexander held Nicholas's glare for a moment, then he lowered the cane. He backed to his chair and fell into it.

Nicholas stood over him. "I was expected to clean up your mess. Then you ordered Timothy to get rid of me because you knew I'd kill you when I found out what you did to Elaine." He glared with contempt at Alexander.

"Where is she?" Alexander asked in a defeated voice.

"What do you care? It's been taken care of. Fixed nice and proper. As you've always demanded. You were my mentor, my teacher. I did anything you asked without question to get your approval. Never in my wildest dreams did I imagine your intent was to turn me into a beast. Just like you."

The muscles under Alexander's eyes twitched. "Don't speak such nonsense. You are destined to be the very best.

You are greatness."

Nicholas bent to face Alexander nose to nose. "I am nothing without Elaine." A sob wracked his body. He pointed to the Steinway. "I only wanted to play the piano. And to be with her."

Alexander straightened up and spewed, "No. You only wanted to play. Never practice. You were never committed to the craft. Perfection was never an obsession to you."

"You're right. The obsession was yours." Nicholas swatted tears from his face. "The manipulation, the control. The tours all over the world you forced me to endure. But I rose to acclaim, didn't I?" Nicholas balled his hands into fists, relishing the pain of his reopened wounds, focusing his rage. "I thought my acclaim would make you proud, but you never believed I deserved it."

Alexander struggled from his chair and brushed past Nicholas. "I suffered for the music at your age. Never considered leaving the keyboard before my cuticles bled. Shoulders so sore I couldn't raise my arms above my head." He swept the expanse of the room with his cane. "When did you ever suffer? I provided you with everything. Never once did you work."

"Why is it so hard for you to accept that the music comes easily to me? I have a gift. My talents were destined. Why did you have to kill Elaine?" Nicholas begged. "Why did you betray me?"

"*I* betrayed *you*? I made everything available to you. Everything. Fame. Performances in the finest auditoriums. Tours around the world. That blasted car. If I hadn't constantly pushed, you would have thrown your talent away."

"No more of your lies." Nicholas took the journal from his jacket pocket. "I found something hidden in that book-case over there. It's a journal my father wrote with the hope that some day I'd find it." He thrust the book toward Alexander. "Go ahead, look at it. There's no doubt the words are his. It proves that in order to have me, you had to destroy him. It's all in there," Nicholas said, dropping the journal to land open-faced on the floor, the fluid handwriting taunting, accusing.

"Your father . . .," Alexander said on an exasperated exhale, his head shaking back and forth, ". . . was an extraordinarily less than average man. I would be surprised at nothing he may have written in a drunken stupor, which was most of the time. His talent, however, was frightening in its intensity. Raw talent, like yours. He fled from his life of music merely because he found perfection to be too much work. He threw away his gift. He threw you away as well."

"I'll never believe that. I think you stole me from him and my mother."

Ignoring Nicholas's words, Alexander continued his rant. "And once you were born, he considered you to be yet another burden. He left because of you. He wanted nothing to do with you."

A sudden, clarifying realization came to Nicholas. "My father was a better pianist than you."

Alexander flinched at the accusation.

Careful not to turn his back on Alexander, Nicholas went to the bar and sloshed an inch of amber liquid into a crystal tumbler. "I share with my father the one thing you couldn't manipulate. The one thing that can't be taught." He drained the drink in one swallow. "Talent."

Alexander clenched his eyes shut when Nicholas said the word.

"Don't you find it odd how Timothy's and my own life have paralleled yours and my father's almost exactly? Tell me, Uncle. I was left for dead, bleeding and abandoned. Was the attempt to kill me Timothy's idea? Or was it a direct order from you?"

After a moment, Alexander limped toward Nicholas. "Miklos . . .," he whispered.

"Nicholas! I'm not your fair Hungarian boy. I'm Nicholas Renfrew Hunt. Son of Charles Ian and Teresa Rosanna Hunt."

Eyes flashing, Alexander charged, cane flailing. Nicholas caught the walking stick mid-swing. Snatching the cane from

Alexander, Nicholas clutched the slender rod like a bat high in the air and prepared to deliver the revenge he burned for.

Sampte wrenched free from Donnelly's grasp. Hawk rushed forward to block him. "One more step and I'll take you out," the deputy said. Sampte stopped, nostrils flaring.

Nicholas tried to summon his wrath, to dispense payback for so many beatings. Instead, he only called forth sorrow. "No." He lowered the cane. "I can't callously cause someone pain. Not even you."

He mimicked Alexander's icy stare, lifted his left knee, and brought the cane down atop it. The staff snapped with a crack. Nicholas gathered the two pieces in one hand and tossed them at Alexander. The sticks bounced off Alexander's chest and danced atop the marble floor.

"I'll never be like you." Exhausted, Nicholas tumbled to the sofa, though his eyes remained on Alexander.

Alexander swayed, catching his balance. He limped across the room and picked up Charles Hunt's journal, then carried it to stand in front of the fireplace that glowed with hot coals. He scanned the scrawled text, flipping each turn of the page with intensity. Then he began to read out loud. "'His evil enveloped my life and I could not break away. Alexander will destroy all that is good in you, Nicholas.' Rubbish. This is nonsense. Surely you don't believe a word of this." Alexander turned to another page. "'Beware when he says the success is all for you. His assurances will be the harshest lie anyone could speak. He thinks of no one but himself. Beware at all times, my son.'" Alexander snapped the book shut.

Nicholas gained satisfaction from the sight of Alexander's shocked face, hair tousled, clothing rumpled.

Alexander tossed the journal into the fireplace. The pungent smell of scorched leather wafted into the room.

"What are you doing?" Nicholas yelled, prompting Hawk and Donnelly to lunge toward the fireplace. Grabbing a poker from its stand, Hawk leaned into the opening and tried to recover the smoldering book.

"Dammit, Donnelly, cover the prisoner," Hawk

commanded.

Donnelly hurried back to Sampte and lifted one hand in a halting position, the other on the butt of his pistol.

Turning from the fueled flames, Alexander looked at the walking stick he had depended upon for as long as Nicholas could remember, now snapped in two, destroyed. Alexander shook his head regretfully as he hobbled to his chair and sat.

For the first time in a decade, Nicholas heard Sampte speak to Alexander in the forbidden cadence of their native homeland. But Hungarian had been the first foreign language Alexander taught him and Nicholas understood every word they said.

"You mustn't do anything foolish," Sampte pleaded.

"If you're not gonna speak English, don't say another word," Hawk warned, smothering the smoking journal with a pillow.

"He's like a son to you," Sampte continued in Hungarian.

"I have nothing now," Alexander said, as if not hearing Sampte. "No more purpose. No one to desire. No one to teach."

Blood surged in Nicholas's ears. He felt his betrayal never-ending. He lifted himself from the sofa, but then found himself unable to move. "That's your own fault," he spouted in Hungarian to Alexander. Everyone in the room spun in his direction.

"Not you, too," Hawk grumbled. "Nicholas, cut it out."

But he couldn't. Alexander's words weren't those of remorse for killing Elaine, or for issuing orders to Sampte and Timothy, commanding them to carry out his gruesome demands. Alexander Kalman cared about no one but himself.

"If it hadn't been for your greed and obsession for perfection from everyone around you, none of this would have happened."

"Yes. This is true," Alexander whispered. "Nothing is good enough. I see that now." He lowered his head, looking exhausted and resigned.

"All right, that's it," Hawk said. "Donnelly get Sampte outta' here."

The trooper attempted to push Sampte toward the door, but the servant planted his feet and didn't budge from his position.

Something about Alexander's defeated manner kept Nicholas's eyes locked on him. He had never witnessed his mentor in defeat. He wanted to relish the man's ruin, but he only felt emptiness.

Alexander slid a hand into his smoking jacket and took something from its pocket. Nicholas immediately recognized Alexander's prized Walther PPK .380 semi-automatic pistol. The reignited fire's light glinted off the polished barrel and its pearl-handled grip.

In one smooth movement, Alexander chambered a round and then raised the gun to his temple.

Sampte lunged for his master. "No!"

Hawk pulled his sidearm, whirled at the commotion, aimed.

Nicholas wrenched his cemented feet from the floor and sprang toward Alexander.

A deafening shot cracked.

The room filled with the resonance of Alexander Kalman's life ending.

74

Eight months had elapsed since Elaine, Alexander and Timothy had been swept from Nicholas's life. Alexander's mansion and all its contents now belonged to Nicholas. Over time, the experiences he endured began to fade, but some nights, he still awoke to nightmares, clutching drenched bed sheets.

Sampte remained in prison where he awaited his sentenceing after he pleaded guilty to killing eighteen people who were directly involved with Alexander Kalman. Zardos had yet to return. Nicholas prayed that his friend, the young Hungarian, had somehow found safe passage back to his homeland, but deep down he knew Sampte should be charged with a nineteenth count of murder.

Deputy Hawk had checked in with Nicholas every week. During their last meeting at a diner not far from the courthouse, the deputy brought a woman in uniform with him. She stood a foot shorter than the deputy, but looked more than qualified to be a cop by the way she commanded the room without saying a word. Nicholas recognized her Native American heritage by her high cheekbones, copper-color skin and long dark hair tied back in a tight ponytail. Hawk proudly introduced her as Inola Walela, the only female cop on the Bryson City police force. Although the two never touched, they sat close together in the booth and exchanged easy smiles and conversation the entire meal. Nicholas hoped the deputy, who had helped him find the justice he so needed, had finally found the love he had been looking for.

It took months for Nicholas to begin feeling comfortable living in the mansion again. At first he limited his movements to the first floor where he set up a training area for his physical therapy exercises, and practiced on the Baldwin piano.

Aranka stayed with him the first few weeks. They would share meals, watch black and white movies from her treasured collection of DVDs, or merely sit and stare out at nothing, content to comfort one another in silence.

Her financial prowess challenged, she had finally traced Alexander's hidden money in various off-shore accounts and had recently transferred all of the assets into a new account—for Nicholas alone.

When Nicholas told Aranka he considered reverting to his birth surname, Hunt, she had cried. He didn't know if her tears were from shame, or the remaining vestiges of love for her brother. But he knew the cloud of Alexander Kalman would always enshroud him, and that booking agents, performers, and audiences would always know him as Nicholas Kalman. He could never outrun his past by merely changing his name.

Finally, Aranka had decided their mourning must end. She hired a contractor and commissioned an interior decorator to refurbish the music room. Aranka forbade Nicholas entry until the task had been completed to her satisfaction.

Now, Nicholas continued to marvel at his new space. Alexander's red velvet chair had been whisked away in the night, replaced by a tiger's eye oak Morris chair. The dark paneling and bookcases had been removed and the walls now gleamed with fresh sky blue paint. Oatmeal-colored Berber carpet covered the cold marble floors. Calming Mediterranean hues upholstered chairs, a small couch and decorative pillows.

Alexander's impressive collection of rare books had been donated to libraries and museums worldwide. The pompous artwork, exchanged for abstract bronzes and canvases.

There remained only one reminder of the former music room: the Steinway still stood regally atop its platform.

Nicholas crossed the room to the instrument and stroked the blistered cover of his father's journal. He kept the book atop the piano at all times and often flipped through its charred edges. He felt his father's presence in the room, but never Alexander's.

Nicholas's preference in performance repertoire changed as well. Rather than Tchaikovsky's crashing concertos and Debussy's preludes, he found comfort in Clementi's upbeat sonatas and spirited symphonies. Nicholas settled behind the Steinway and played a few bars of his now favorite composer's Opus 25, Number 5 while he waited for Jessica to arrive.

Even though they had seen each other quite a few times and spoke on the phone every day, she remained at a distance and always refused to come to his house. Today, he insisted she visit.

Nicholas still missed Elaine, desperately at times. His feelings for Jessica were different from those he had felt for the lover he would never forget. Theirs was a love doomed from the beginning, one so passionate and reckless it seemed dream-like. This new relationship filled him with hope for the future.

Hearing a car on the drive, he went to the window and peered down to see Jessica's familiar Taurus. He had tried to buy her a new automobile, even drove her to the local dealership, but she refused with such veracity that Nicholas hadn't dared to bring up the subject again. Last week he custom ordered a silver Jaguar convertible. He hoped she would like the sleek sports car, but knew it would take a lot of convincing for her to actually take possession of the extravagant gift—one of many he planned to give her.

He smoothed his hair and straightened his cashmere turtleneck sweater. Crossing the room, he twirled a bottle of champagne in an ice bucket atop a brass bar cart and wondered if she would be as nervous as he.

Nicholas's newest hire, Arabelle Duncan, a local mother of four college-aged boys who fussed over Nicholas like her own child, peeked her head into the room. "You ready, sugar?"

He nodded, his heart beating a little faster.

Arabelle waved Jessica into the room, winked at

Nicholas, then left them alone.

He hurried to Jessica and enveloped her in his arms. "I'm so glad you came."

Jessica whistled her approval. "Quite a snazzy place you've got here." She walked all around the music room, then stepped onto the terrace and scanned the endless horizon.

"I wish you would have come before now."

She shrugged. "It didn't feel right."

"But it does now?"

She smiled. "I'm here, aren't I?"

He returned the smile.

Taking in the room, her eyes sparkling, she said, "I've noticed this place from the highway. Never imagined I'd see the inside, though."

"Come and sit down. I'll get us a drink."

While Jessica settled on the plush sofa, Nicholas poured champagne into awaiting flutes. Handing a glass to Jessica, he sat down beside her. They raised their glasses and clinked them together. He noticed her hand tremble slightly when she lifted the delicate hand-blown glass to her lips.

"Don't be nervous," he whispered.

"I'm sorry. I don't know why, but I am."

They sipped in silence for a little while.

"So, your classes are over?"

"Last week."

"I'm looking forward to your graduation ceremony."

"I smiled when I received your RSVP. I'm excited for you to meet my Aunt Sarah."

Nicholas beamed. "It will be my honor."

"What were you so anxious to talk to me about, Nicholas?"

"I can't stop thinking about you." He reached for her hand. "I miss you. And I want to be with you."

Jessica blushed. She rubbed the top of his hand with her thumb.

"I know you've heard of the National Theatre in Prague."

"Of course. Josef Svoboda designed his greatest masterpieces for that theatre."

"I'm scheduled to perform there next month."

Jessica's mouth dropped open. "Really?"

He waited a beat before he continued. "I'd like you to come with me."

Jessica sat looking at her lap a long time. "Are you asking me to change my life? To start a new one with you?"

"Would that be so bad?"

Her eyes beaded with tears, then her gaze went to the bubbles in her drink.

Nicholas reached out. With delicate fingertips, he tilted her chin so that he could look into eyes the exact shade of emeralds. "Will you come with me?"

She waited so long to respond, he had convinced himself she would say no, run from the room, never return.

Jessica traced the fading scar along the side of Nicholas's face with the tip of her finger and said, "You know I will."

ACKNOWLEDGEMENTS

Although every effort has been made to present you, the reader, true-to-life experiences, this is a work of fiction, therefore, some of the locations have been changed, altered or added. As well, all characters within *Staccato* are figments of this writer's imagination.

I offer my appreciation to the talented writers: Virginia Nosky, Sharon Anderson, Sam Barone, Marcia Fine, Judy Starbuck, Marty Roselius, Heidi Horchler, Martin Cox, and members of the Scottsdale Writers Group. Thank you all for keeping me on track.

Countless hours of research were accomplished in order to select the ideal musical compositions showcased on these pages. As well, the world-class pianist Michael Glenn Williams assisted me with the behind-the-scenes glimpses of a professional touring musician. Mr. Williams requested I pass along that his personal mentors in no way resemble the nemesis I alone created.

DNA elements within this novel were graciously verified by Tracie D. Fife, Crime Scene Specialist Supervisor, Scottsdale Police Department.

For inspiration, I turned to Frank Conroy's masterpiece *Body & Soul*.

I am grateful to Mike Simpson and his dedicated and talented team at *Second Wind Publishing*, especially Pat Bertram, for providing me the opportunity to present my debut novel.

I also wish to thank my family who have stood beside me during this journey to publication. Your encouragement means more to me than you possibly realize.